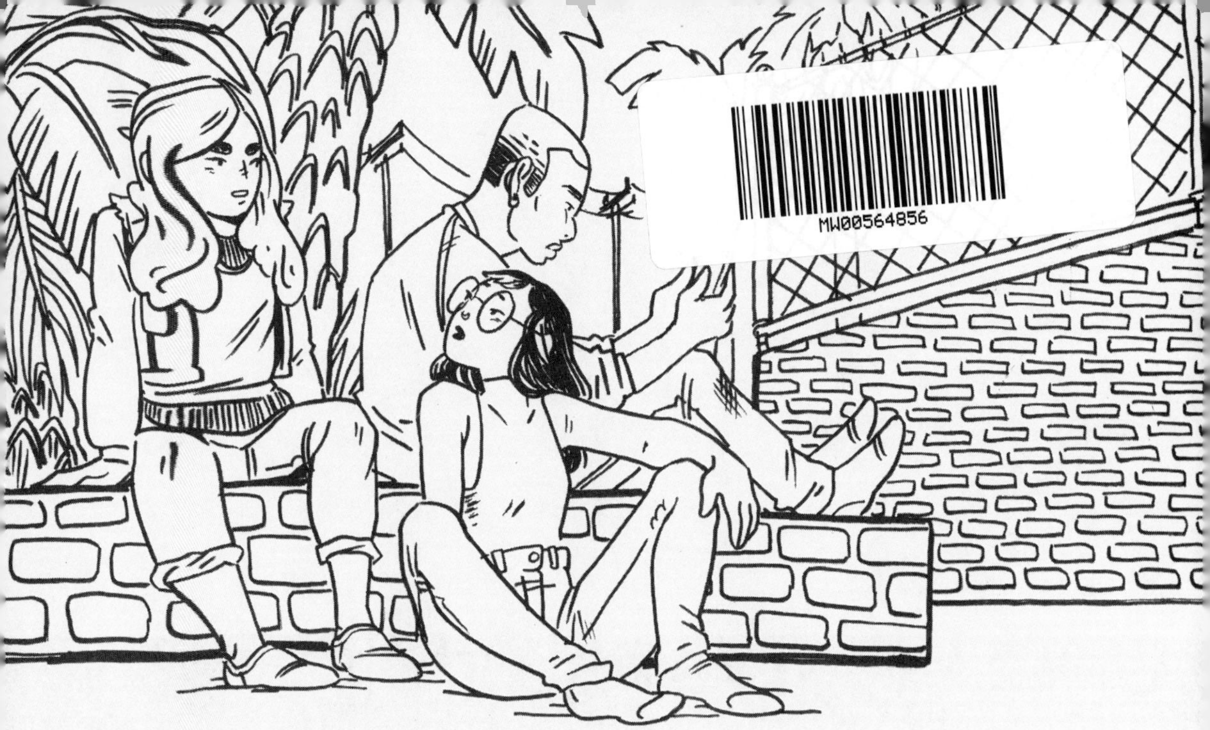

FUCK OFF SQUAD

NICOLE GOUX DAVE BAKER

 PUBLISHED BY SILVER SPROCKET, SILVERSPROCKET.NET ISBN: 9781945509261 ; SILVER #091. LAYOUT BY MIKE LOPEZ (POSTLOPEZ.COM)
PRINTED IN CANADA.

FUCK OFF
SQUAD

PART 2

FEVER
COAST

PART 1

TEENAGE SWITCHBLADE

PART 3

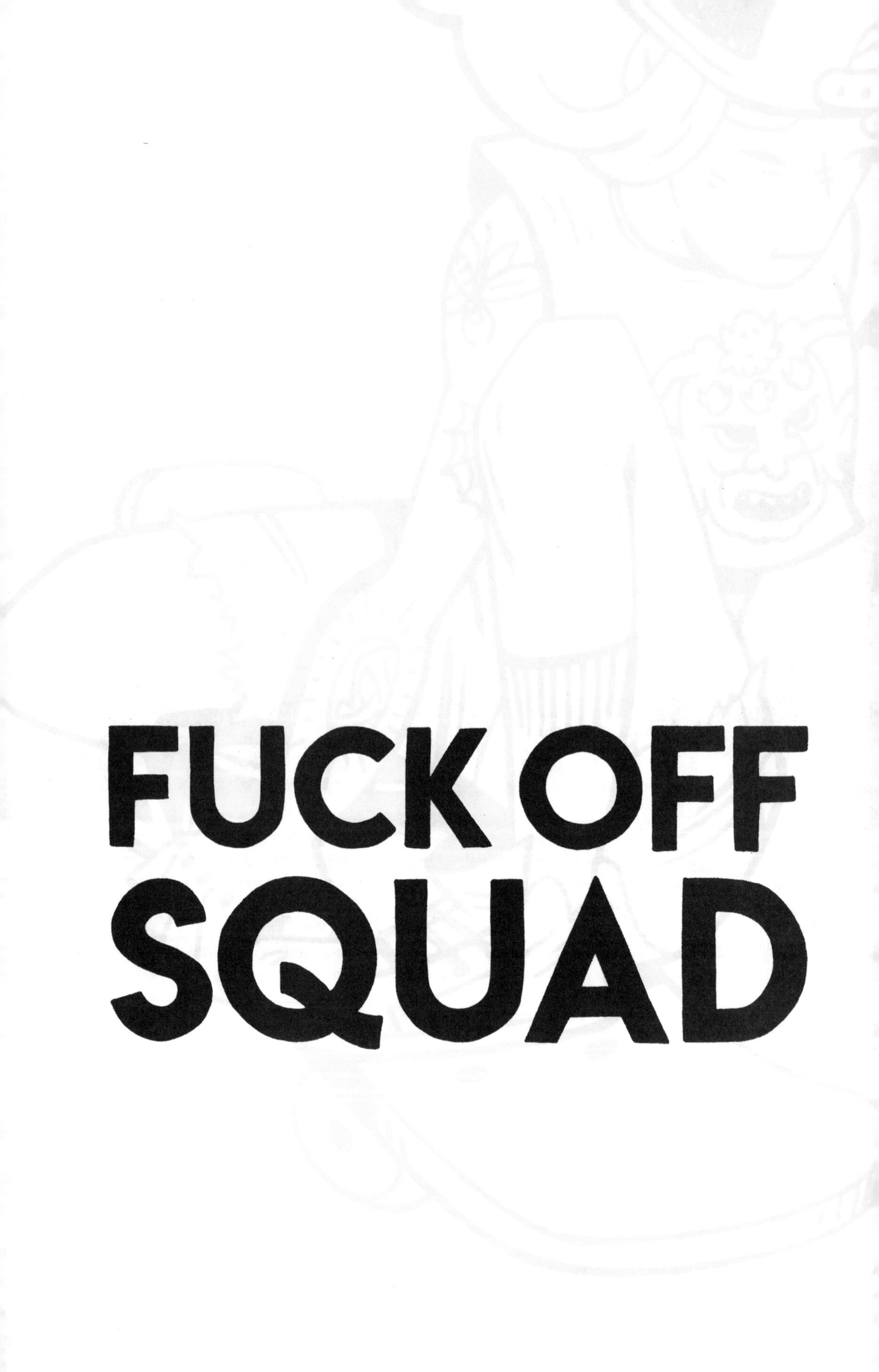

FUCK OFF SQUAD

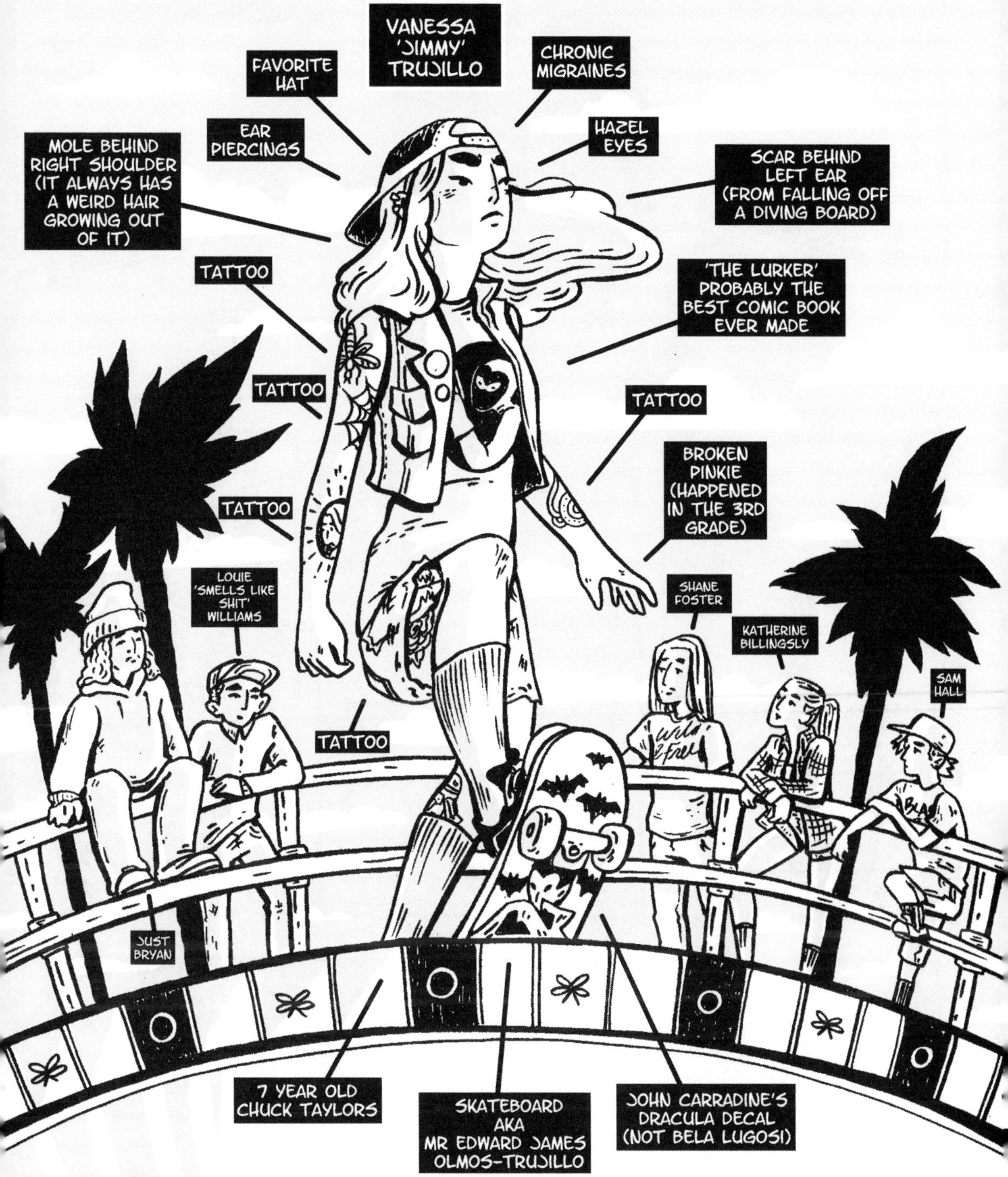
VANESSA 'JIMMY' TRUJILLO
FAVORITE HAT
CHRONIC MIGRAINES
EAR PIERCINGS
HAZEL EYES
MOLE BEHIND RIGHT SHOULDER (IT ALWAYS HAS A WEIRD HAIR GROWING OUT OF IT)
SCAR BEHIND LEFT EAR (FROM FALLING OFF A DIVING BOARD)
TATTOO
'THE LURKER' PROBABLY THE BEST COMIC BOOK EVER MADE
TATTOO
TATTOO
BROKEN PINKIE (HAPPENED IN THE 3RD GRADE)
TATTOO
LOUIE 'SMELLS LIKE SHIT' WILLIAMS
SHANE FOSTER
KATHERINE BILLINGSLY
SAM HALL
TATTOO
JUST BRYAN
7 YEAR OLD CHUCK TAYLORS
SKATEBOARD AKA MR EDWARD JAMES OLMOS-TRUJILLO
JOHN CARRADINE'S DRACULA DECAL (NOT BELA LUGOSI)

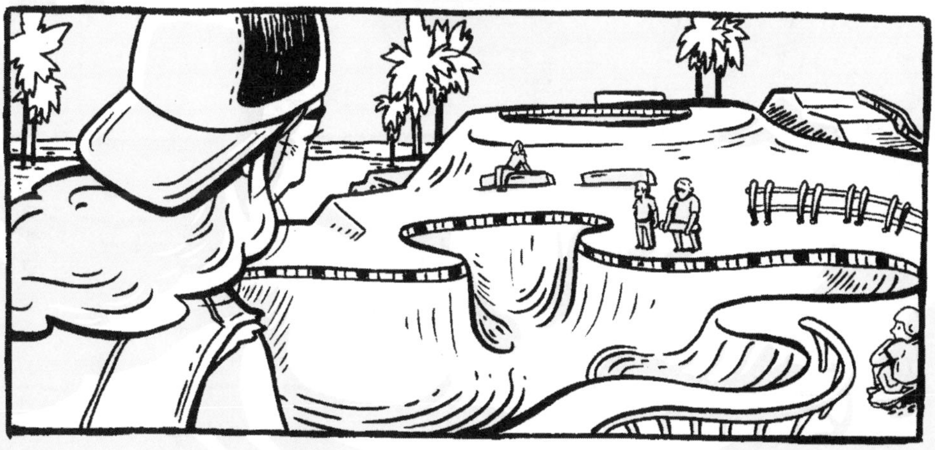

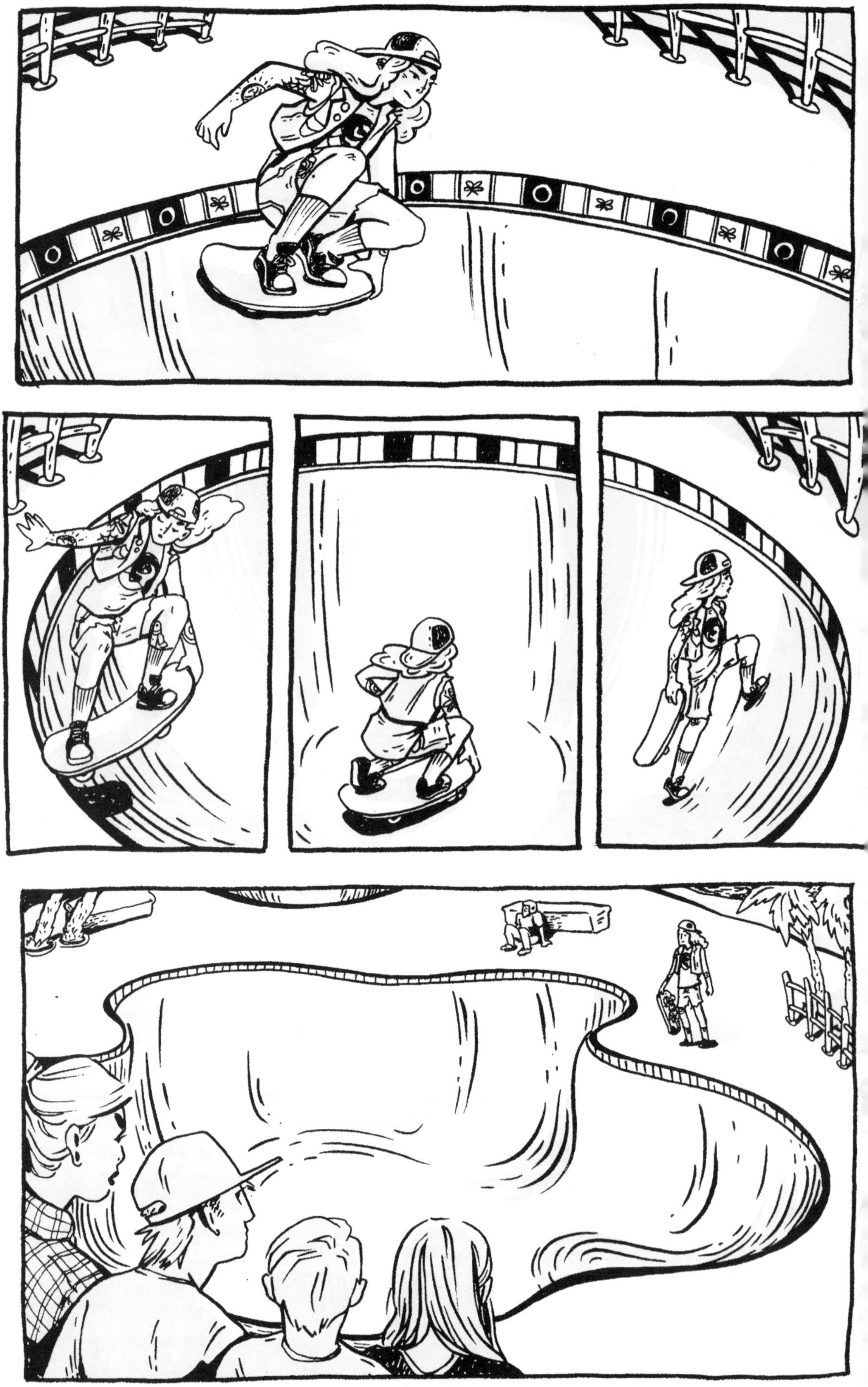

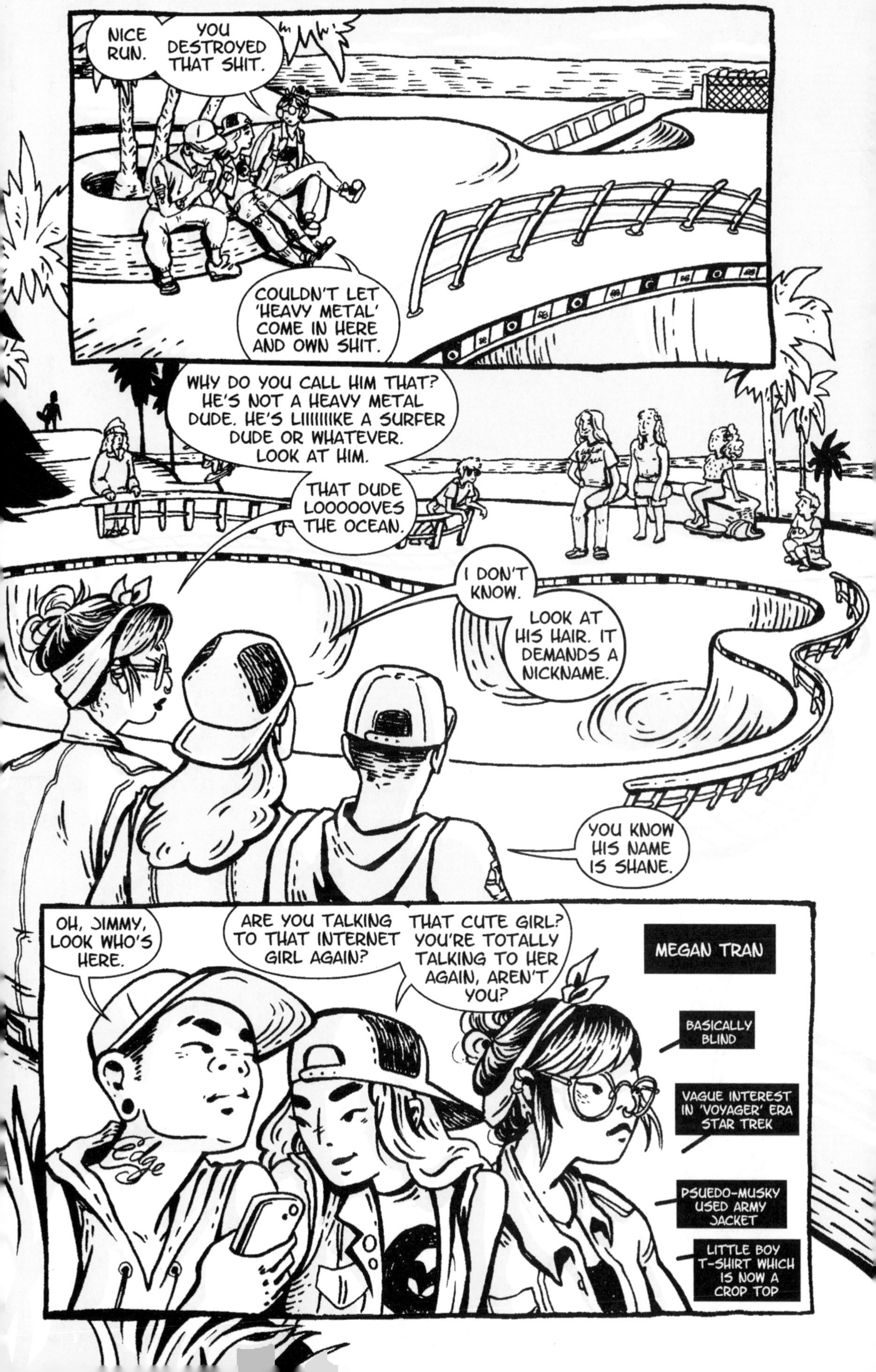
NICE RUN.
YOU DESTROYED THAT SHIT.
COULDN'T LET 'HEAVY METAL' COME IN HERE AND OWN SHIT.
WHY DO YOU CALL HIM THAT? HE'S NOT A HEAVY METAL DUDE. HE'S LIIIIIIIKE A SURFER DUDE OR WHATEVER. LOOK AT HIM.
THAT DUDE LOOOOOVES THE OCEAN.
I DON'T KNOW.
LOOK AT HIS HAIR. IT DEMANDS A NICKNAME.
YOU KNOW HIS NAME IS SHANE.
OH, JIMMY, LOOK WHO'S HERE.
ARE YOU TALKING TO THAT INTERNET GIRL AGAIN?
THAT CUTE GIRL? YOU'RE TOTALLY TALKING TO HER AGAIN, AREN'T YOU?
MEGAN TRAN
BASICALLY BLIND
VAGUE INTEREST IN 'VOYAGER' ERA STAR TREK
PSUEDO-MUSKY USED ARMY JACKET
LITTLE BOY T-SHIRT WHICH IS NOW A CROP TOP
Edge

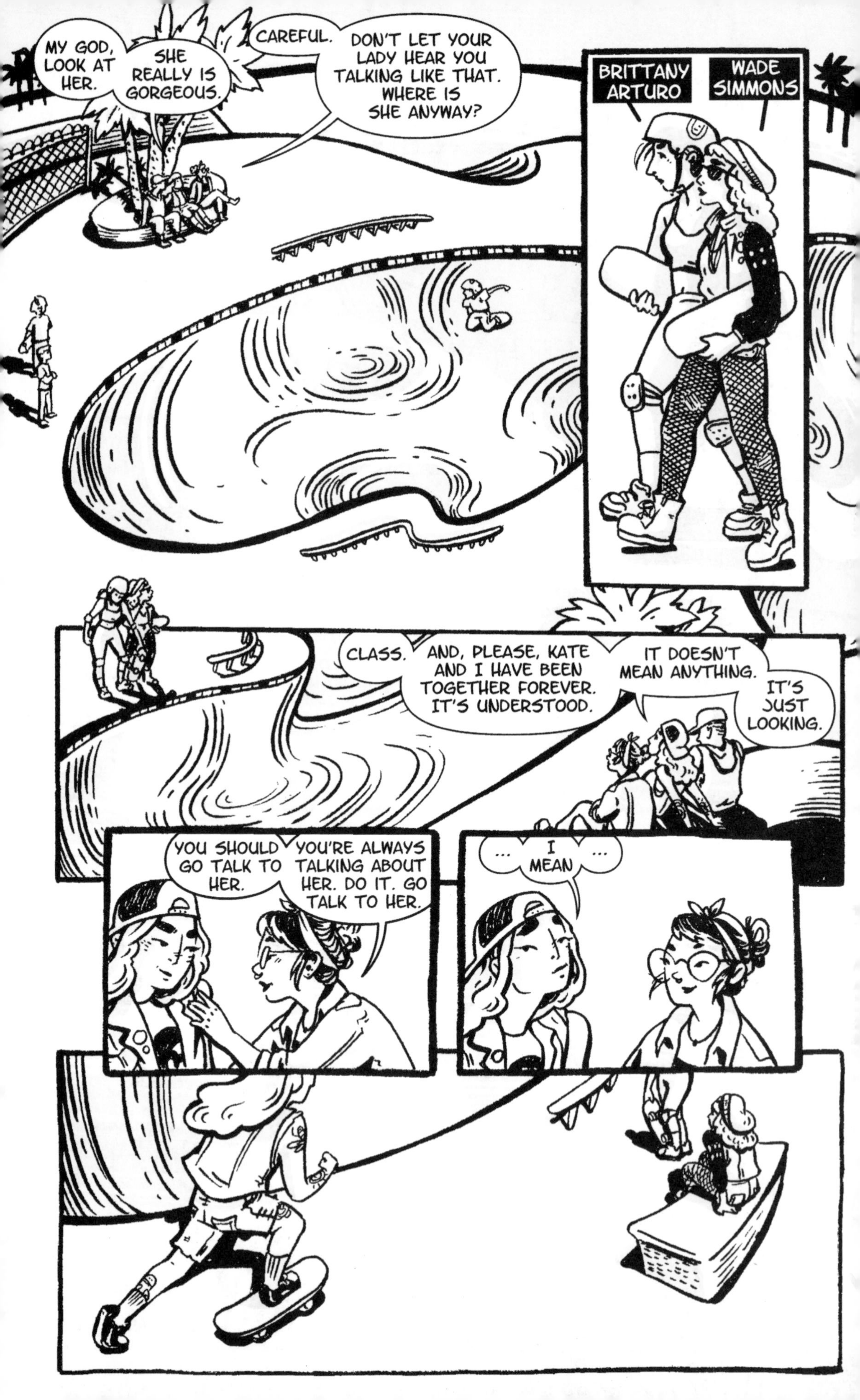
MY GOD, LOOK AT HER.
SHE REALLY IS GORGEOUS.
CAREFUL.
DON'T LET YOUR LADY HEAR YOU TALKING LIKE THAT. WHERE IS SHE ANYWAY?
BRITTANY ARTURO
WADE SIMMONS
CLASS.
AND, PLEASE, KATE AND I HAVE BEEN TOGETHER FOREVER. IT'S UNDERSTOOD.
IT DOESN'T MEAN ANYTHING.
IT'S JUST LOOKING.
YOU SHOULD GO TALK TO HER.
YOU'RE ALWAYS TALKING ABOUT HER. DO IT. GO TALK TO HER.
...
I MEAN
...

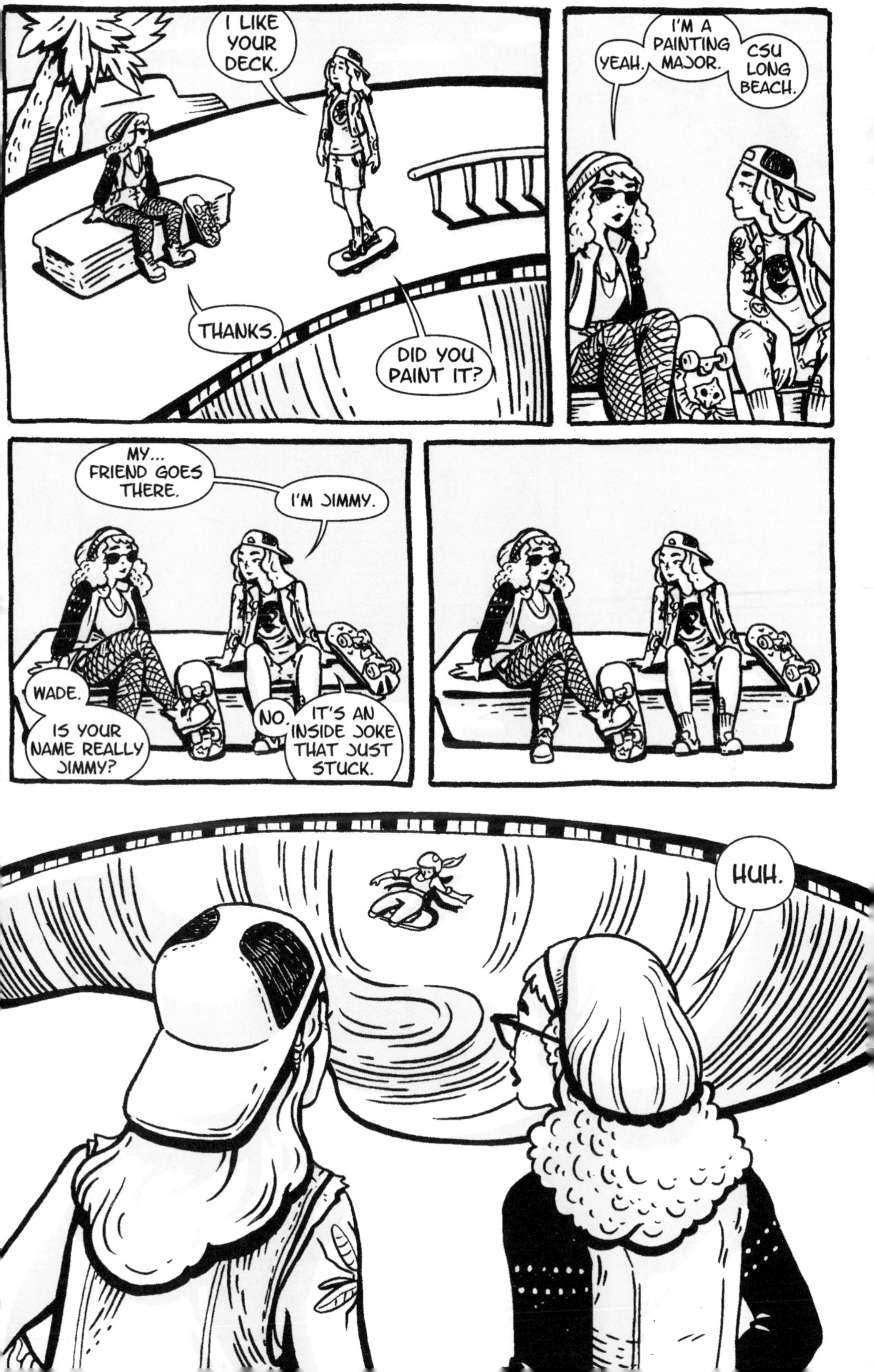
I LIKE YOUR DECK.
THANKS.
DID YOU PAINT IT?
YEAH.
I'M A PAINTING MAJOR.
CSU LONG BEACH.
MY... FRIEND GOES THERE.
I'M JIMMY.
WADE.
IS YOUR NAME REALLY JIMMY?
NO.
IT'S AN INSIDE JOKE THAT JUST STUCK.
HUH.

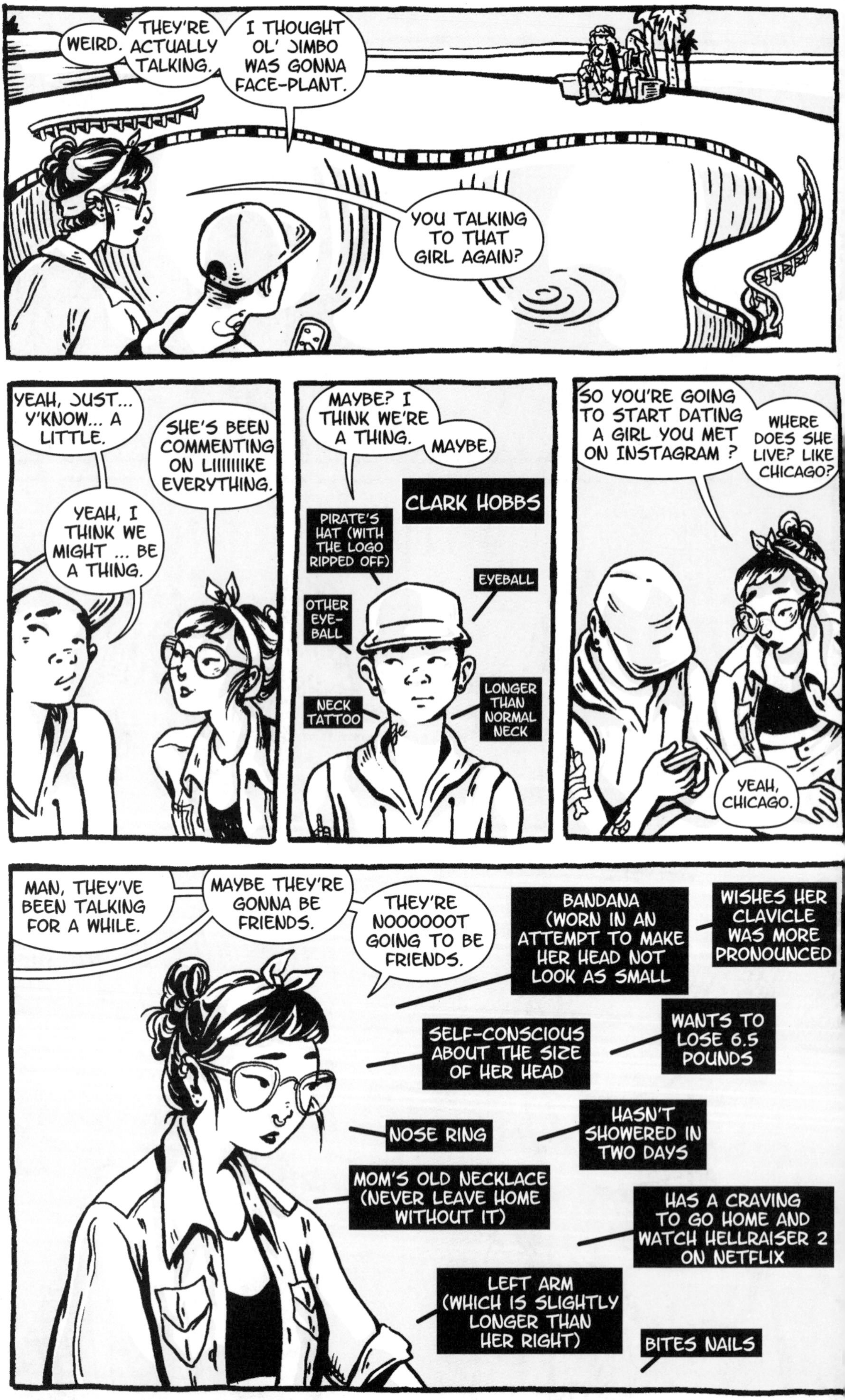
WEIRD.
THEY'RE ACTUALLY TALKING.
I THOUGHT OL' JIMBO WAS GONNA FACE-PLANT.
YOU TALKING TO THAT GIRL AGAIN?
YEAH, JUST... Y'KNOW... A LITTLE.
SHE'S BEEN COMMENTING ON LIIIIIIKE EVERYTHING.
YEAH, I THINK WE MIGHT ... BE A THING.
MAYBE? I THINK WE'RE A THING.
MAYBE.
CLARK HOBBS
PIRATE'S HAT (WITH THE LOGO RIPPED OFF)
EYEBALL
OTHER EYE-BALL
NECK TATTOO
LONGER THAN NORMAL NECK
SO YOU'RE GOING TO START DATING A GIRL YOU MET ON INSTAGRAM ?
WHERE DOES SHE LIVE? LIKE CHICAGO?
YEAH, CHICAGO.
MAN, THEY'VE BEEN TALKING FOR A WHILE.
MAYBE THEY'RE GONNA BE FRIENDS.
THEY'RE NOOOOOOT GOING TO BE FRIENDS.
BANDANA (WORN IN AN ATTEMPT TO MAKE HER HEAD NOT LOOK AS SMALL
WISHES HER CLAVICLE WAS MORE PRONOUNCED
SELF-CONSCIOUS ABOUT THE SIZE OF HER HEAD
WANTS TO LOSE 6.5 POUNDS
NOSE RING
HASN'T SHOWERED IN TWO DAYS
MOM'S OLD NECKLACE (NEVER LEAVE HOME WITHOUT IT)
HAS A CRAVING TO GO HOME AND WATCH HELLRAISER 2 ON NETFLIX
LEFT ARM (WHICH IS SLIGHTLY LONGER THAN HER RIGHT)
BITES NAILS

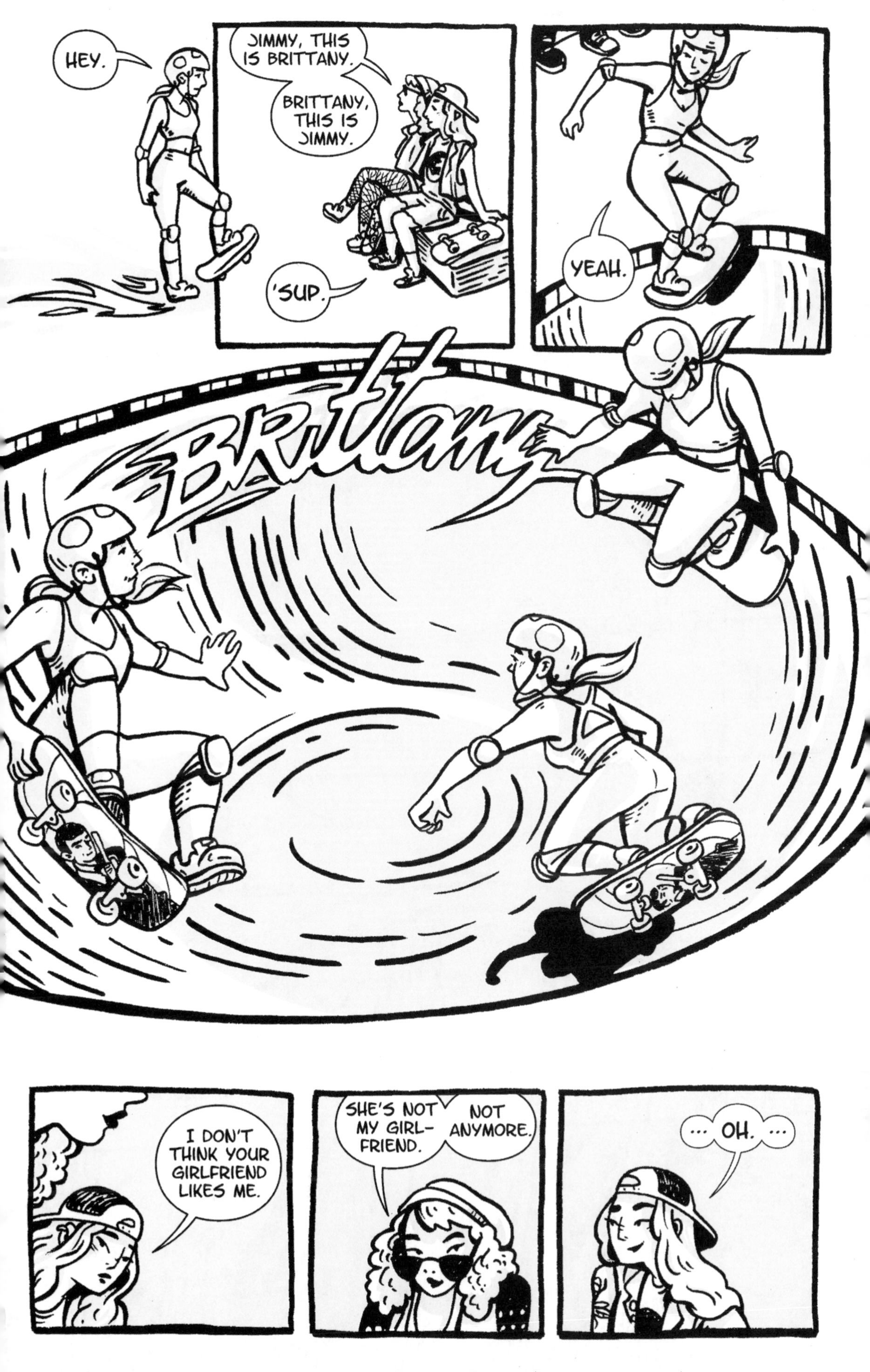
HEY.
JIMMY, THIS IS BRITTANY.
BRITTANY, THIS IS JIMMY.
'SUP.
YEAH.
BRITTANY
I DON'T THINK YOUR GIRLFRIEND LIKES ME.
SHE'S NOT MY GIRL-FRIEND.
NOT ANYMORE.
... OH. ...

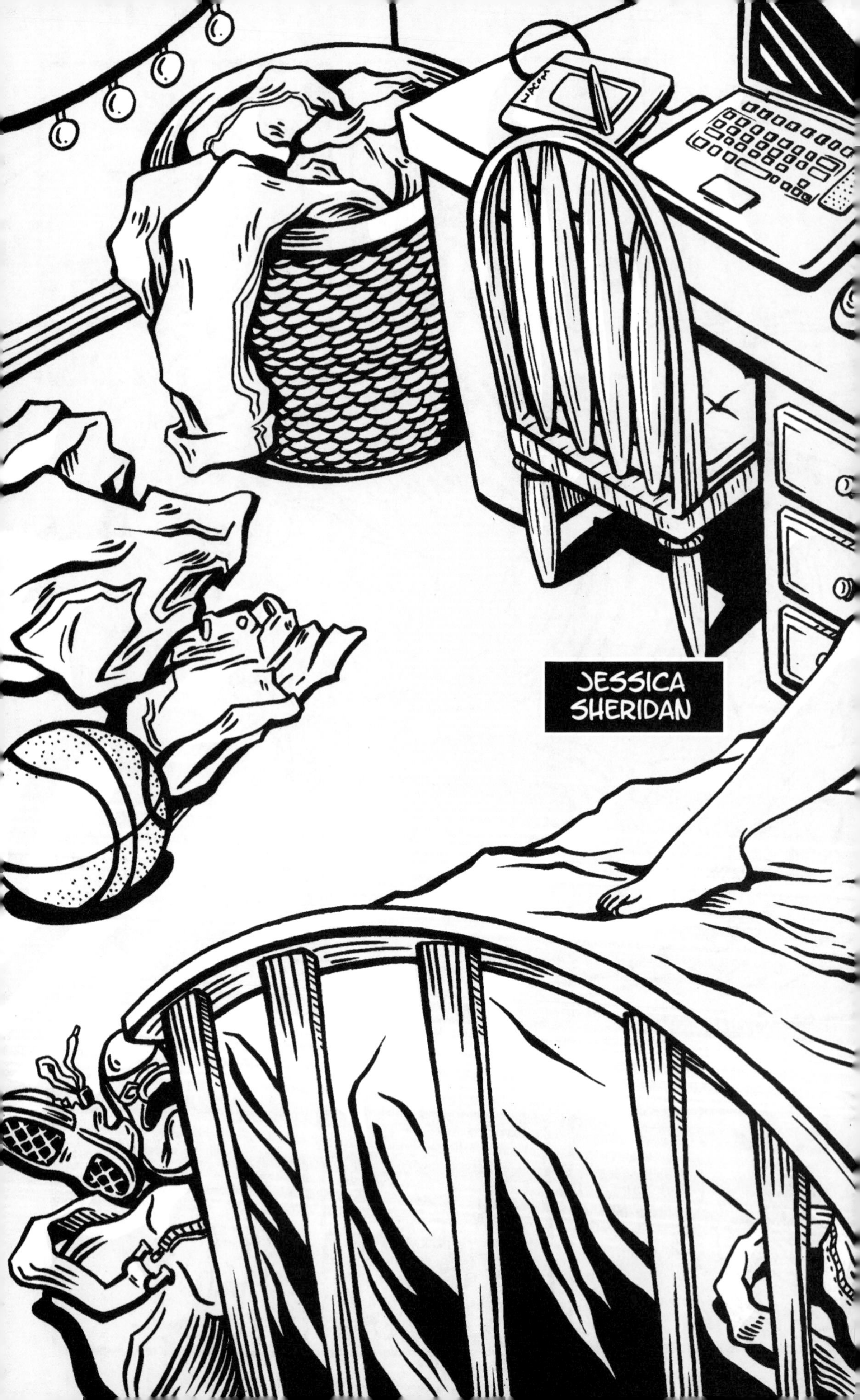
JESSICA SHERIDAN

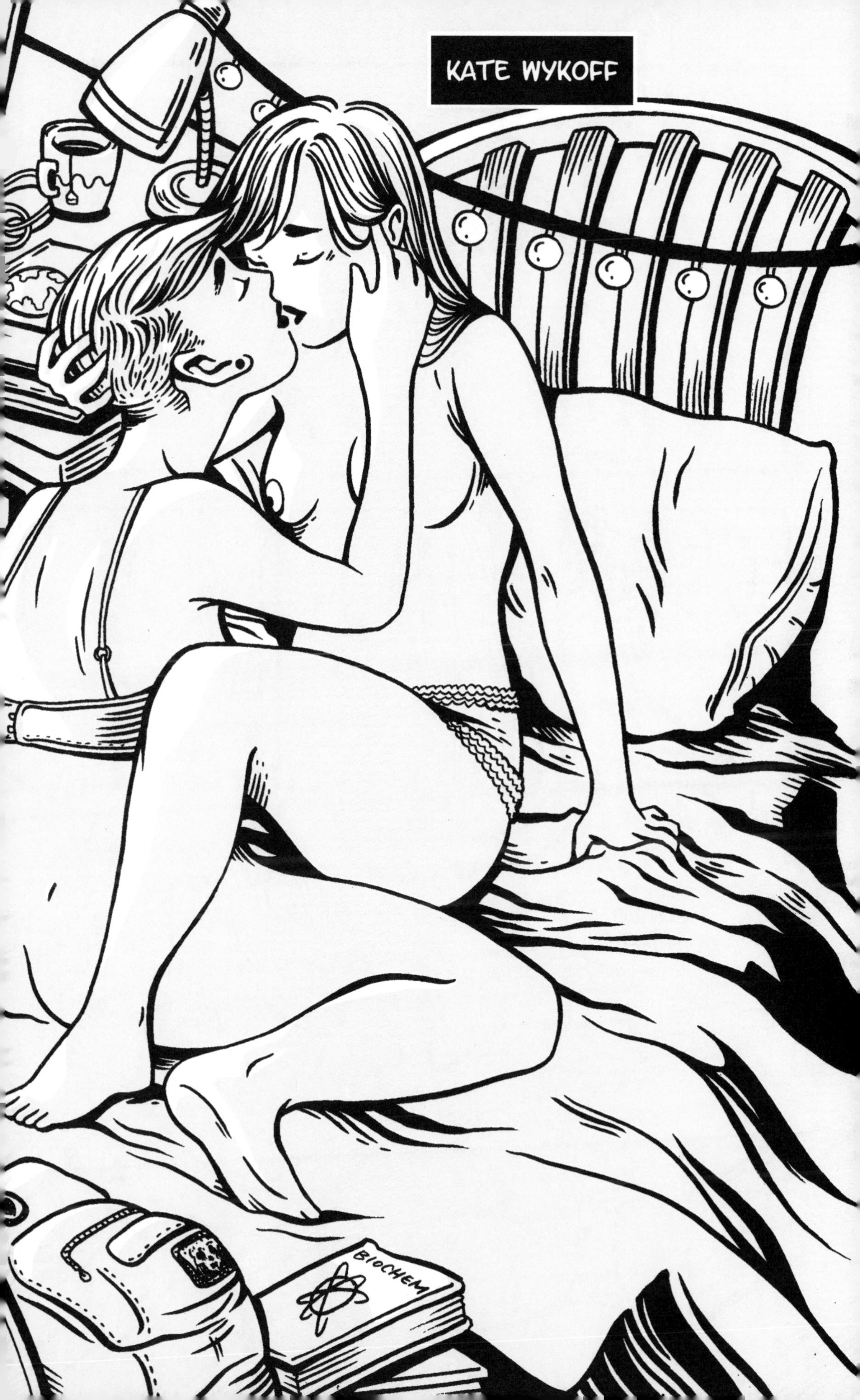
KATE WYKOFF
BIOCHEM

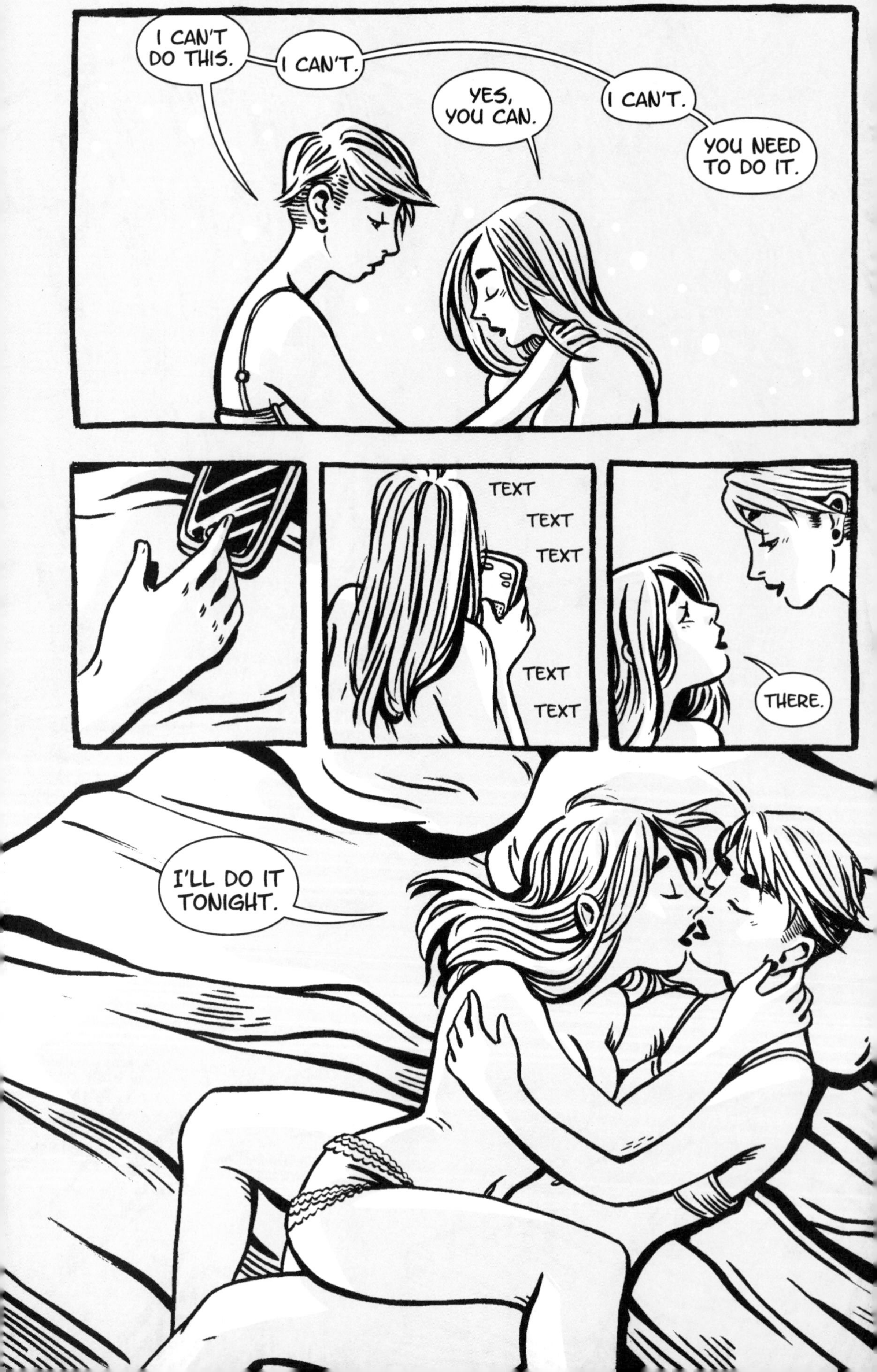
I CAN'T DO THIS.
I CAN'T.
YES, YOU CAN.
I CAN'T.
YOU NEED TO DO IT.
TEXT
TEXT
TEXT
TEXT
TEXT
THERE.
I'LL DO IT TONIGHT.

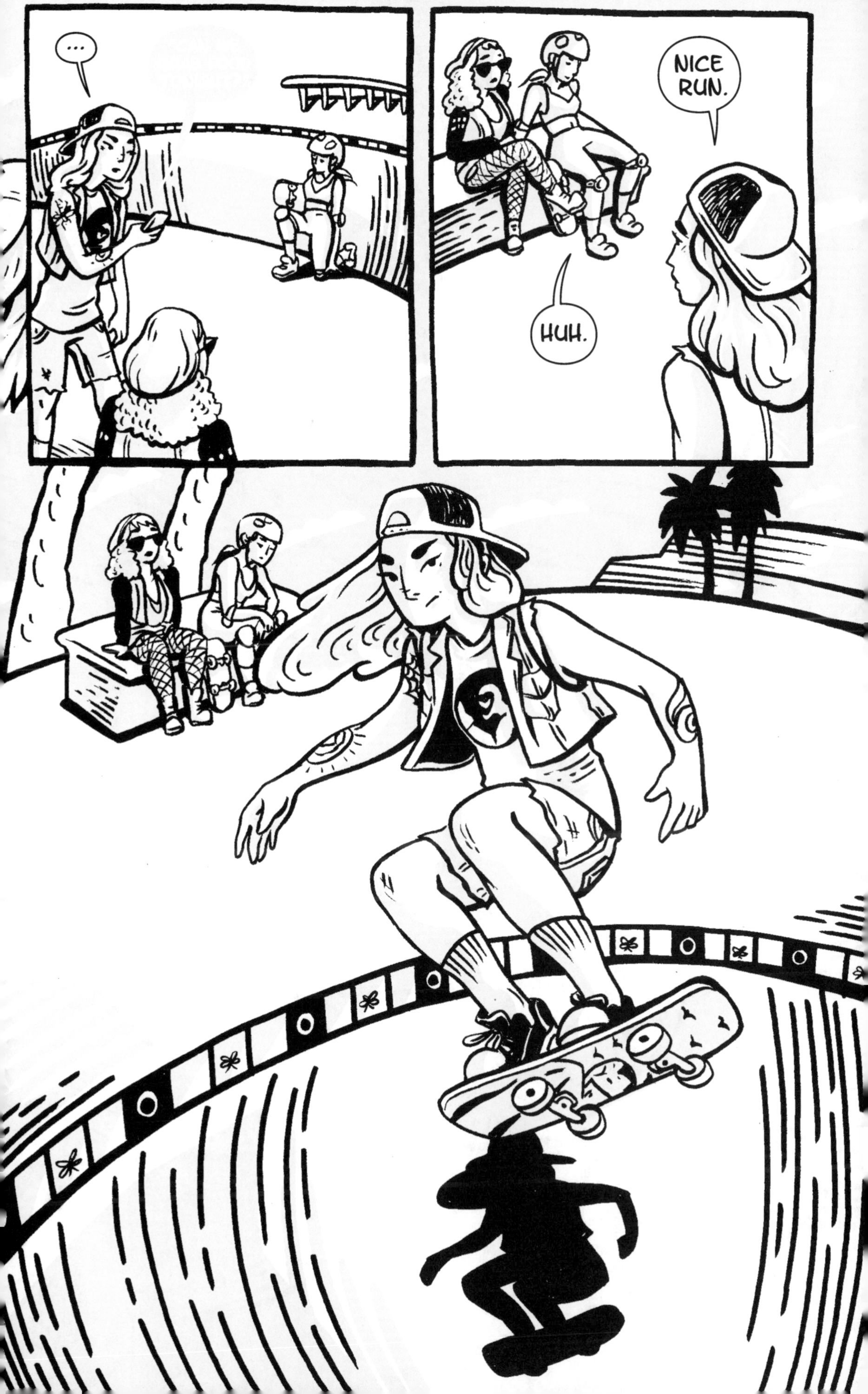
...
NICE RUN.
HUH.

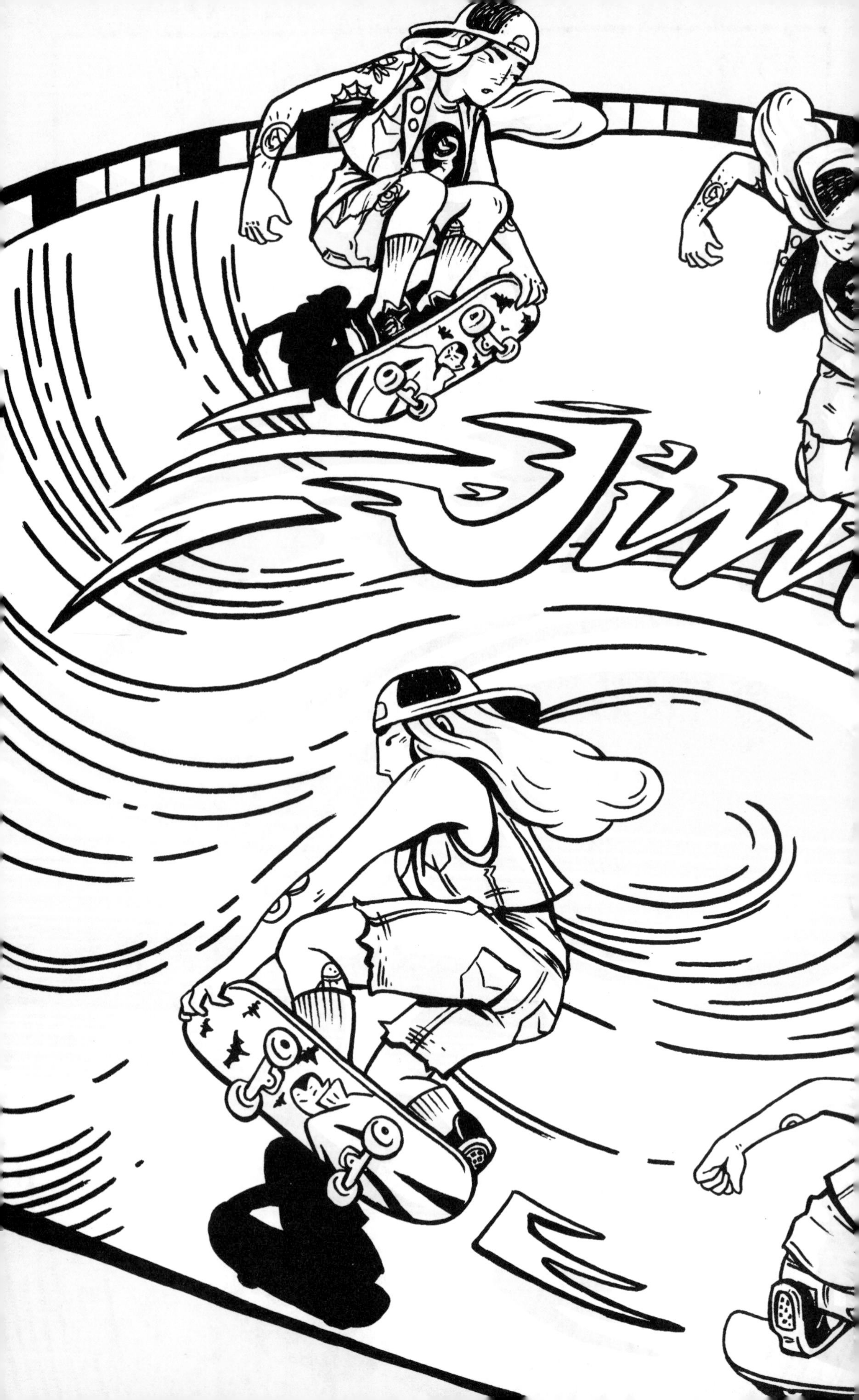

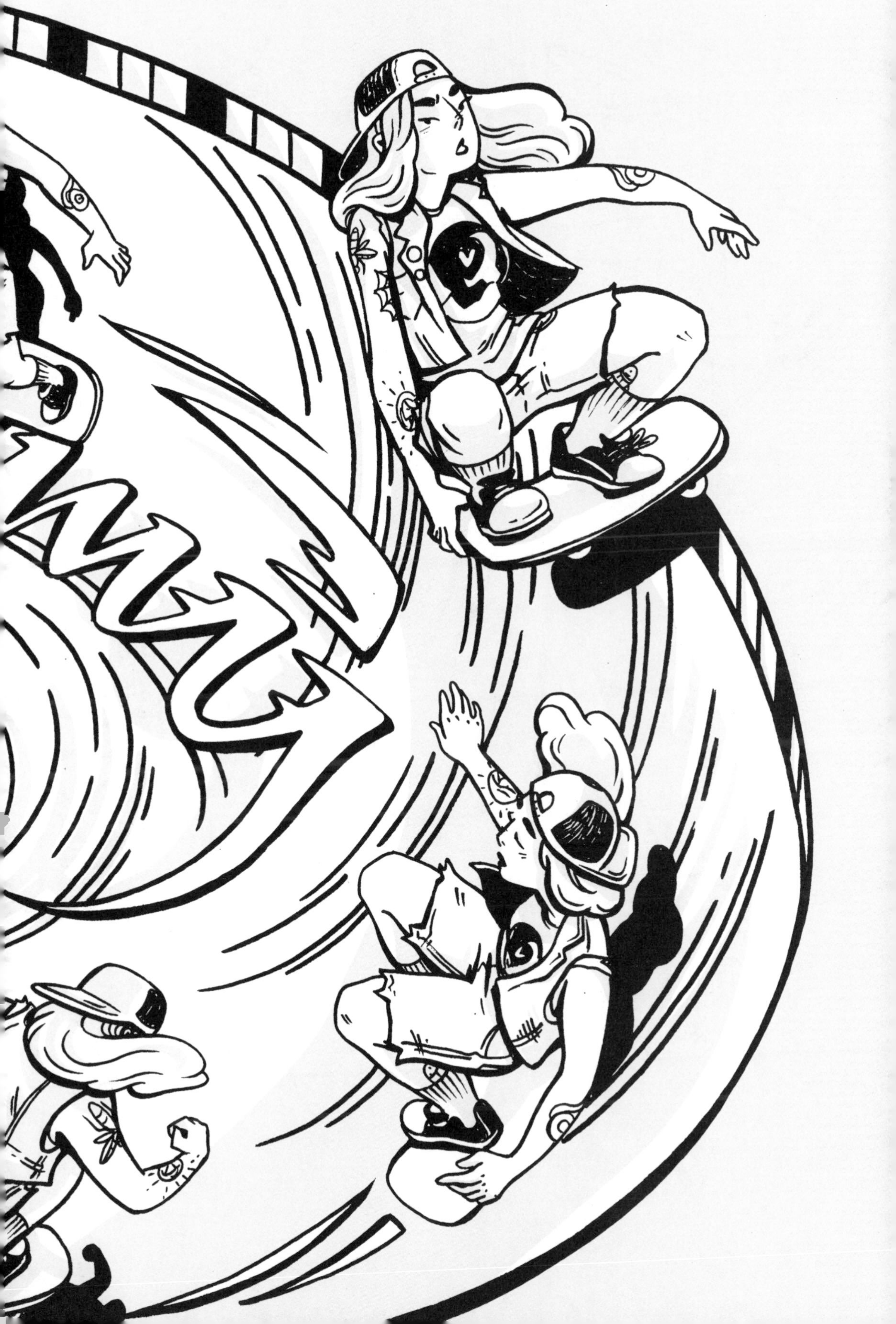

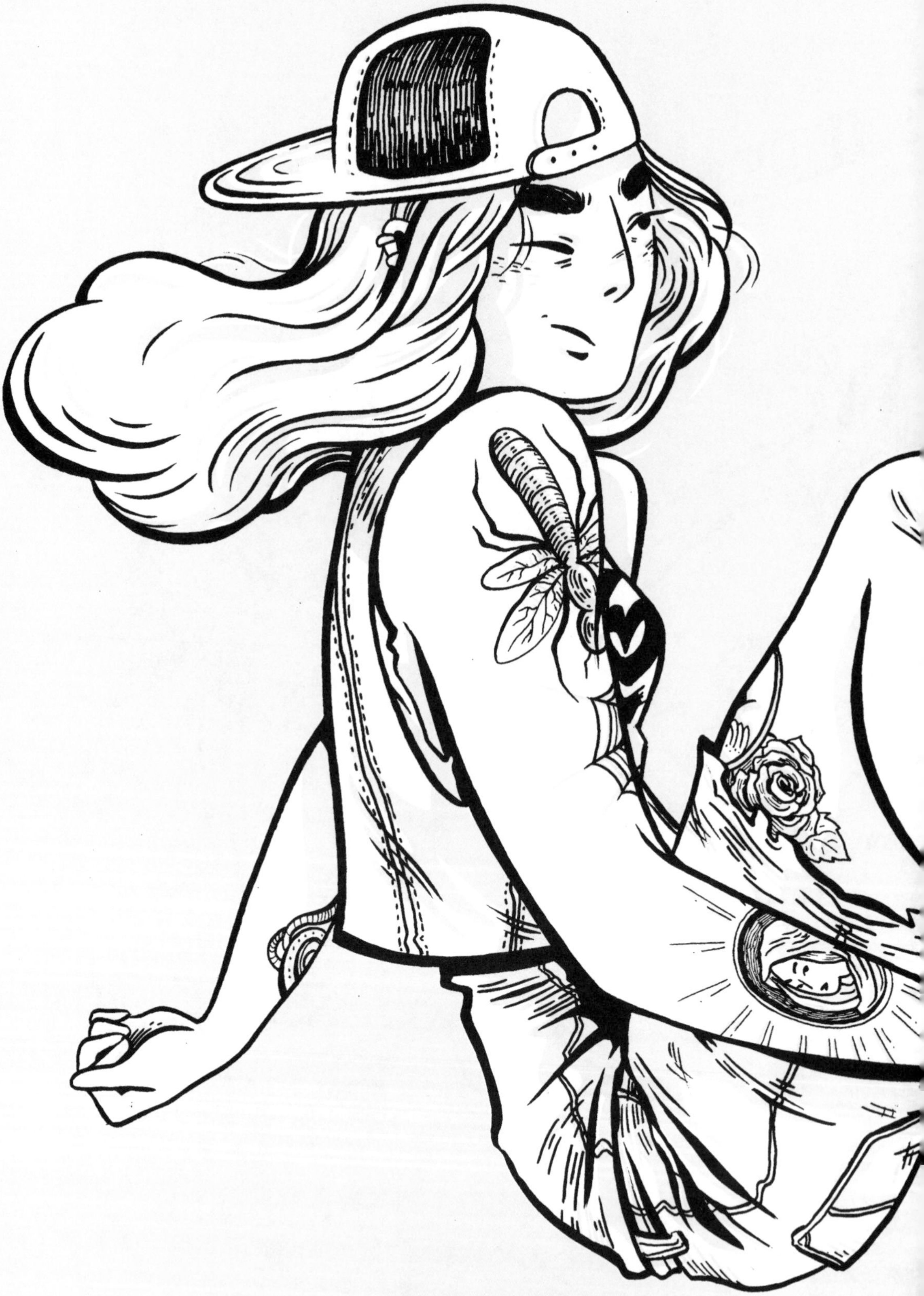

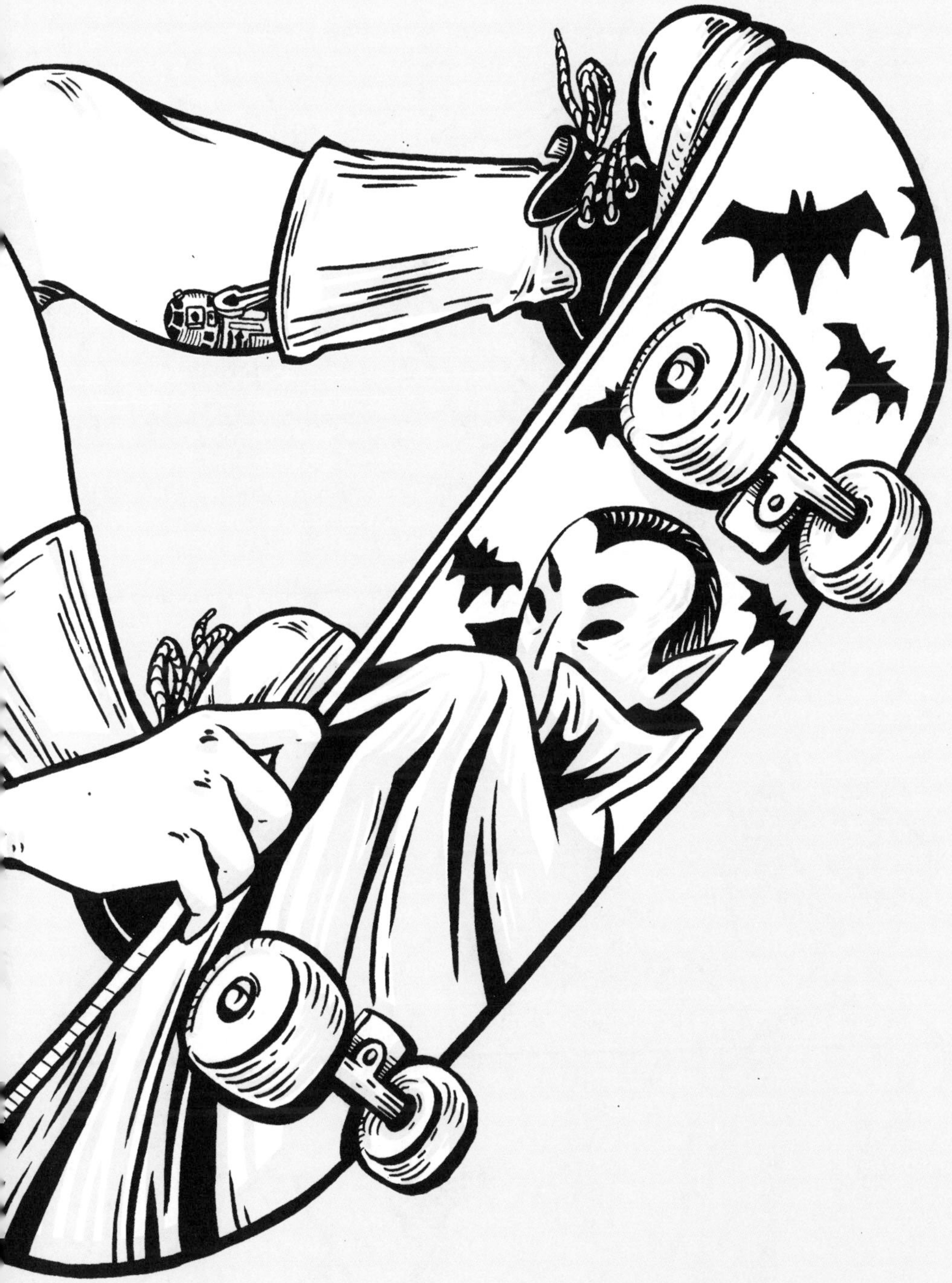

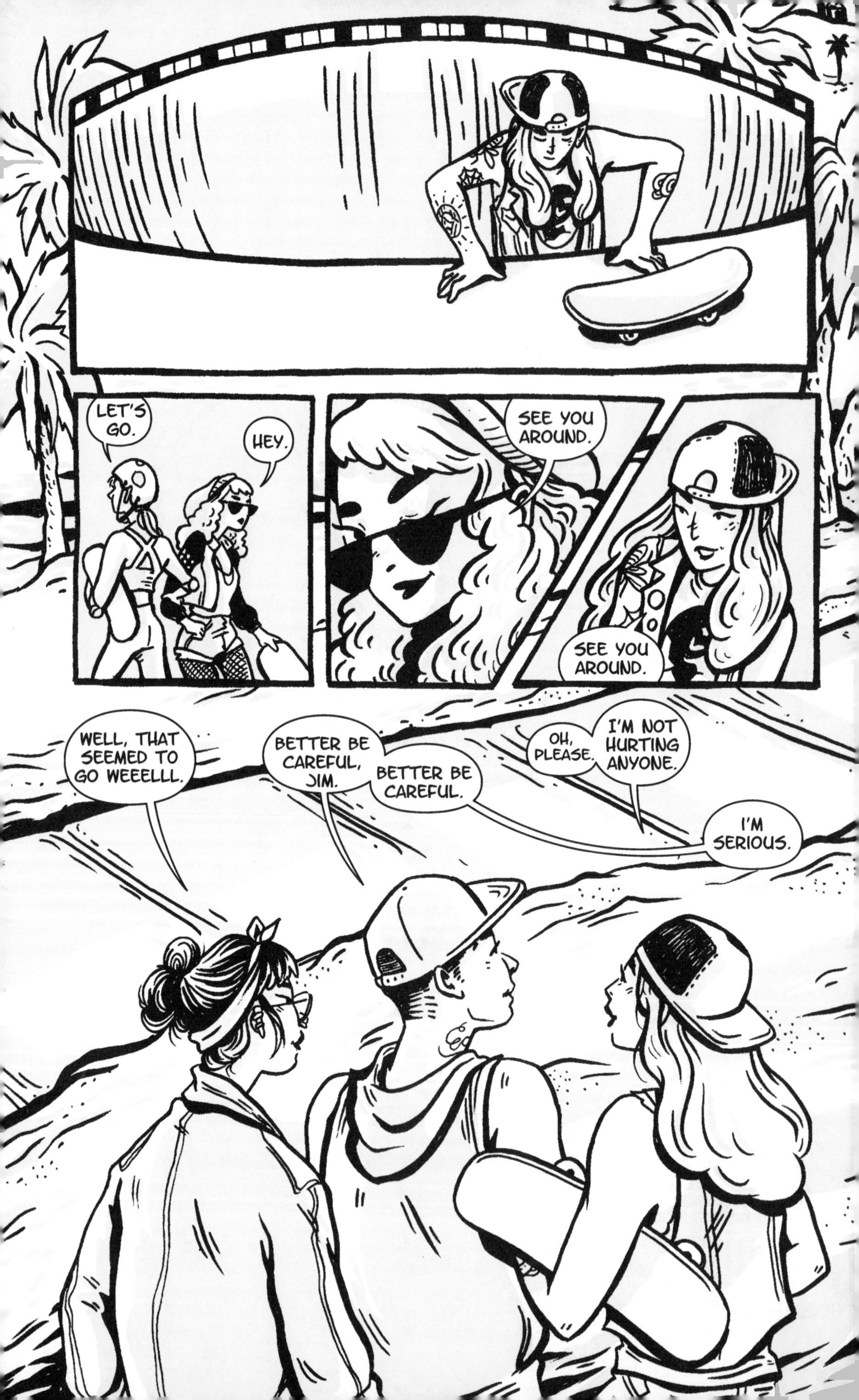
LET'S GO.
HEY.
SEE YOU AROUND.
SEE YOU AROUND.
WELL, THAT SEEMED TO GO WEEELLL.
BETTER BE CAREFUL, JIM.
BETTER BE CAREFUL.
OH, PLEASE.
I'M NOT HURTING ANYONE.
I'M SERIOUS.

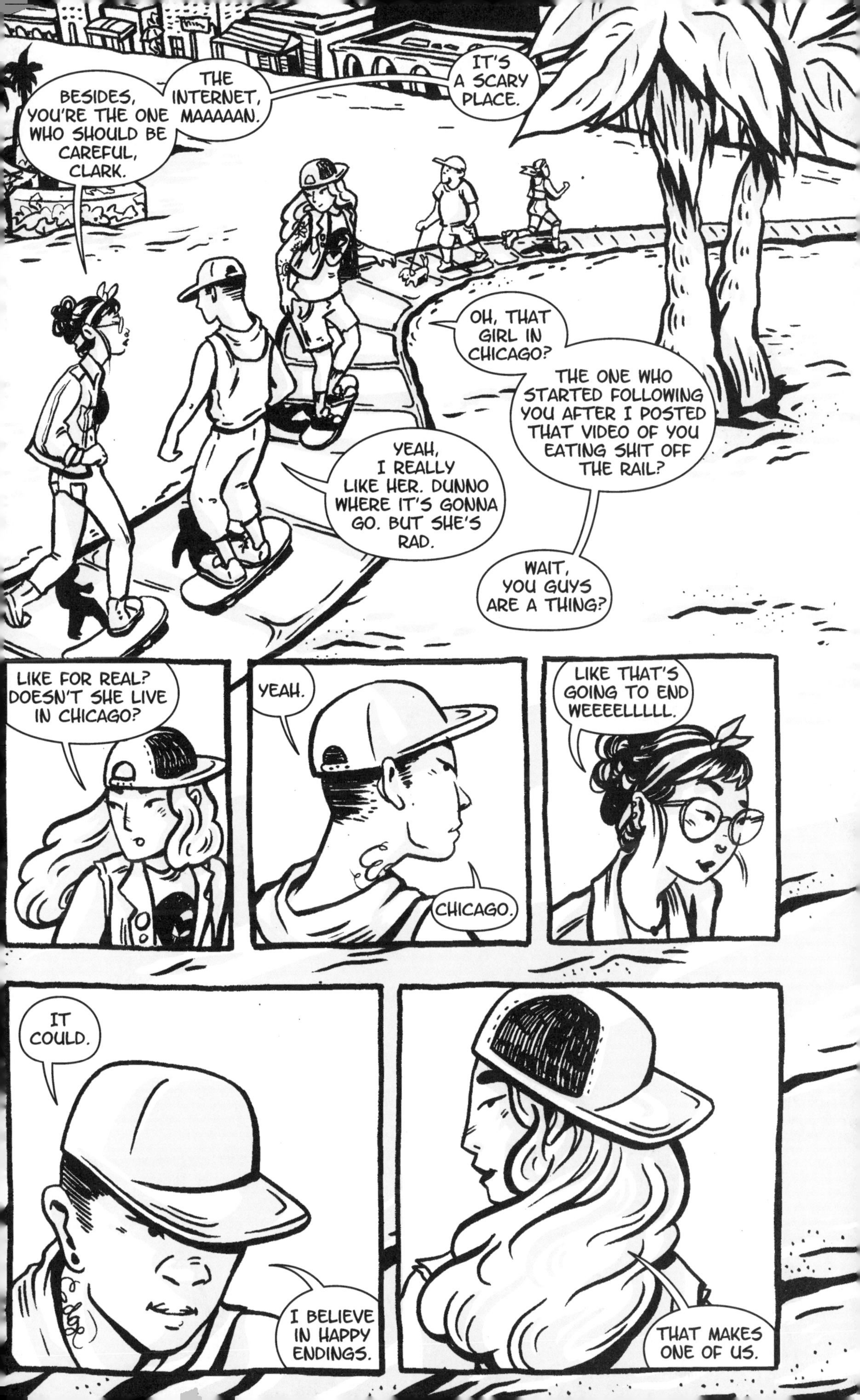
BESIDES, YOU'RE THE ONE WHO SHOULD BE CAREFUL, CLARK.
THE INTERNET, MAAAAAN.
IT'S A SCARY PLACE.
OH, THAT GIRL IN CHICAGO?
THE ONE WHO STARTED FOLLOWING YOU AFTER I POSTED THAT VIDEO OF YOU EATING SHIT OFF THE RAIL?
YEAH, I REALLY LIKE HER. DUNNO WHERE IT'S GONNA GO. BUT SHE'S RAD.
WAIT, YOU GUYS ARE A THING?
LIKE FOR REAL? DOESN'T SHE LIVE IN CHICAGO?
YEAH.
CHICAGO.
LIKE THAT'S GOING TO END WEEEELLLLL.
IT COULD.
I BELIEVE IN HAPPY ENDINGS.
THAT MAKES ONE OF US.

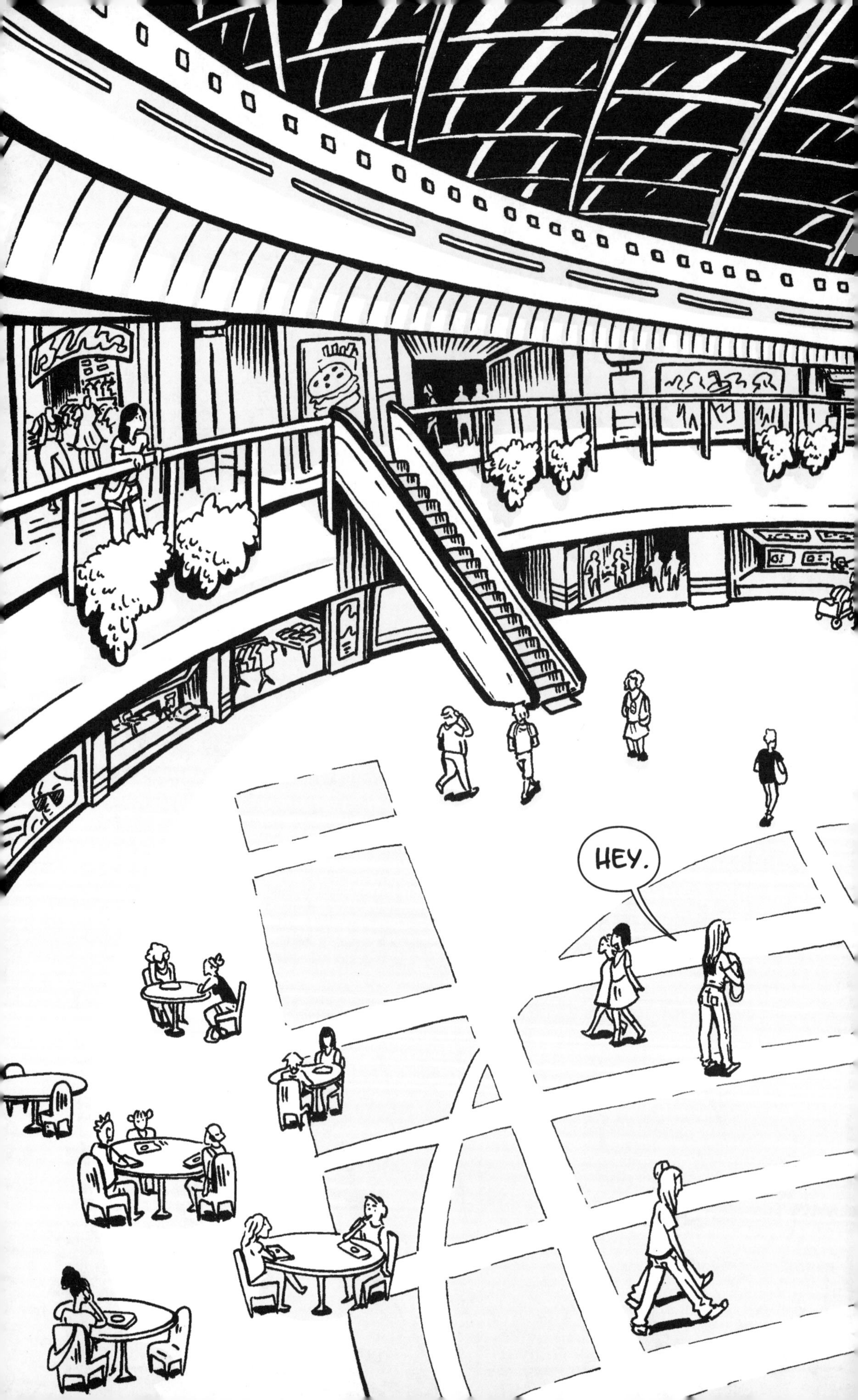
HEY.

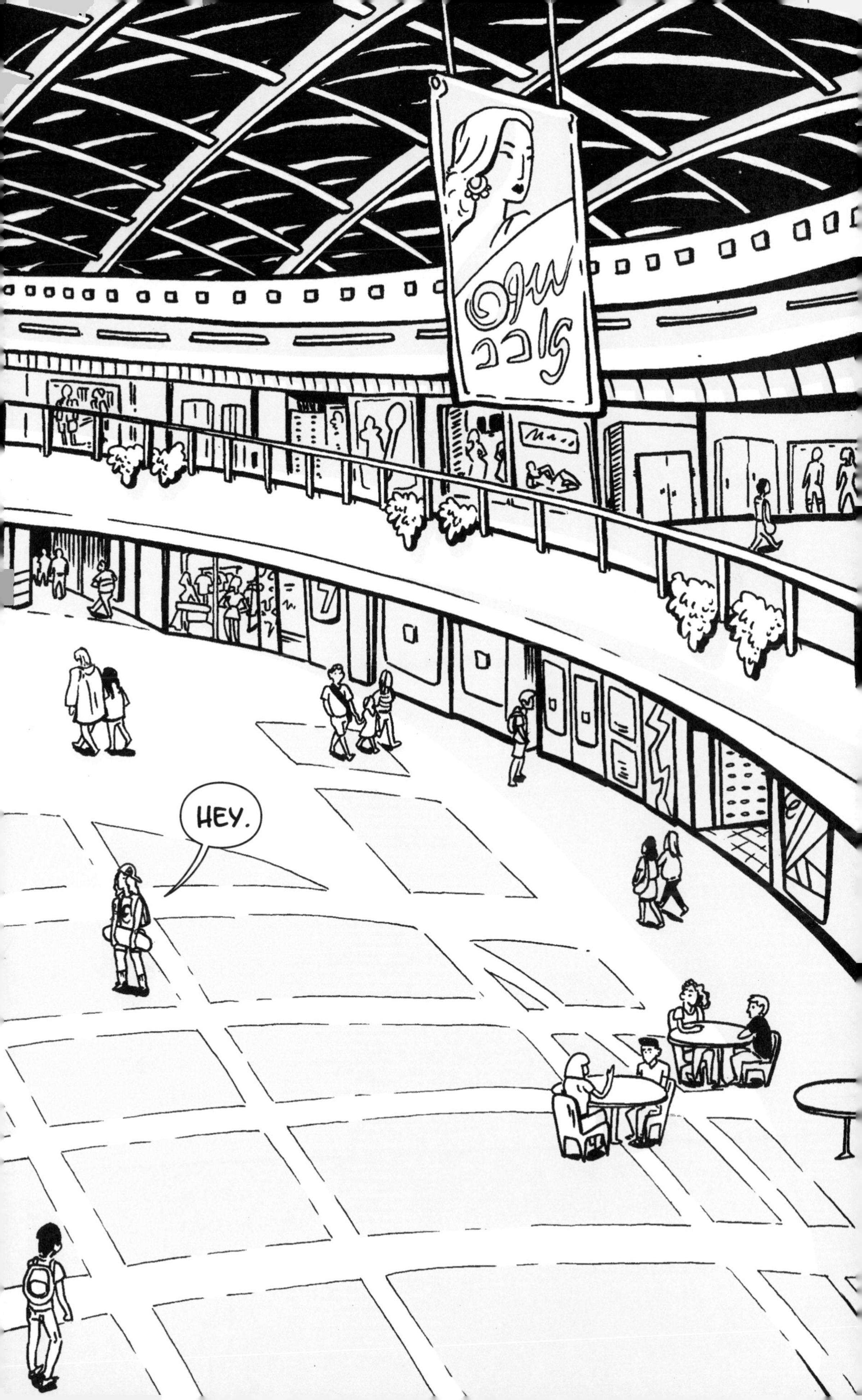
HEY.

TEENAGE SWITCHBLADE

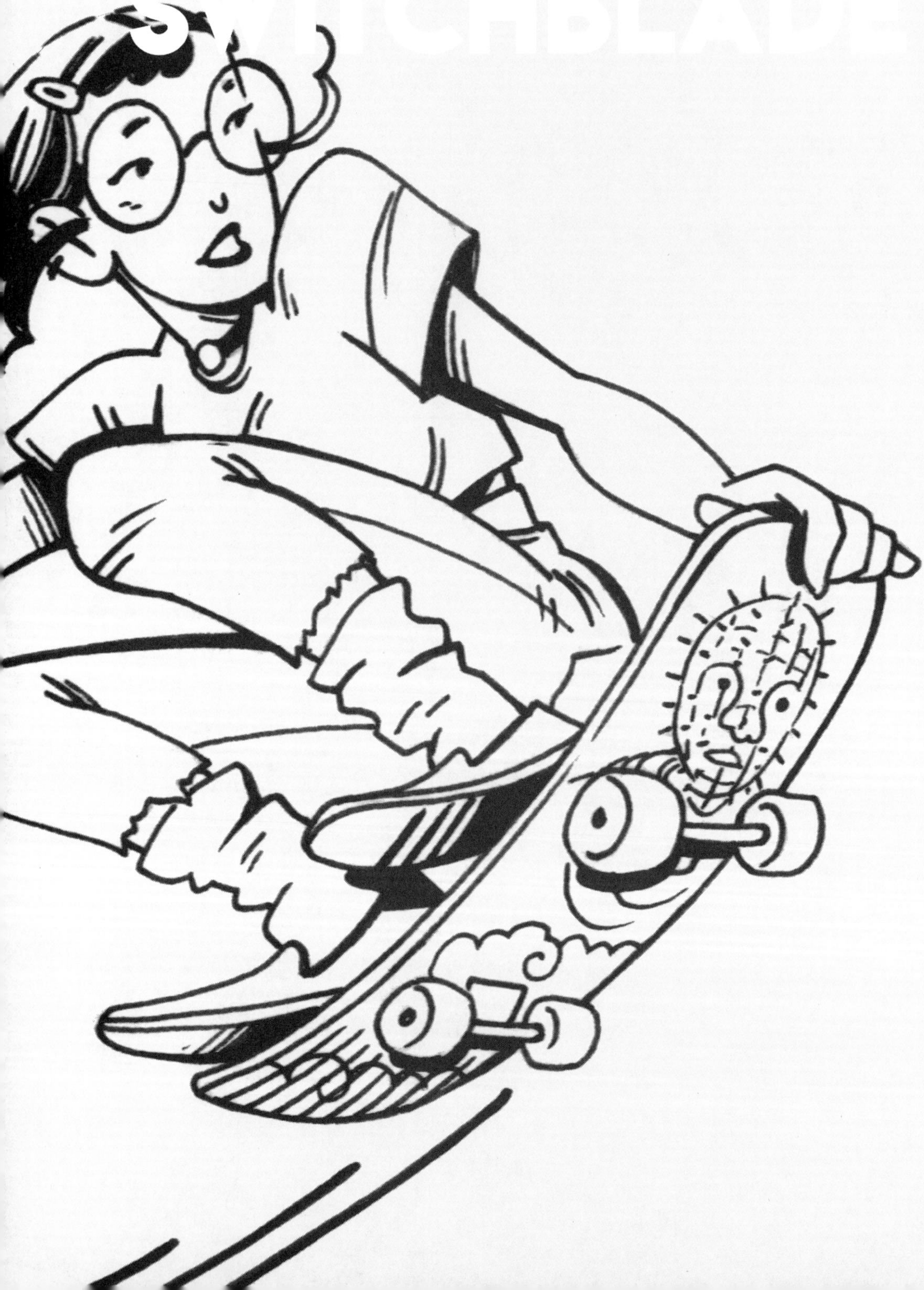

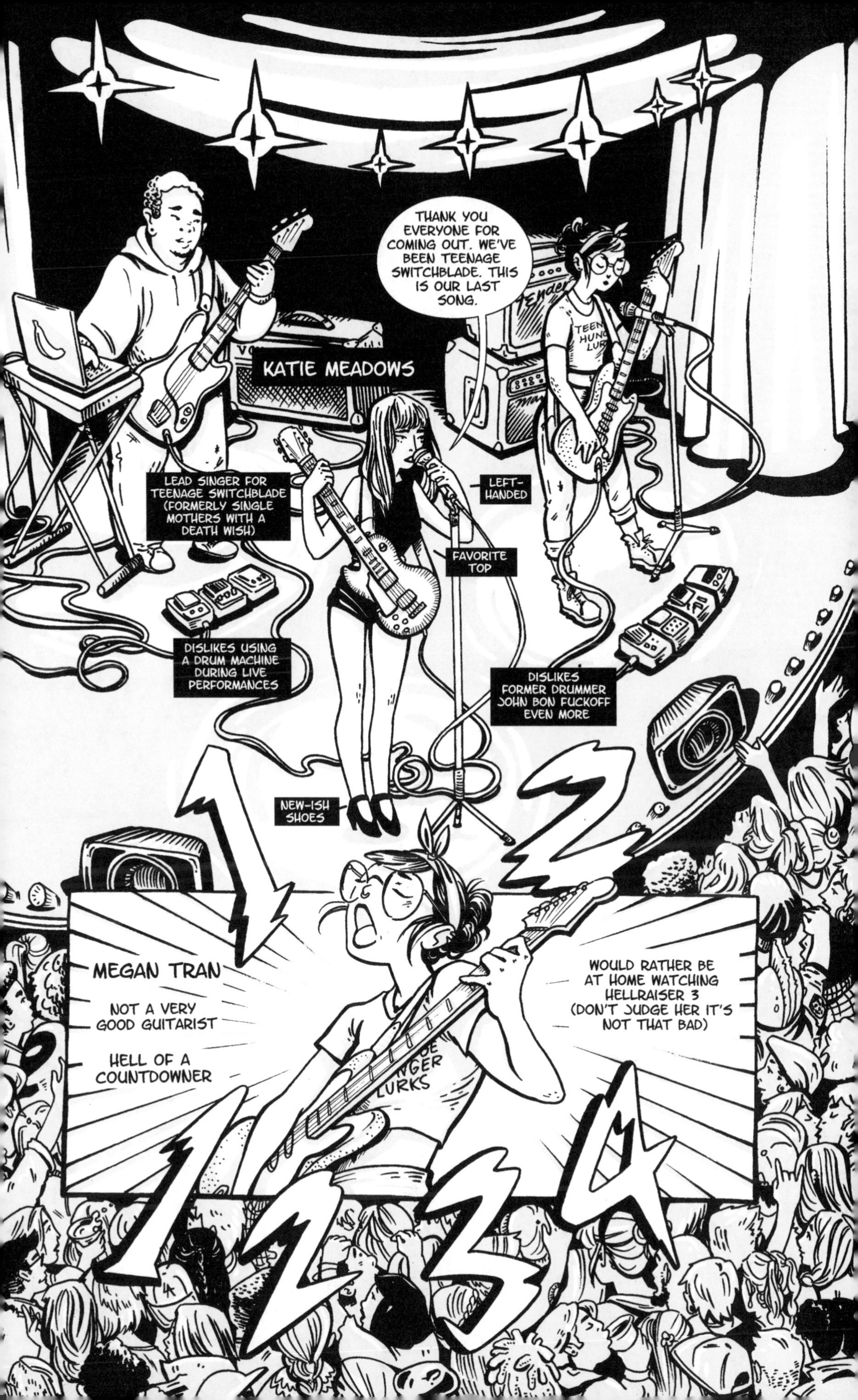
THANK YOU EVERYONE FOR COMING OUT. WE'VE BEEN TEENAGE SWITCHBLADE. THIS IS OUR LAST SONG.
KATIE MEADOWS
LEAD SINGER FOR TEENAGE SWITCHBLADE (FORMERLY SINGLE MOTHERS WITH A DEATH WISH)
LEFT-HANDED
FAVORITE TOP
DISLIKES USING A DRUM MACHINE DURING LIVE PERFORMANCES
DISLIKES FORMER DRUMMER JOHN BON FUCKOFF EVEN MORE
NEW-ISH SHOES
MEGAN TRAN
NOT A VERY GOOD GUITARIST
HELL OF A COUNTDOWNER
WOULD RATHER BE AT HOME WATCHING HELLRAISER 3 (DON'T JUDGE HER IT'S NOT THAT BAD)
1 2 3 4

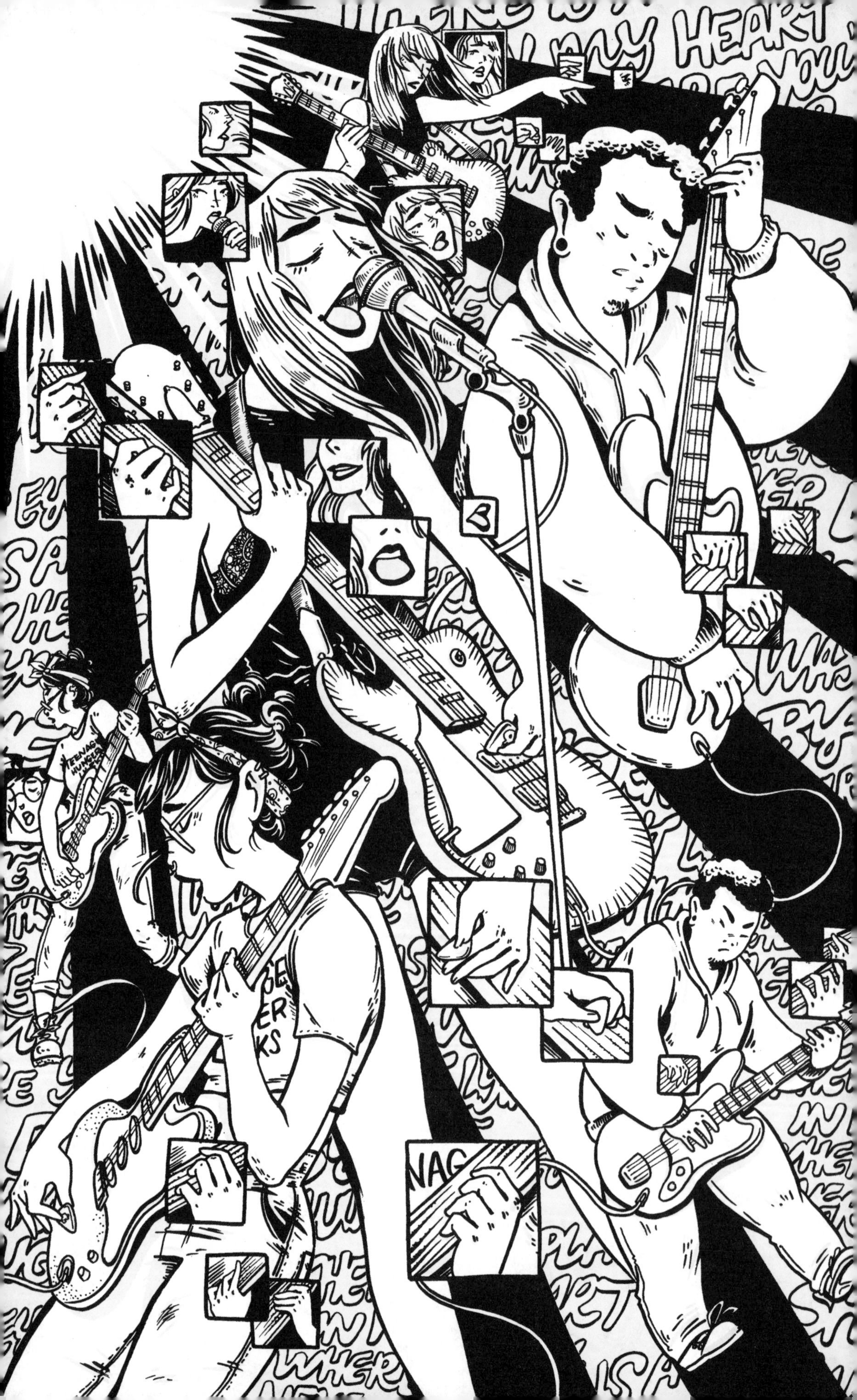
MY HEART

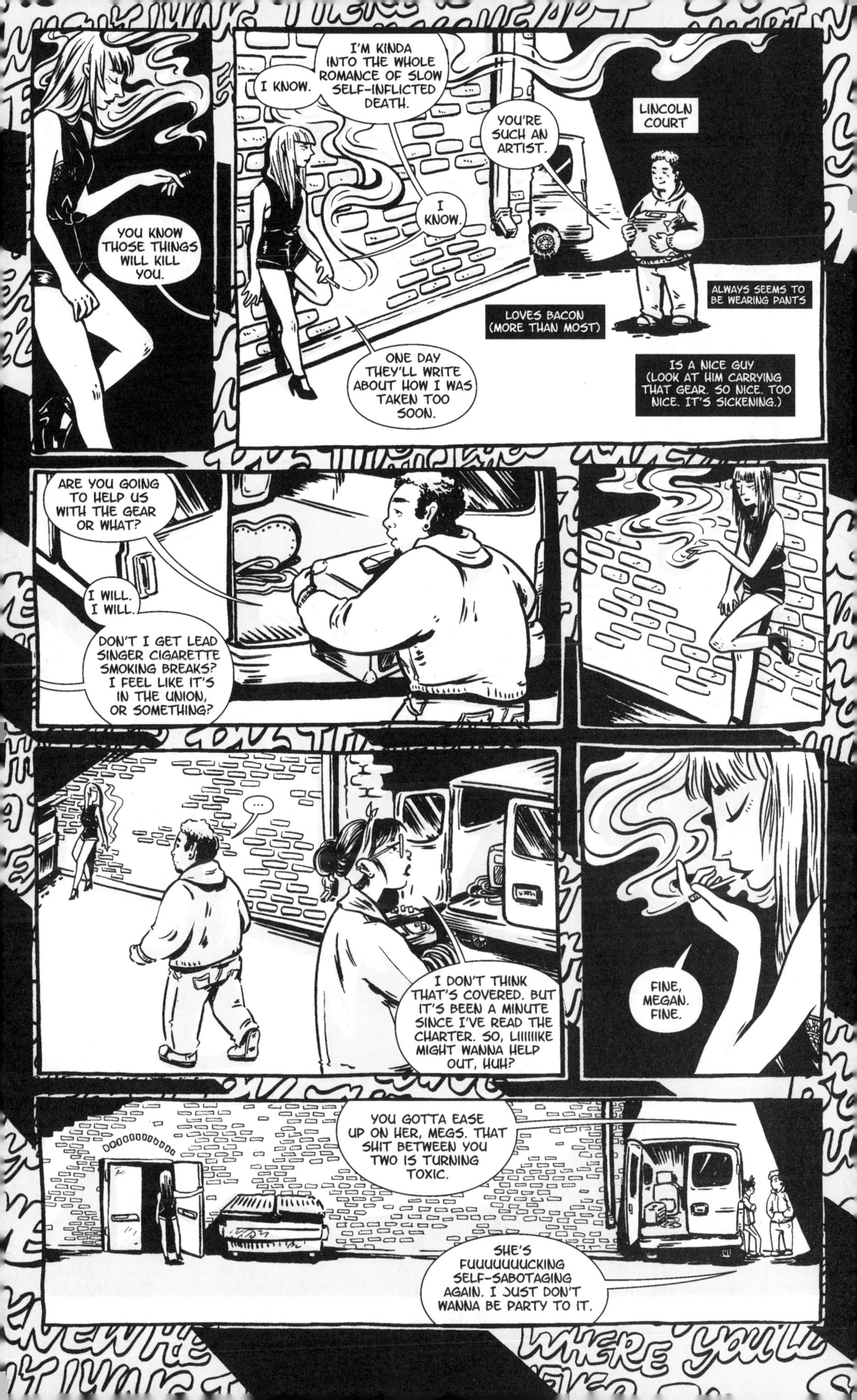
YOU KNOW THOSE THINGS WILL KILL YOU.
I KNOW.
I'M KINDA INTO THE WHOLE ROMANCE OF SLOW SELF-INFLICTED DEATH.
YOU'RE SUCH AN ARTIST.
I KNOW.
ONE DAY THEY'LL WRITE ABOUT HOW I WAS TAKEN TOO SOON.
LINCOLN COURT
ALWAYS SEEMS TO BE WEARING PANTS
LOVES BACON (MORE THAN MOST)
IS A NICE GUY (LOOK AT HIM CARRYING THAT GEAR. SO NICE. TOO NICE. IT'S SICKENING.)
ARE YOU GOING TO HELP US WITH THE GEAR OR WHAT?
I WILL. I WILL.
DON'T I GET LEAD SINGER CIGARETTE SMOKING BREAKS? I FEEL LIKE IT'S IN THE UNION, OR SOMETHING?
...
I DON'T THINK THAT'S COVERED. BUT IT'S BEEN A MINUTE SINCE I'VE READ THE CHARTER. SO, LIIIIIIKE MIGHT WANNA HELP OUT, HUH?
FINE, MEGAN. FINE.
YOU GOTTA EASE UP ON HER, MEGS. THAT SHIT BETWEEN YOU TWO IS TURNING TOXIC.
SHE'S FUUUUUUCKING SELF-SABOTAGING AGAIN. I JUST DON'T WANNA BE PARTY TO IT.

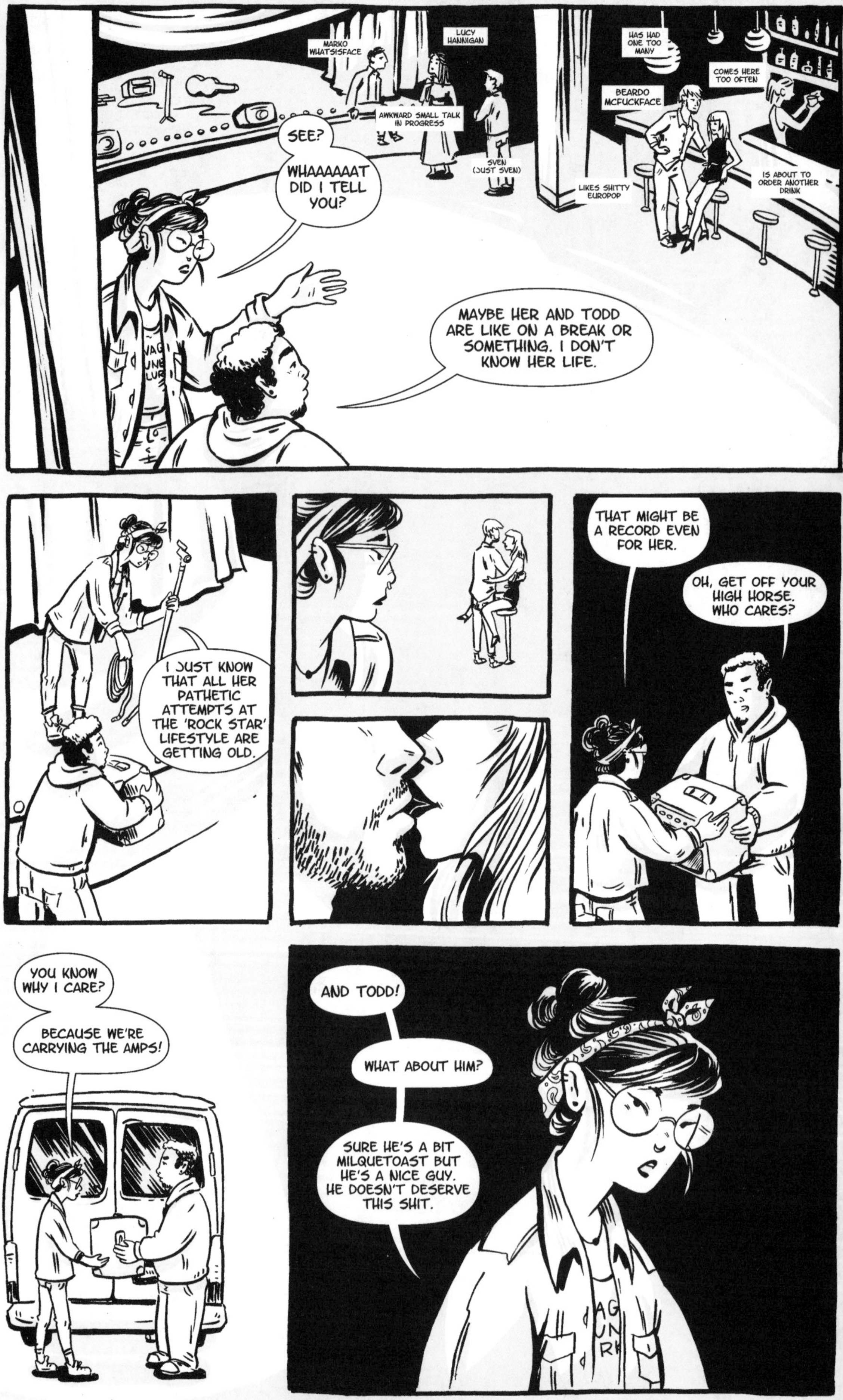
MARKO WHATSISFACE
LUCY HANNIGAN
HAS HAD ONE TOO MANY
COMES HERE TOO OFTEN
BEARDO MCFUCKFACE
AWKWARD SMALL TALK IN PROGRESS
SEE?
WHAAAAAAT DID I TELL YOU?
SVEN (JUST SVEN)
LIKES SHITTY EUROPOP
IS ABOUT TO ORDER ANOTHER DRINK
MAYBE HER AND TODD ARE LIKE ON A BREAK OR SOMETHING. I DON'T KNOW HER LIFE.
I JUST KNOW THAT ALL HER PATHETIC ATTEMPTS AT THE 'ROCK STAR' LIFESTYLE ARE GETTING OLD.
THAT MIGHT BE A RECORD EVEN FOR HER.
OH, GET OFF YOUR HIGH HORSE. WHO CARES?
YOU KNOW WHY I CARE?
BECAUSE WE'RE CARRYING THE AMPS!
AND TODD!
WHAT ABOUT HIM?
SURE HE'S A BIT MILQUETOAST BUT HE'S A NICE GUY. HE DOESN'T DESERVE THIS SHIT.

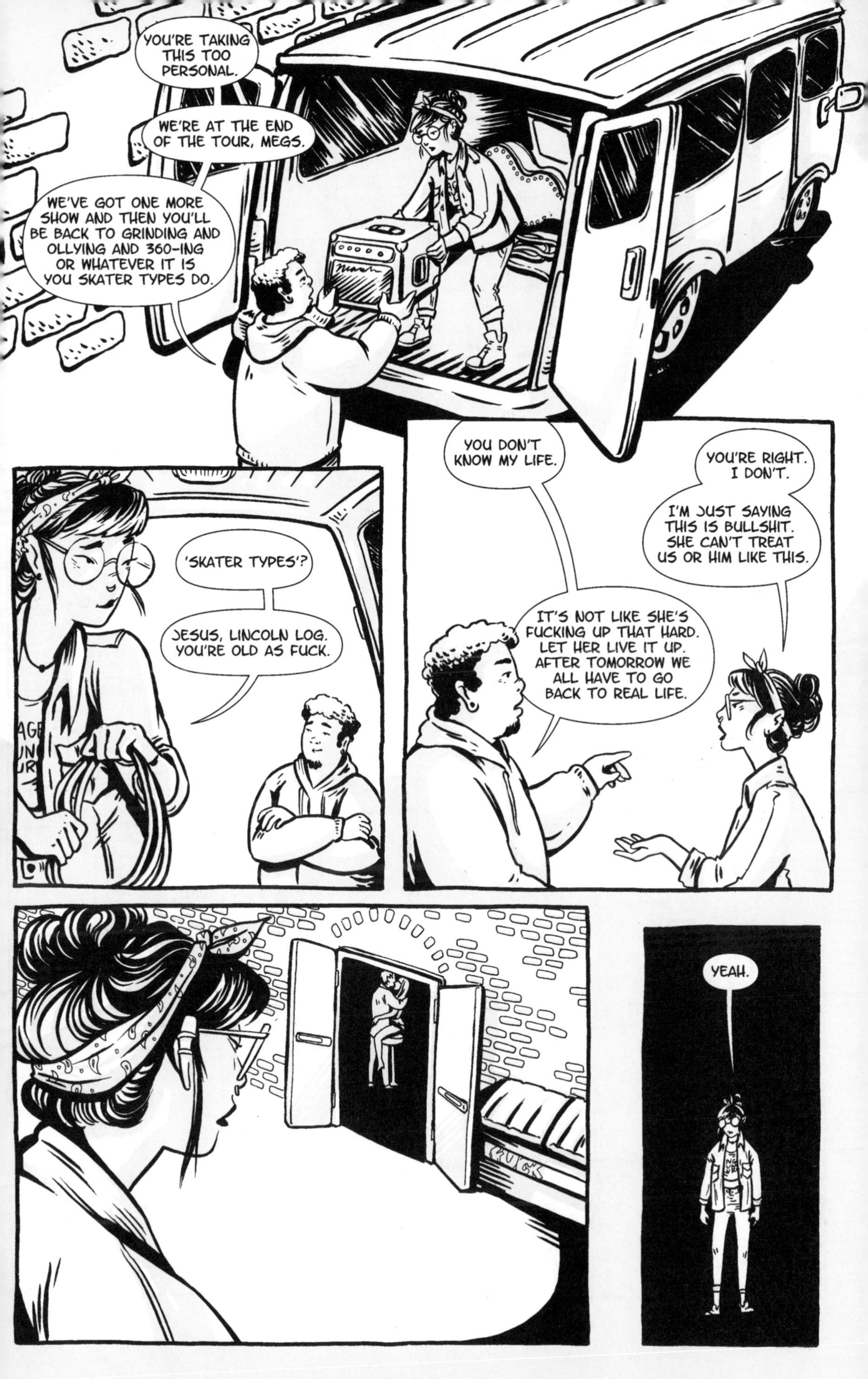
YOU'RE TAKING THIS TOO PERSONAL.
WE'RE AT THE END OF THE TOUR, MEGS.
WE'VE GOT ONE MORE SHOW AND THEN YOU'LL BE BACK TO GRINDING AND OLLYING AND 360-ING OR WHATEVER IT IS YOU SKATER TYPES DO.
'SKATER TYPES'?
JESUS, LINCOLN LOG. YOU'RE OLD AS FUCK.
YOU DON'T KNOW MY LIFE.
YOU'RE RIGHT. I DON'T.
I'M JUST SAYING THIS IS BULLSHIT. SHE CAN'T TREAT US OR HIM LIKE THIS.
IT'S NOT LIKE SHE'S FUCKING UP THAT HARD. LET HER LIVE IT UP. AFTER TOMORROW WE ALL HAVE TO GO BACK TO REAL LIFE.
YEAH.

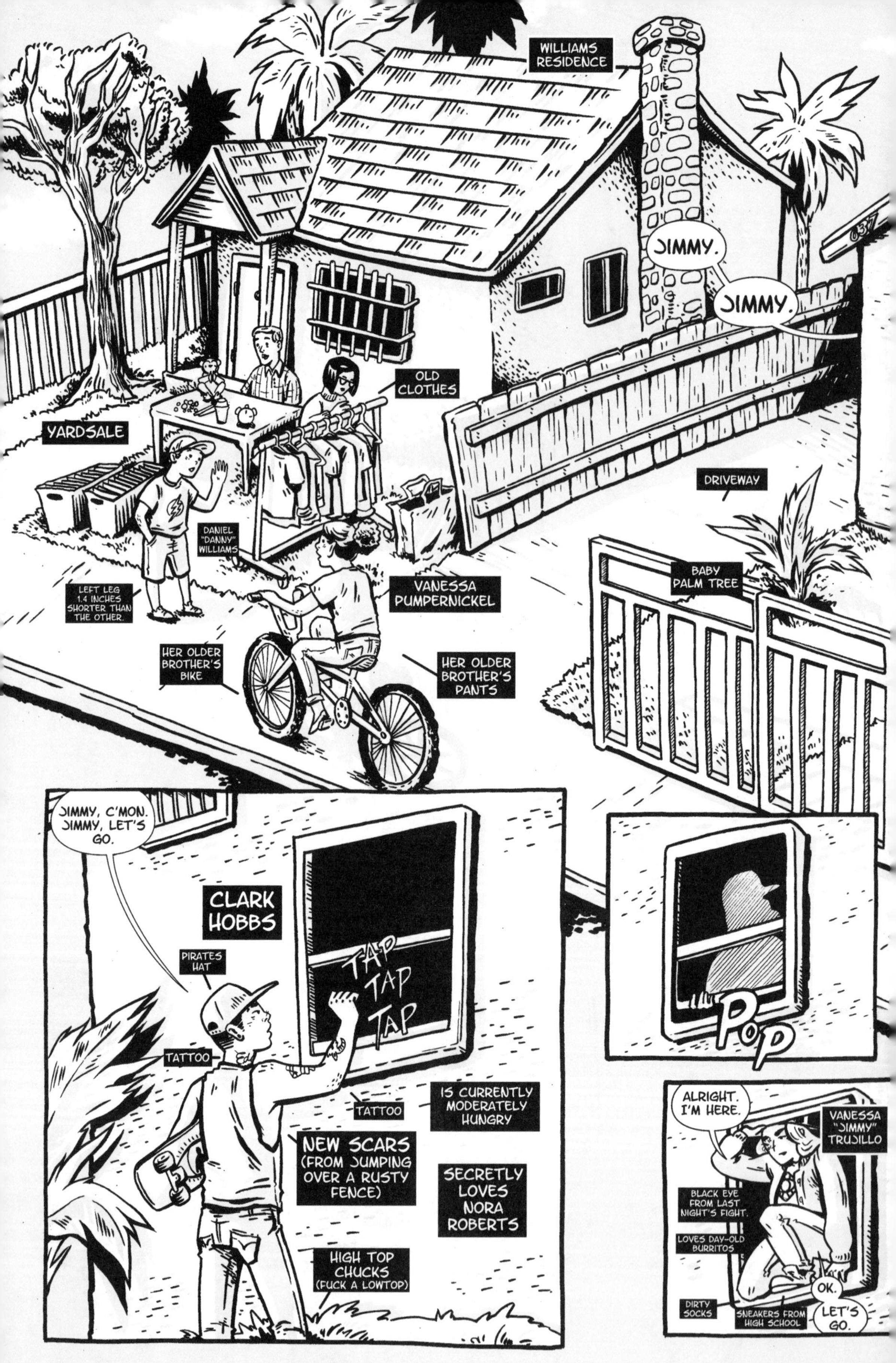

WILLIAMS RESIDENCE
JIMMY.
JIMMY.
YARDSALE
OLD CLOTHES
DRIVEWAY
DANIEL "DANNY" WILLIAMS
LEFT LEG 1.4 INCHES SHORTER THAN THE OTHER.
VANESSA PUMPERNICKEL
BABY PALM TREE
HER OLDER BROTHER'S BIKE
HER OLDER BROTHER'S PANTS
JIMMY, C'MON. JIMMY, LET'S GO.
CLARK HOBBS
PIRATES HAT
TAP TAP TAP
TATTOO
TATTOO
IS CURRENTLY MODERATELY HUNGRY
NEW SCARS (FROM JUMPING OVER A RUSTY FENCE)
SECRETLY LOVES NORA ROBERTS
HIGH TOP CHUCKS (FUCK A LOWTOP)
POP
ALRIGHT. I'M HERE.
VANESSA "JIMMY" TRUJILLO
BLACK EYE FROM LAST NIGHT'S FIGHT.
LOVES DAY-OLD BURRITOS
DIRTY SOCKS
SNEAKERS FROM HIGH SCHOOL
OK.
LET'S GO.

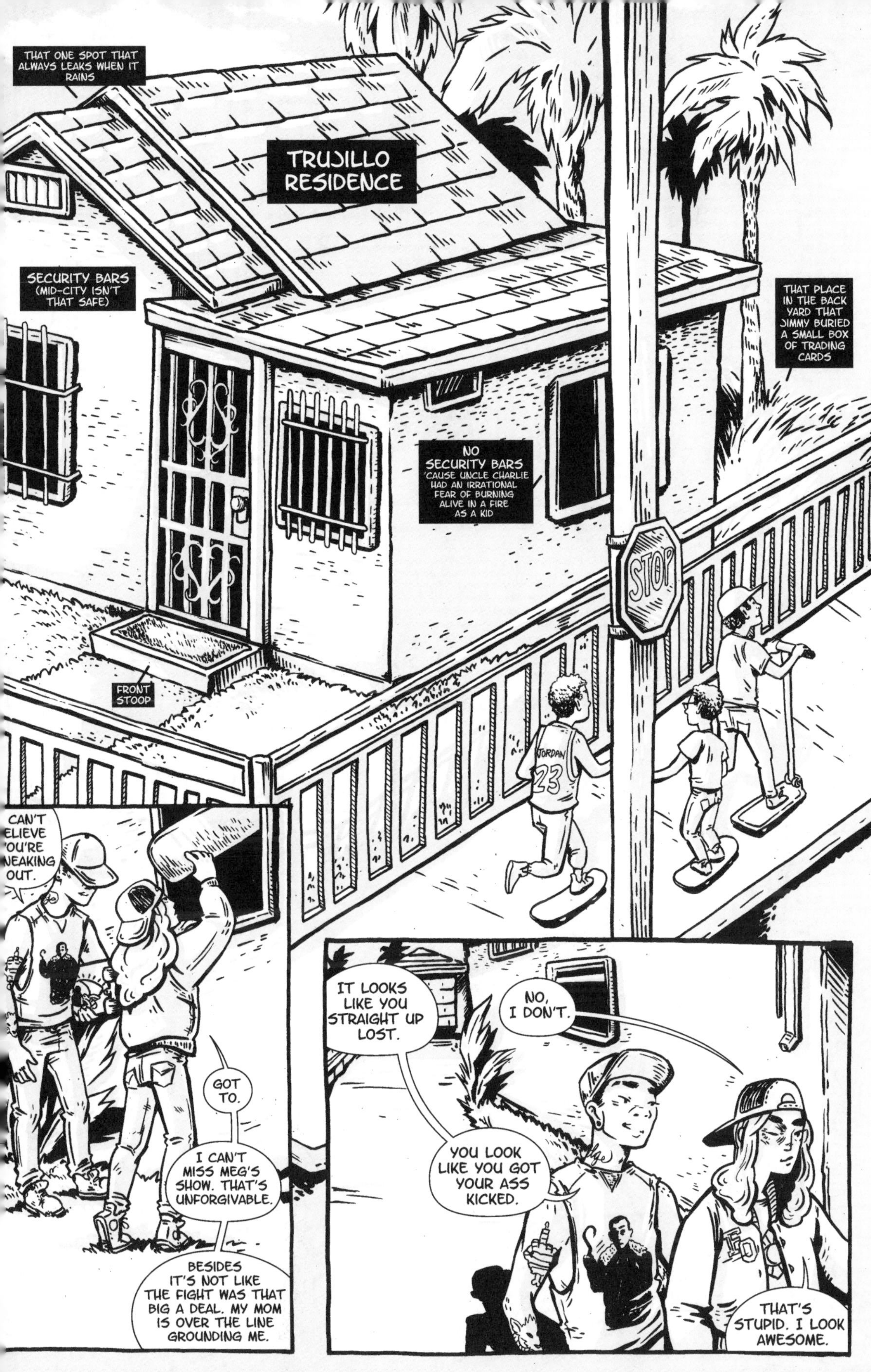
THAT ONE SPOT THAT ALWAYS LEAKS WHEN IT RAINS
TRUJILLO RESIDENCE
SECURITY BARS (MID-CITY ISN'T THAT SAFE)
THAT PLACE IN THE BACK YARD THAT JIMMY BURIED A SMALL BOX OF TRADING CARDS
NO SECURITY BARS 'CAUSE UNCLE CHARLIE HAD AN IRRATIONAL FEAR OF BURNING ALIVE IN A FIRE AS A KID
STOP
FRONT STOOP
JORDAN 23
CAN'T ELIEVE OU'RE NEAKING OUT.
GOT TO.
I CAN'T MISS MEG'S SHOW. THAT'S UNFORGIVABLE.
BESIDES IT'S NOT LIKE THE FIGHT WAS THAT BIG A DEAL. MY MOM IS OVER THE LINE GROUNDING ME.
IT LOOKS LIKE YOU STRAIGHT UP LOST.
NO, I DON'T.
YOU LOOK LIKE YOU GOT YOUR ASS KICKED.
THAT'S STUPID. I LOOK AWESOME.

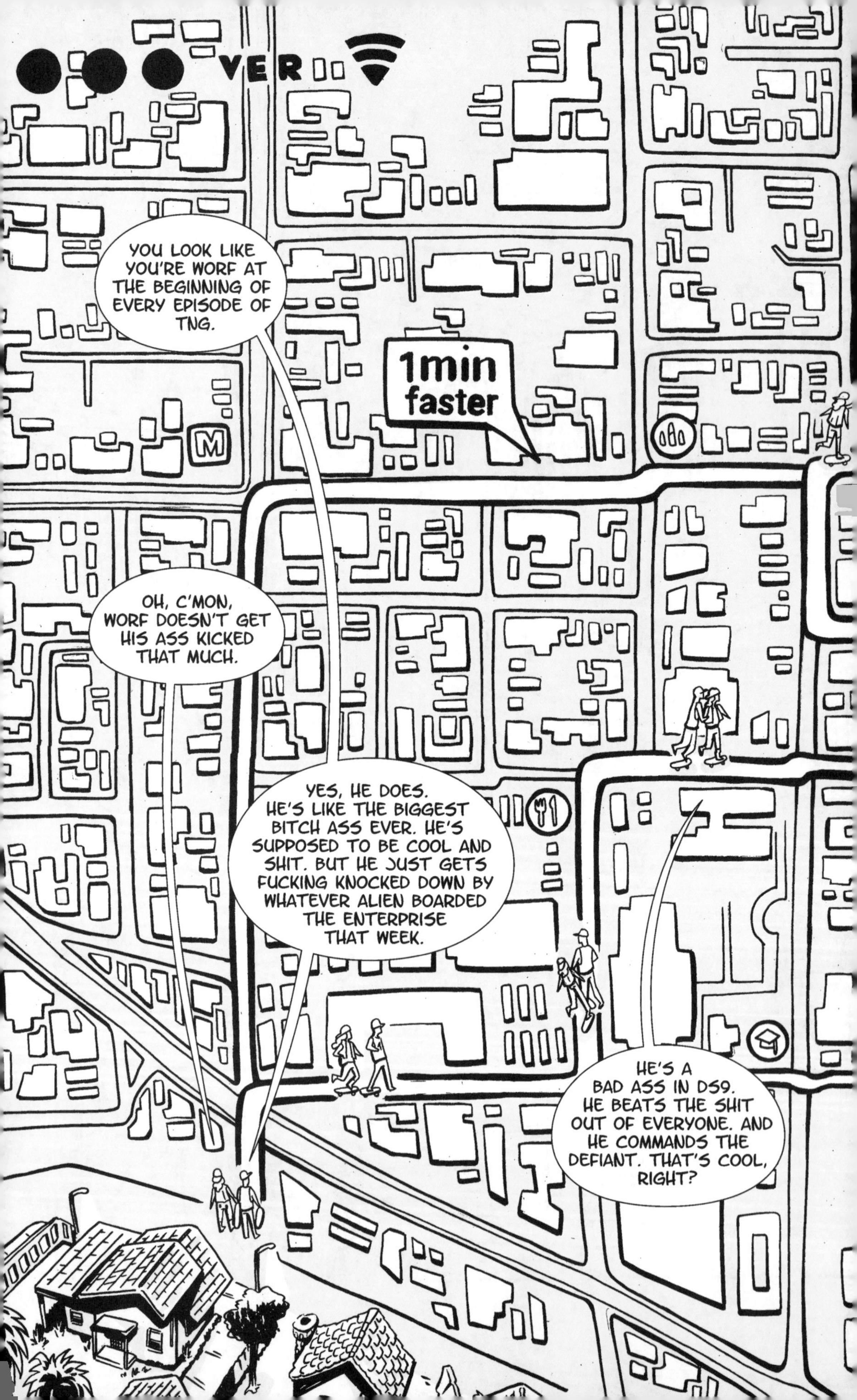
VER
YOU LOOK LIKE YOU'RE WORF AT THE BEGINNING OF EVERY EPISODE OF TNG.
1min faster
OH, C'MON, WORF DOESN'T GET HIS ASS KICKED THAT MUCH.
YES, HE DOES. HE'S LIKE THE BIGGEST BITCH ASS EVER. HE'S SUPPOSED TO BE COOL AND SHIT. BUT HE JUST GETS FUCKING KNOCKED DOWN BY WHATEVER ALIEN BOARDED THE ENTERPRISE THAT WEEK.
HE'S A BAD ASS IN DS9. HE BEATS THE SHIT OUT OF EVERYONE. AND HE COMMANDS THE DEFIANT. THAT'S COOL, RIGHT?

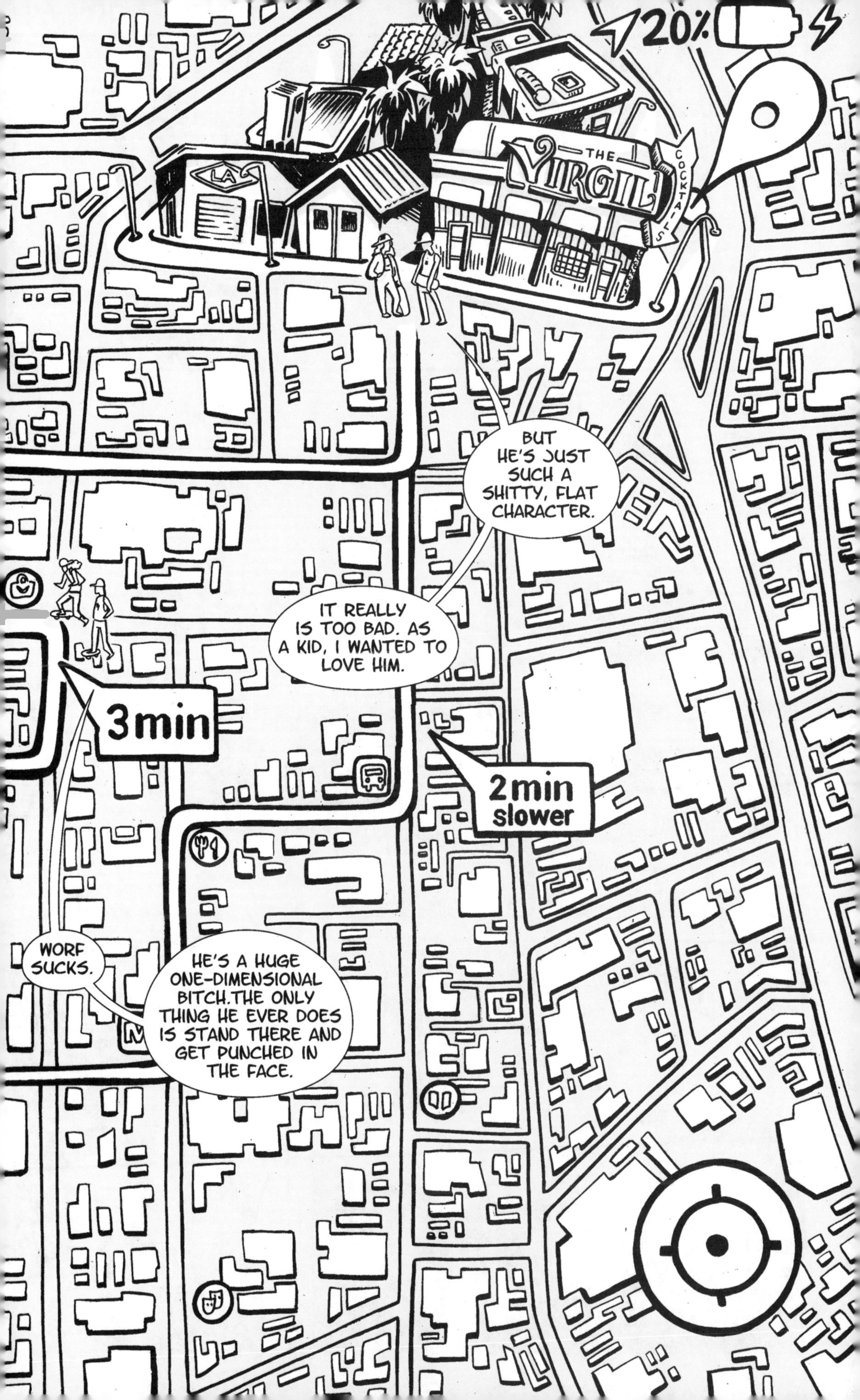
20%
THE VIRGIL
COCKTAILS
LA
BUT HE'S JUST SUCH A SHITTY, FLAT CHARACTER.
IT REALLY IS TOO BAD. AS A KID, I WANTED TO LOVE HIM.
3min
2min slower
WORF SUCKS.
HE'S A HUGE ONE-DIMENSIONAL BITCH. THE ONLY THING HE EVER DOES IS STAND THERE AND GET PUNCHED IN THE FACE.

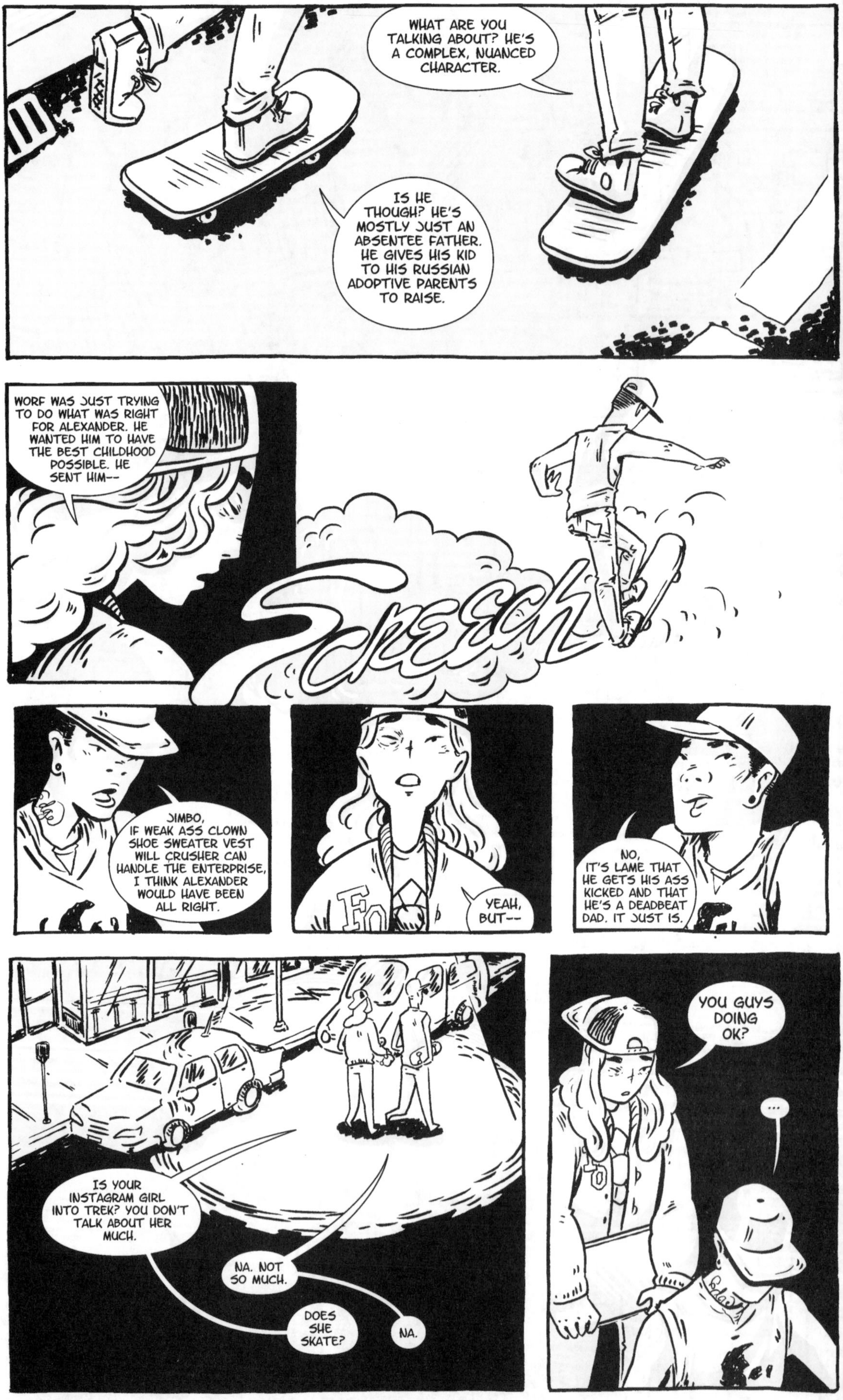
WHAT ARE YOU TALKING ABOUT? HE'S A COMPLEX, NUANCED CHARACTER.
IS HE THOUGH? HE'S MOSTLY JUST AN ABSENTEE FATHER. HE GIVES HIS KID TO HIS RUSSIAN ADOPTIVE PARENTS TO RAISE.
WORF WAS JUST TRYING TO DO WHAT WAS RIGHT FOR ALEXANDER. HE WANTED HIM TO HAVE THE BEST CHILDHOOD POSSIBLE. HE SENT HIM--
SCREECH
JIMBO, IF WEAK ASS CLOWN SHOE SWEATER VEST WILL CRUSHER CAN HANDLE THE ENTERPRISE, I THINK ALEXANDER WOULD HAVE BEEN ALL RIGHT.
YEAH, BUT--
NO, IT'S LAME THAT HE GETS HIS ASS KICKED AND THAT HE'S A DEADBEAT DAD. IT JUST IS.
IS YOUR INSTAGRAM GIRL INTO TREK? YOU DON'T TALK ABOUT HER MUCH.
NA. NOT SO MUCH.
DOES SHE SKATE?
NA.
YOU GUYS DOING OK?
...

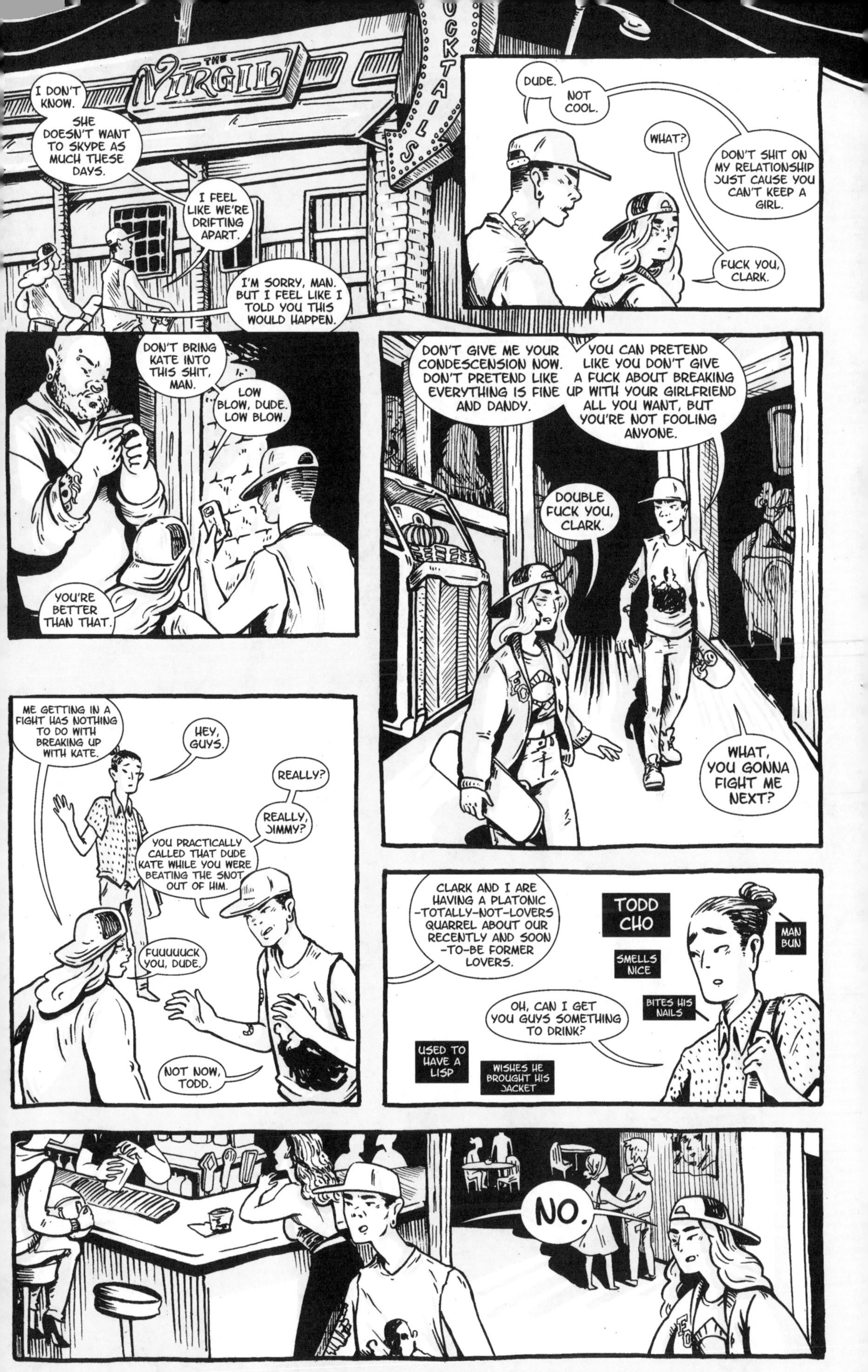
THE VIRGIL
COCKTAILS
I DON'T KNOW.
SHE DOESN'T WANT TO SKYPE AS MUCH THESE DAYS.
I FEEL LIKE WE'RE DRIFTING APART.
I'M SORRY, MAN. BUT I FEEL LIKE I TOLD YOU THIS WOULD HAPPEN.
DUDE.
NOT COOL.
WHAT?
DON'T SHIT ON MY RELATIONSHIP JUST CAUSE YOU CAN'T KEEP A GIRL.
FUCK YOU, CLARK.
DON'T BRING KATE INTO THIS SHIT, MAN.
LOW BLOW, DUDE. LOW BLOW.
YOU'RE BETTER THAN THAT.
DON'T GIVE ME YOUR CONDESCENSION NOW. DON'T PRETEND LIKE EVERYTHING IS FINE AND DANDY.
YOU CAN PRETEND LIKE YOU DON'T GIVE A FUCK ABOUT BREAKING UP WITH YOUR GIRLFRIEND ALL YOU WANT, BUT YOU'RE NOT FOOLING ANYONE.
DOUBLE FUCK YOU, CLARK.
WHAT, YOU GONNA FIGHT ME NEXT?
ME GETTING IN A FIGHT HAS NOTHING TO DO WITH BREAKING UP WITH KATE.
HEY, GUYS.
REALLY?
REALLY, JIMMY?
YOU PRACTICALLY CALLED THAT DUDE KATE WHILE YOU WERE BEATING THE SNOT OUT OF HIM.
FUUUUUCK YOU, DUDE.
NOT NOW, TODD.
CLARK AND I ARE HAVING A PLATONIC -TOTALLY-NOT-LOVERS QUARREL ABOUT OUR RECENTLY AND SOON -TO-BE FORMER LOVERS.
TODD CHO
MAN BUN
SMELLS NICE
BITES HIS NAILS
OH, CAN I GET YOU GUYS SOMETHING TO DRINK?
USED TO HAVE A LISP
WISHES HE BROUGHT HIS JACKET
NO.

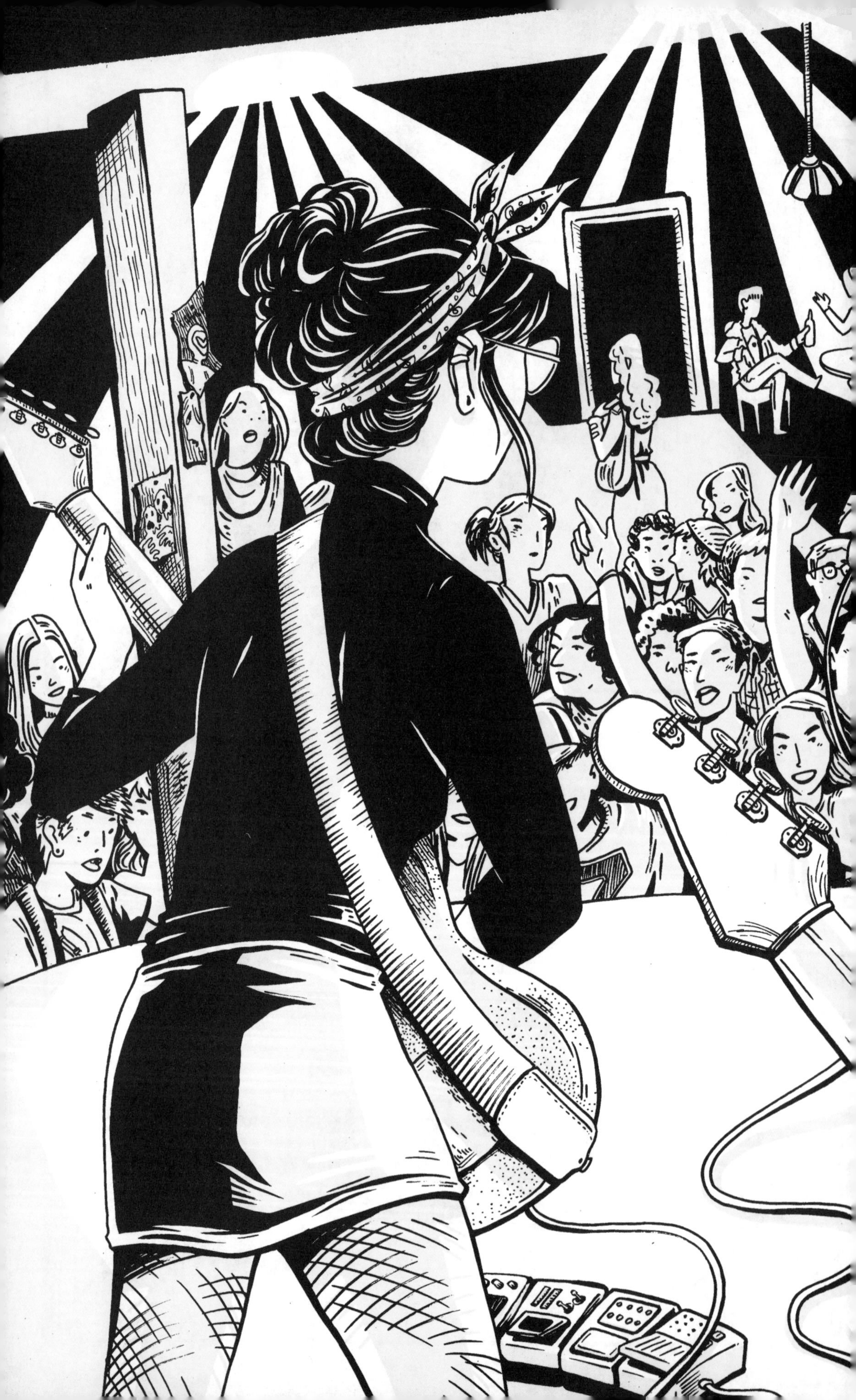

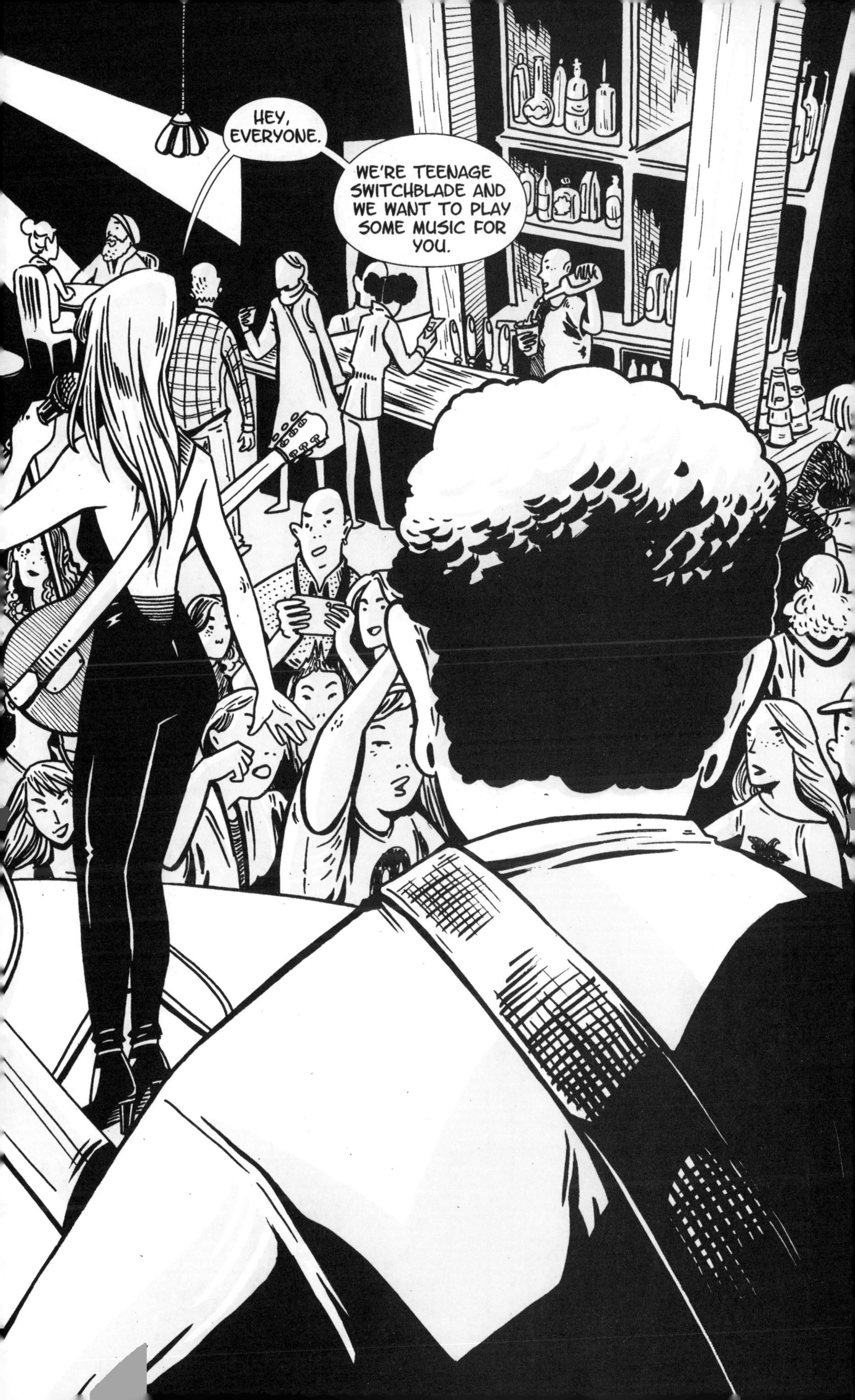
HEY, EVERYONE.
WE'RE TEENAGE SWITCHBLADE AND WE WANT TO PLAY SOME MUSIC FOR YOU.

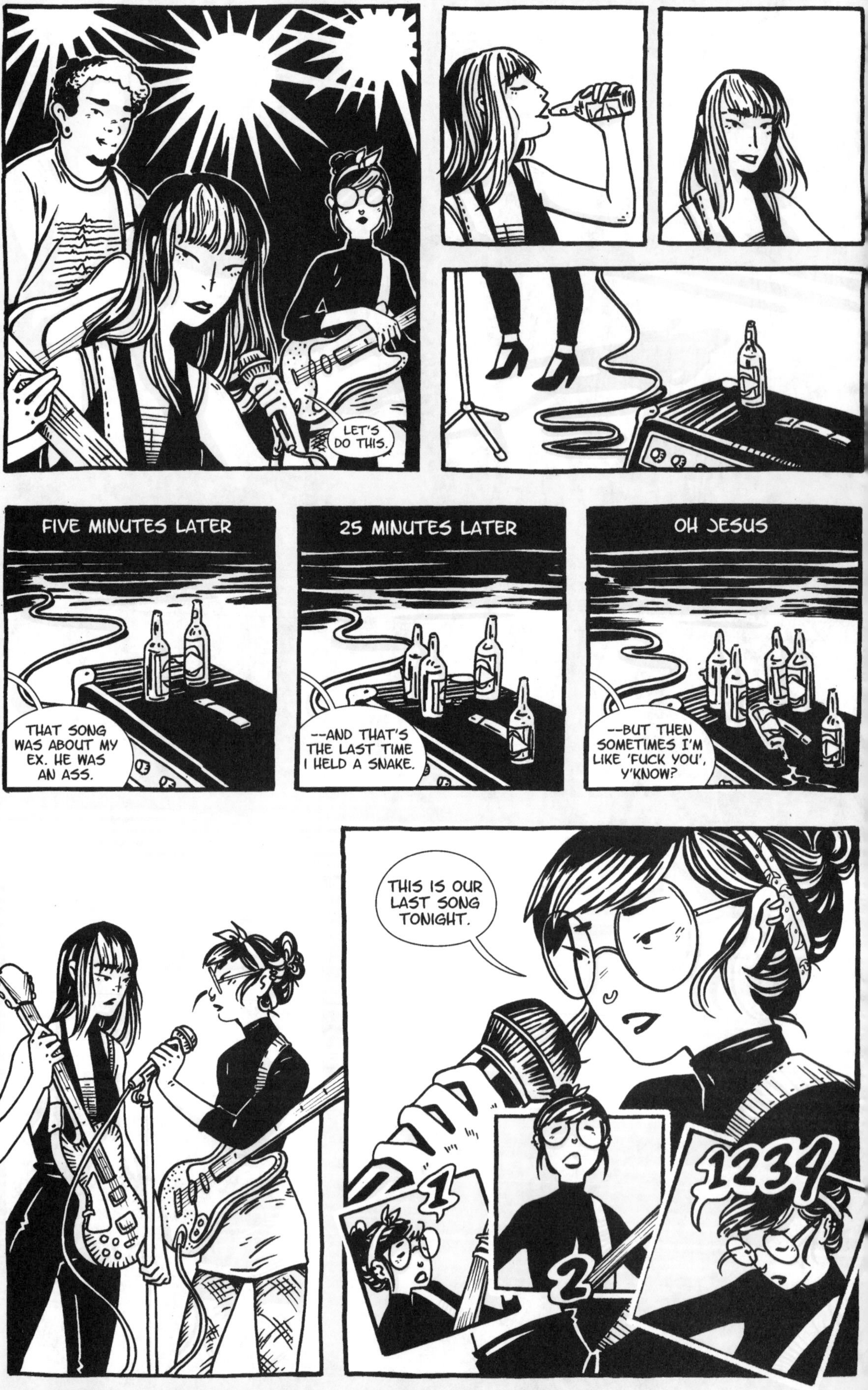
LET'S DO THIS.
FIVE MINUTES LATER
THAT SONG WAS ABOUT MY EX. HE WAS AN ASS.
25 MINUTES LATER
--AND THAT'S THE LAST TIME I HELD A SNAKE.
OH JESUS
--BUT THEN SOMETIMES I'M LIKE 'FUCK YOU', Y'KNOW?
THIS IS OUR LAST SONG TONIGHT.
1
2
1234

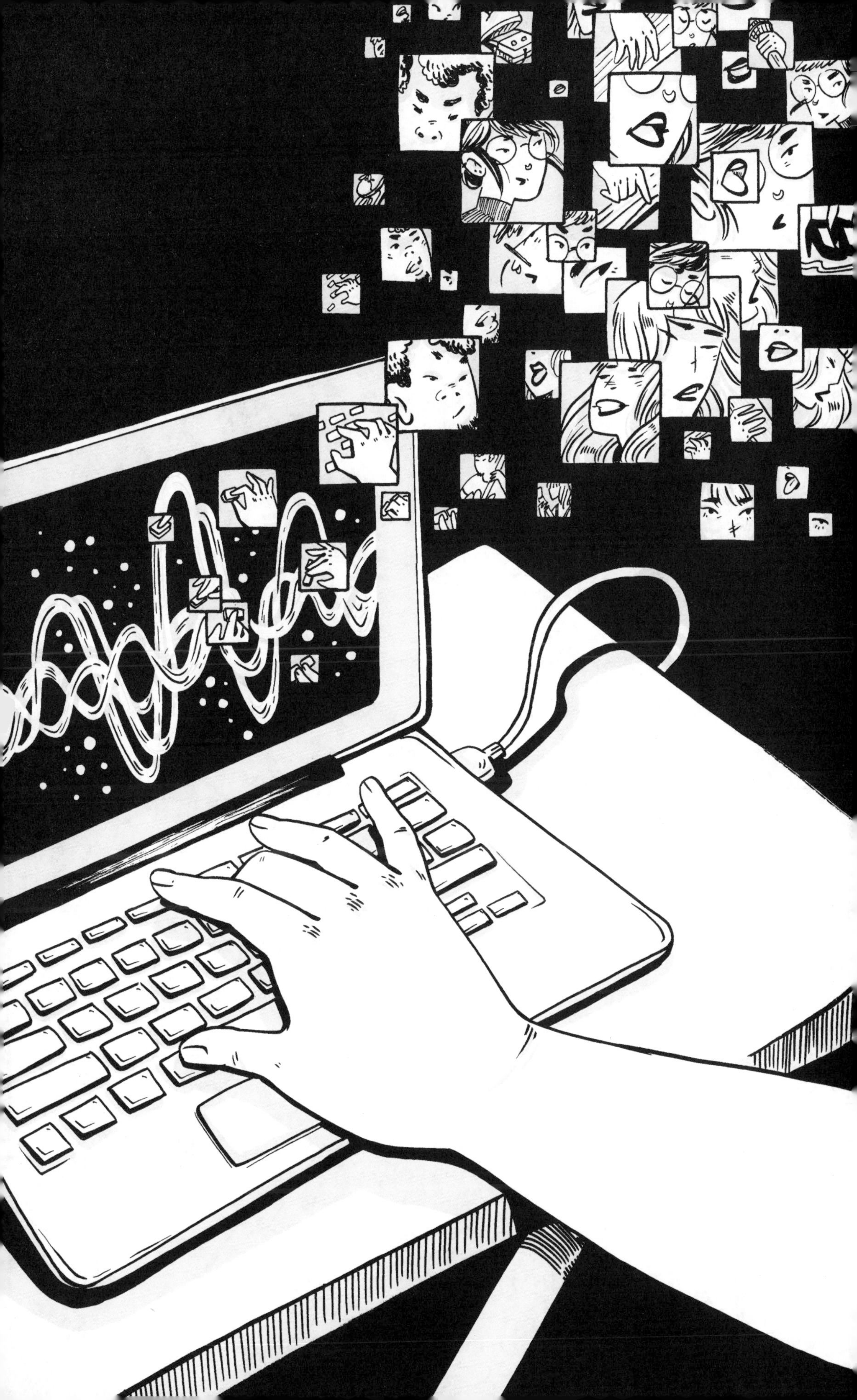

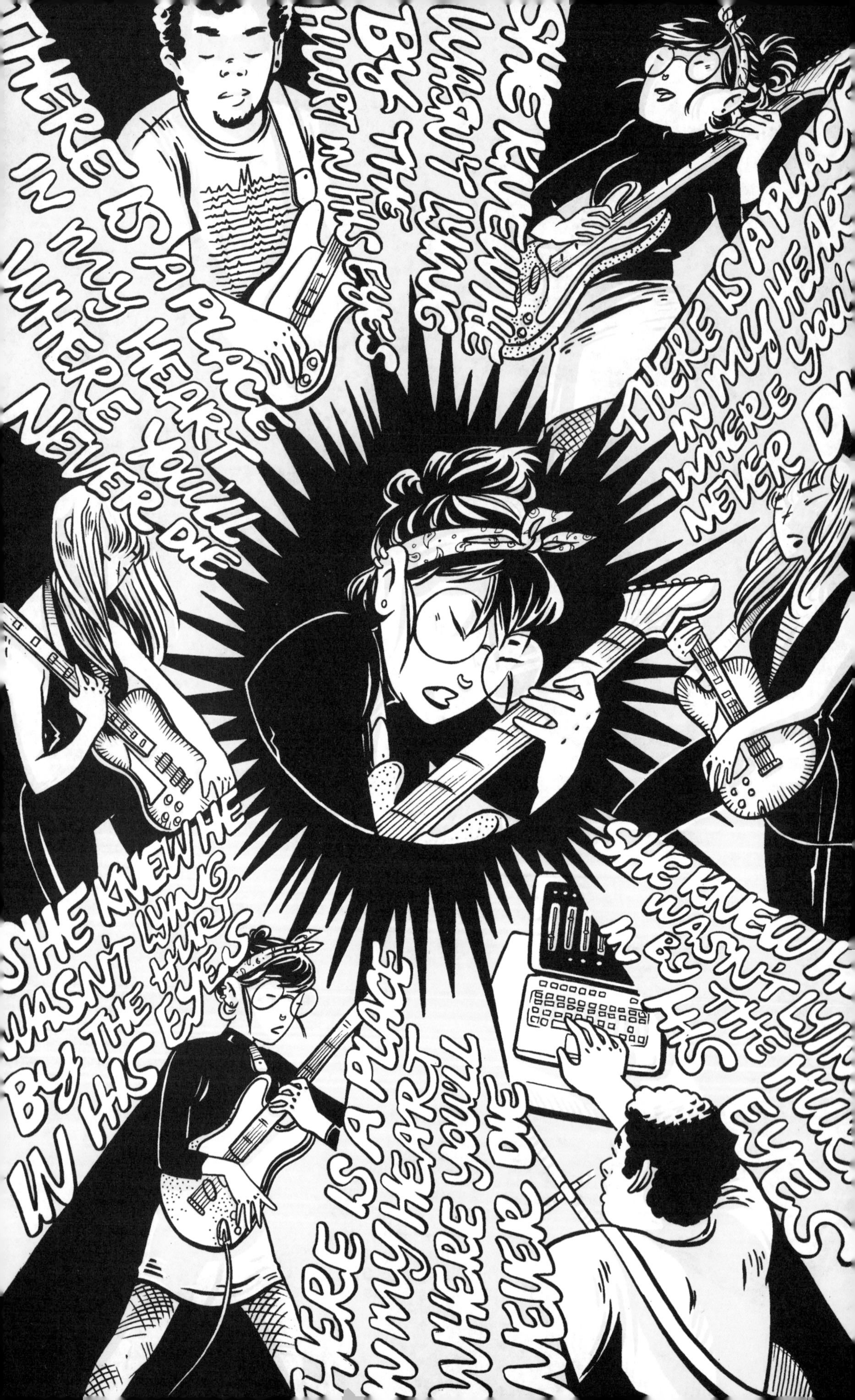

THERE IS A PLACE IN MY HEART WHERE YOU'LL NEVER DIE
SHE KNEW HE WASN'T LYING BY THE HURT IN HIS EYES
THERE IS A PLACE IN MY HEART WHERE YOU'LL NEVER D
SHE KNEW HE WASN'T LYING BY THE HURT IN HIS EYES
THERE IS A PLACE IN MY HEART WHERE YOU'LL NEVER DIE
SHE KNEW HE WASN'T LYING BY THE HURT IN HIS EYES

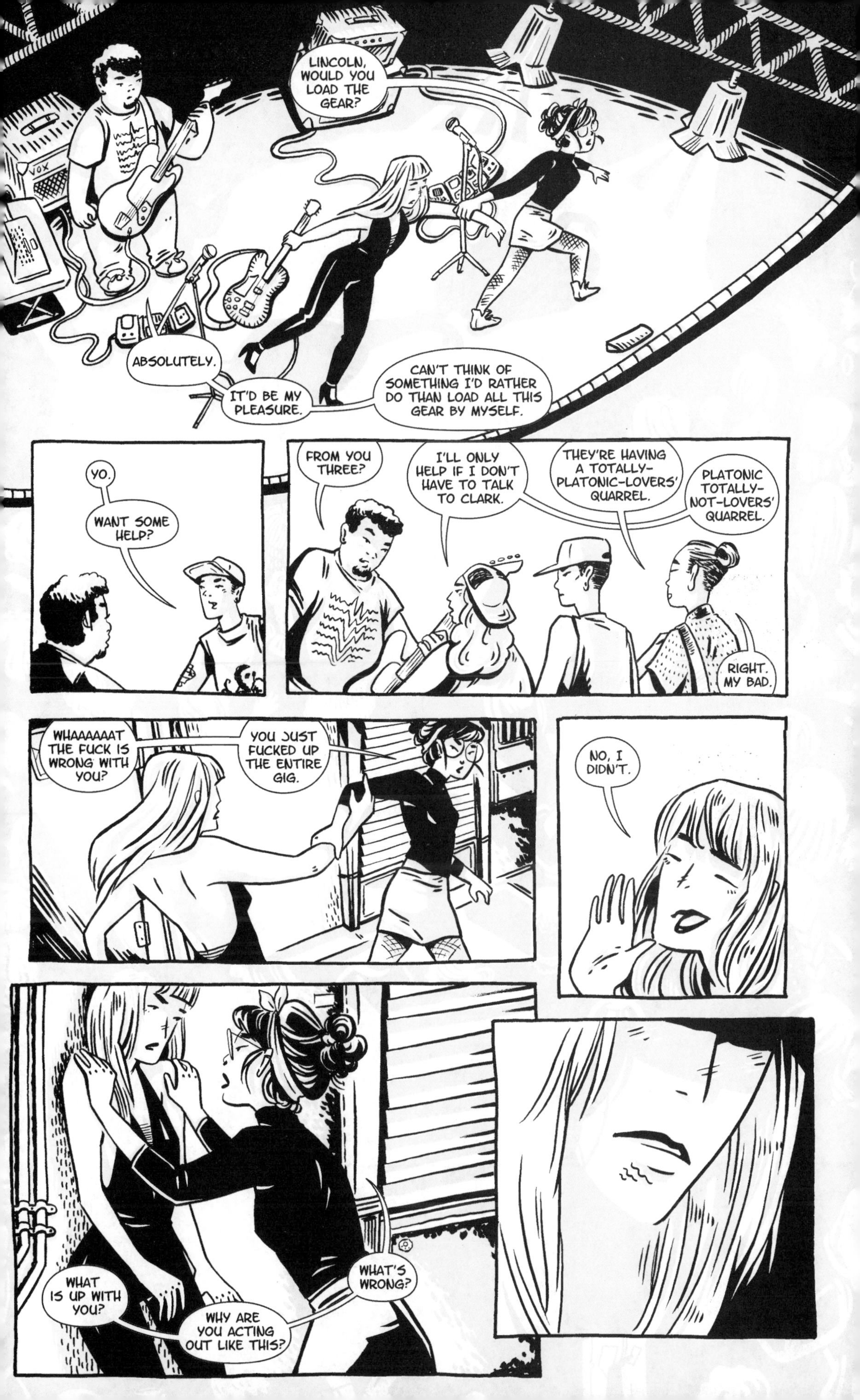
LINCOLN, WOULD YOU LOAD THE GEAR?
ABSOLUTELY.
IT'D BE MY PLEASURE.
CAN'T THINK OF SOMETHING I'D RATHER DO THAN LOAD ALL THIS GEAR BY MYSELF.
YO.
WANT SOME HELP?
FROM YOU THREE?
I'LL ONLY HELP IF I DON'T HAVE TO TALK TO CLARK.
THEY'RE HAVING A TOTALLY-PLATONIC-LOVERS' QUARREL.
PLATONIC TOTALLY-NOT-LOVERS' QUARREL.
RIGHT. MY BAD.
WHAAAAAAT THE FUCK IS WRONG WITH YOU?
YOU JUST FUCKED UP THE ENTIRE GIG.
NO, I DIDN'T.
WHAT IS UP WITH YOU?
WHY ARE YOU ACTING OUT LIKE THIS?
WHAT'S WRONG?

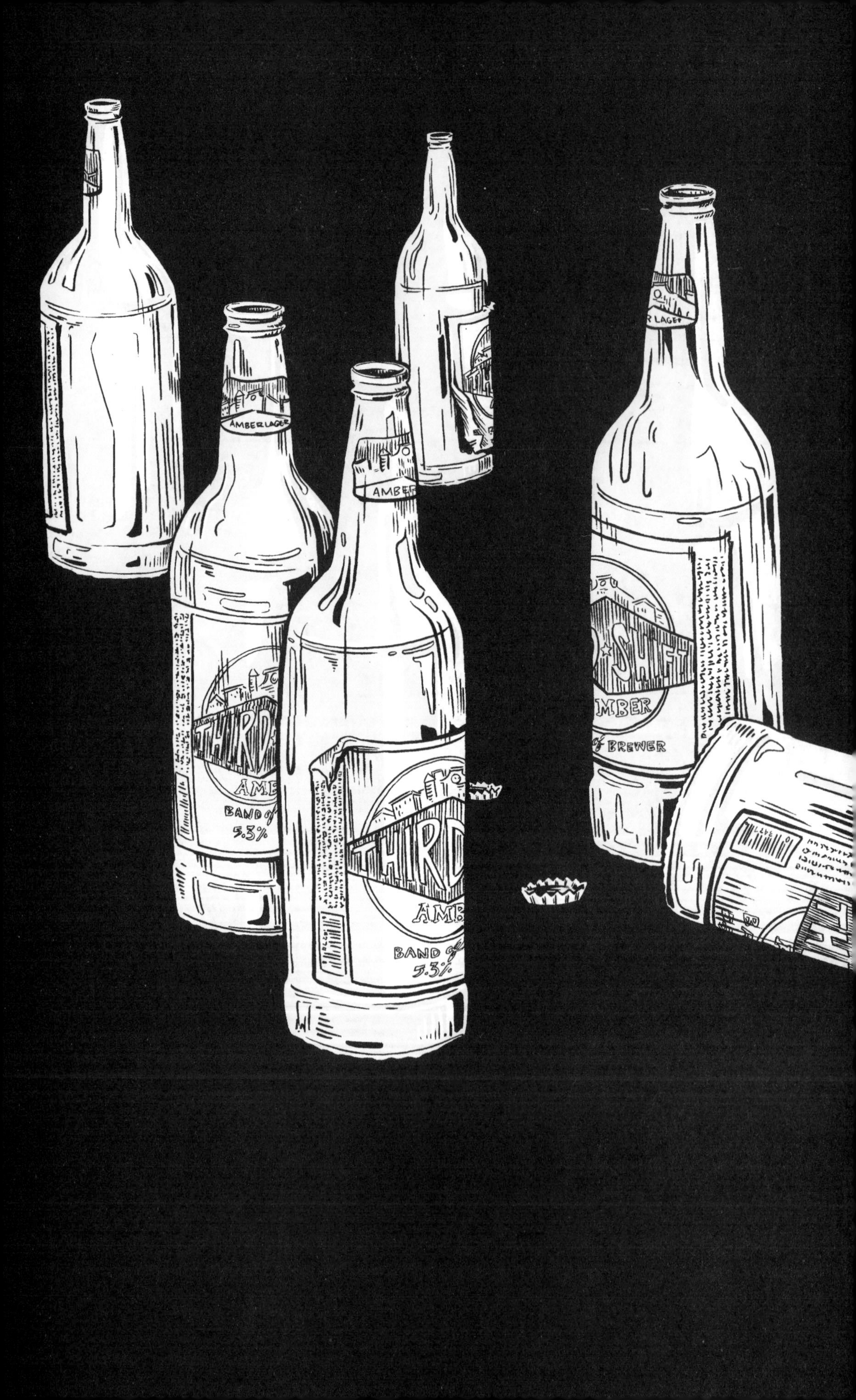
AMBERLAGER
THIRD
BAND of
5.3%
AMBER
BREWER

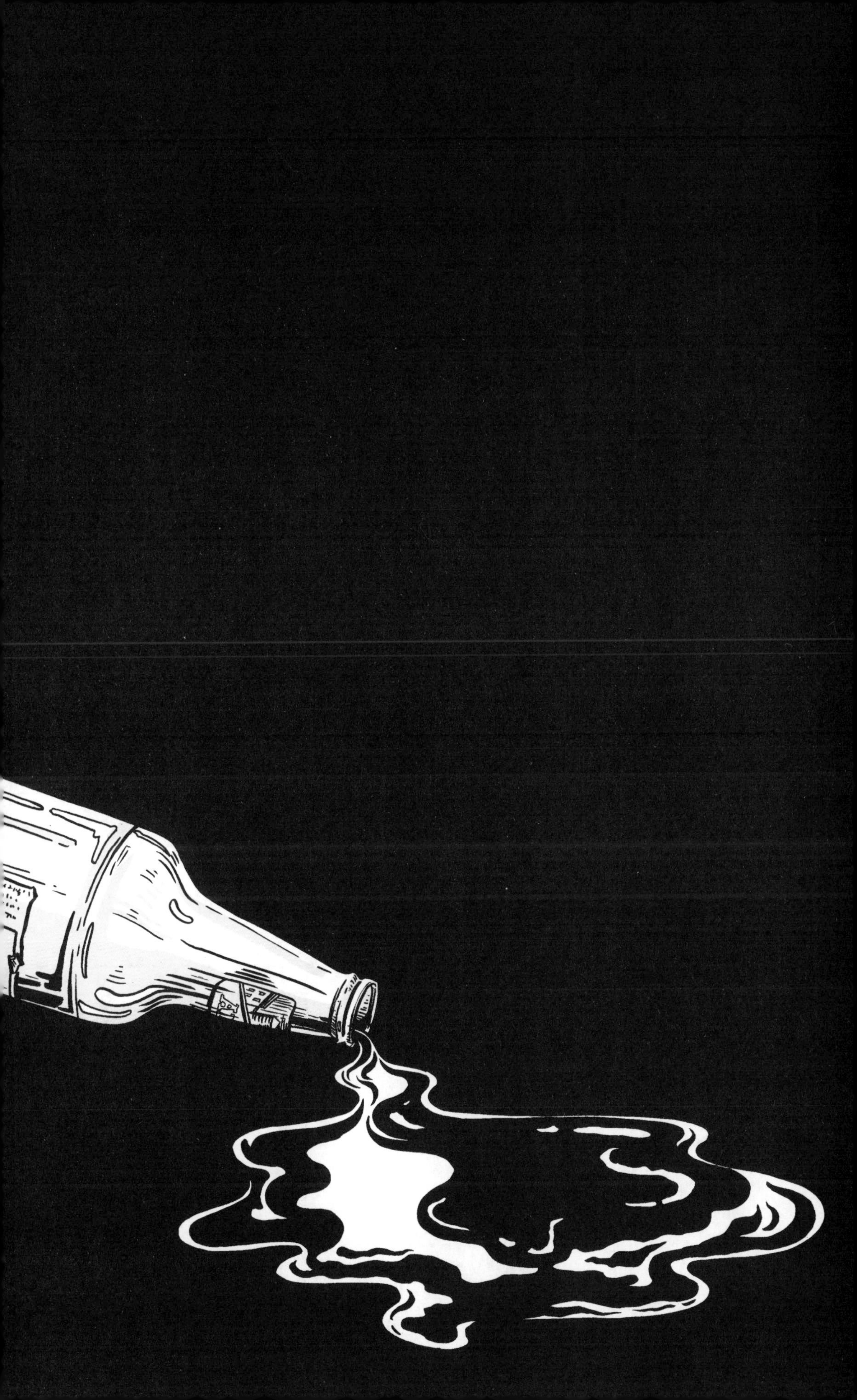

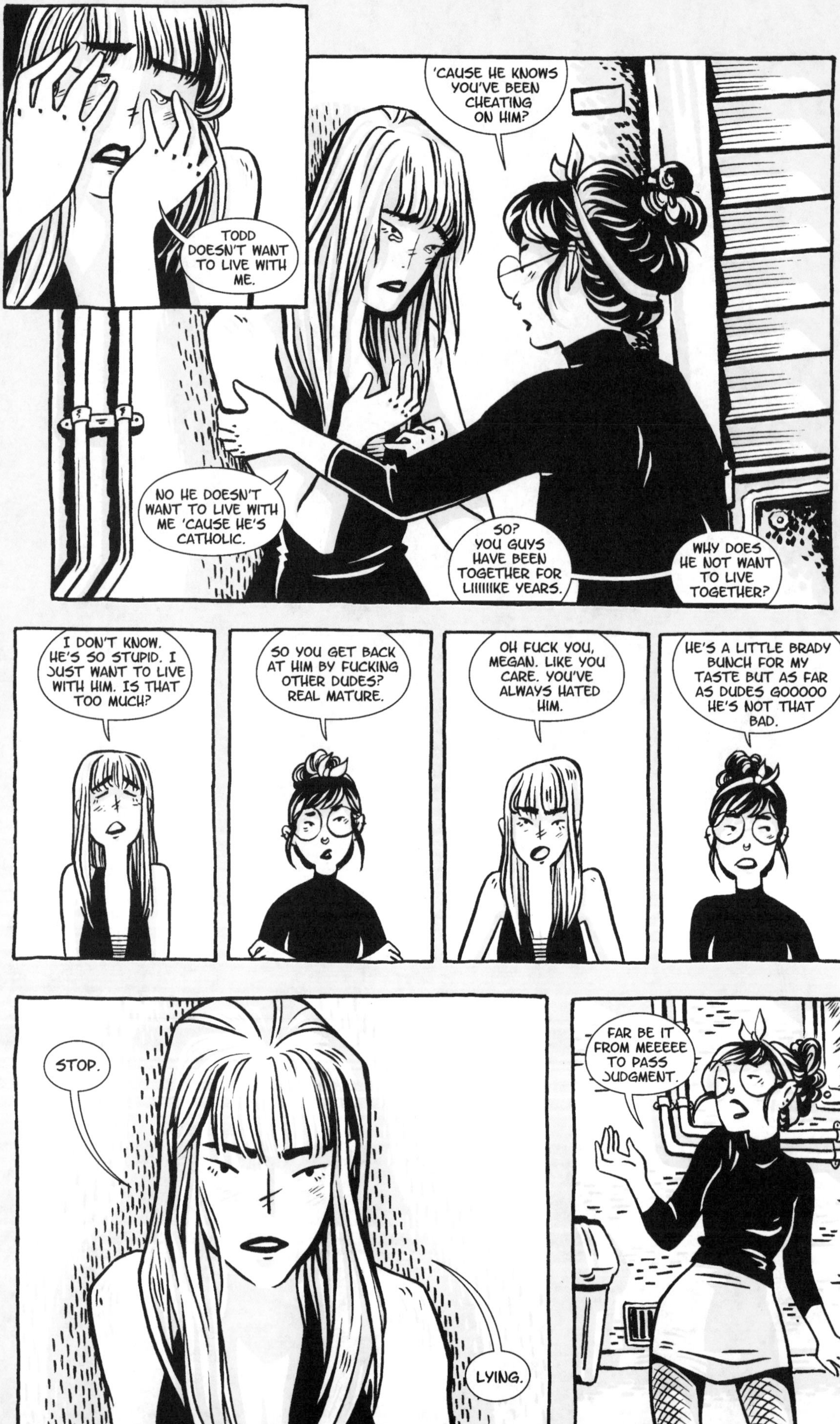
TODD DOESN'T WANT TO LIVE WITH ME.
'CAUSE HE KNOWS YOU'VE BEEN CHEATING ON HIM?
NO HE DOESN'T WANT TO LIVE WITH ME 'CAUSE HE'S CATHOLIC.
SO? YOU GUYS HAVE BEEN TOGETHER FOR LIIIIIIKE YEARS.
WHY DOES HE NOT WANT TO LIVE TOGETHER?
I DON'T KNOW. HE'S SO STUPID. I JUST WANT TO LIVE WITH HIM. IS THAT TOO MUCH?
SO YOU GET BACK AT HIM BY FUCKING OTHER DUDES? REAL MATURE.
OH FUCK YOU, MEGAN. LIKE YOU CARE. YOU'VE ALWAYS HATED HIM.
HE'S A LITTLE BRADY BUNCH FOR MY TASTE BUT AS FAR AS DUDES GOOOOO HE'S NOT THAT BAD.
STOP.
LYING.
FAR BE IT FROM MEEEEE TO PASS JUDGMENT.

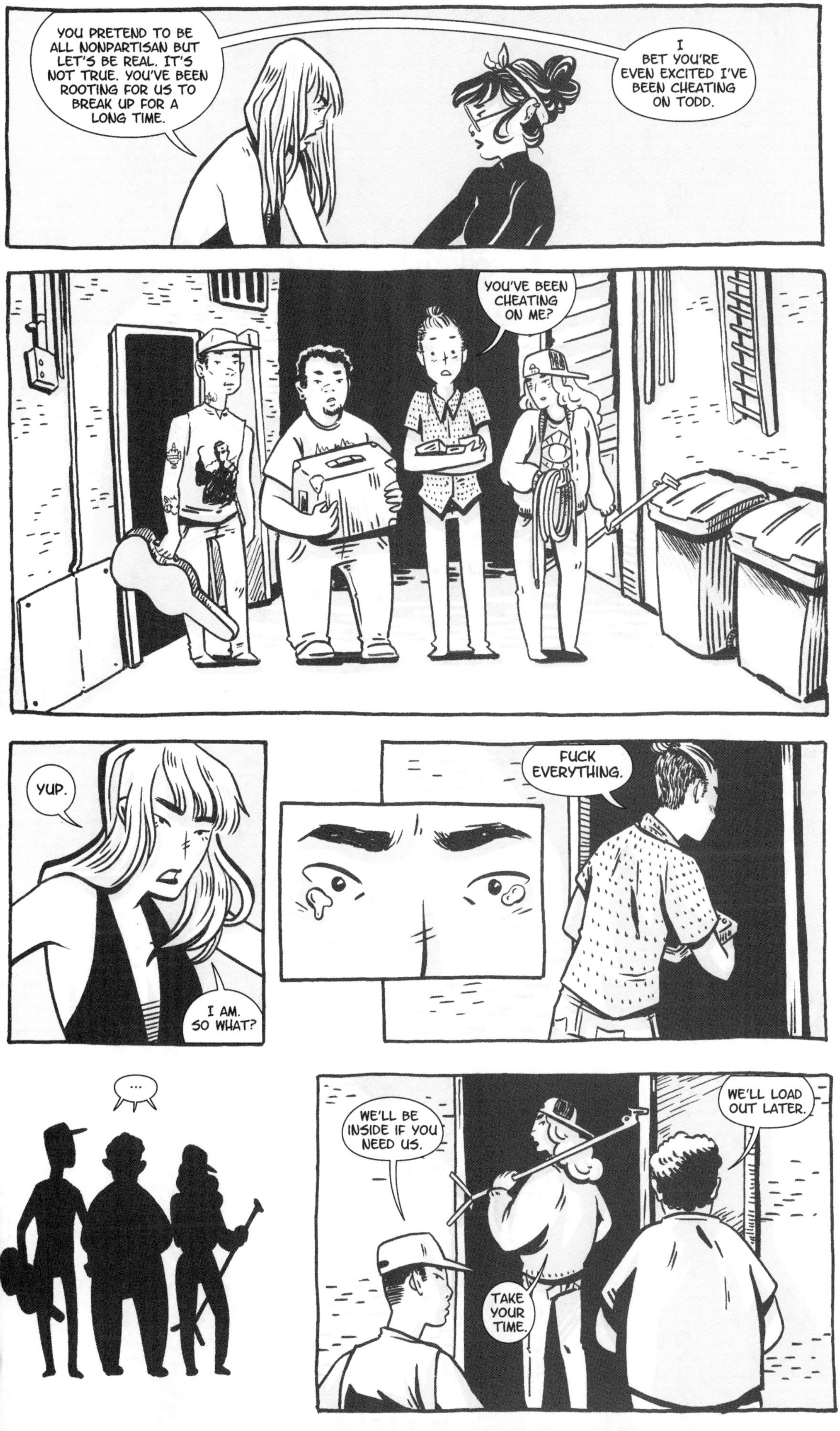
YOU PRETEND TO BE ALL NONPARTISAN BUT LET'S BE REAL. IT'S NOT TRUE. YOU'VE BEEN ROOTING FOR US TO BREAK UP FOR A LONG TIME.
I BET YOU'RE EVEN EXCITED I'VE BEEN CHEATING ON TODD.
YOU'VE BEEN CHEATING ON ME?
YUP.
I AM. SO WHAT?
FUCK EVERYTHING.
...
WE'LL BE INSIDE IF YOU NEED US.
TAKE YOUR TIME.
WE'LL LOAD OUT LATER.

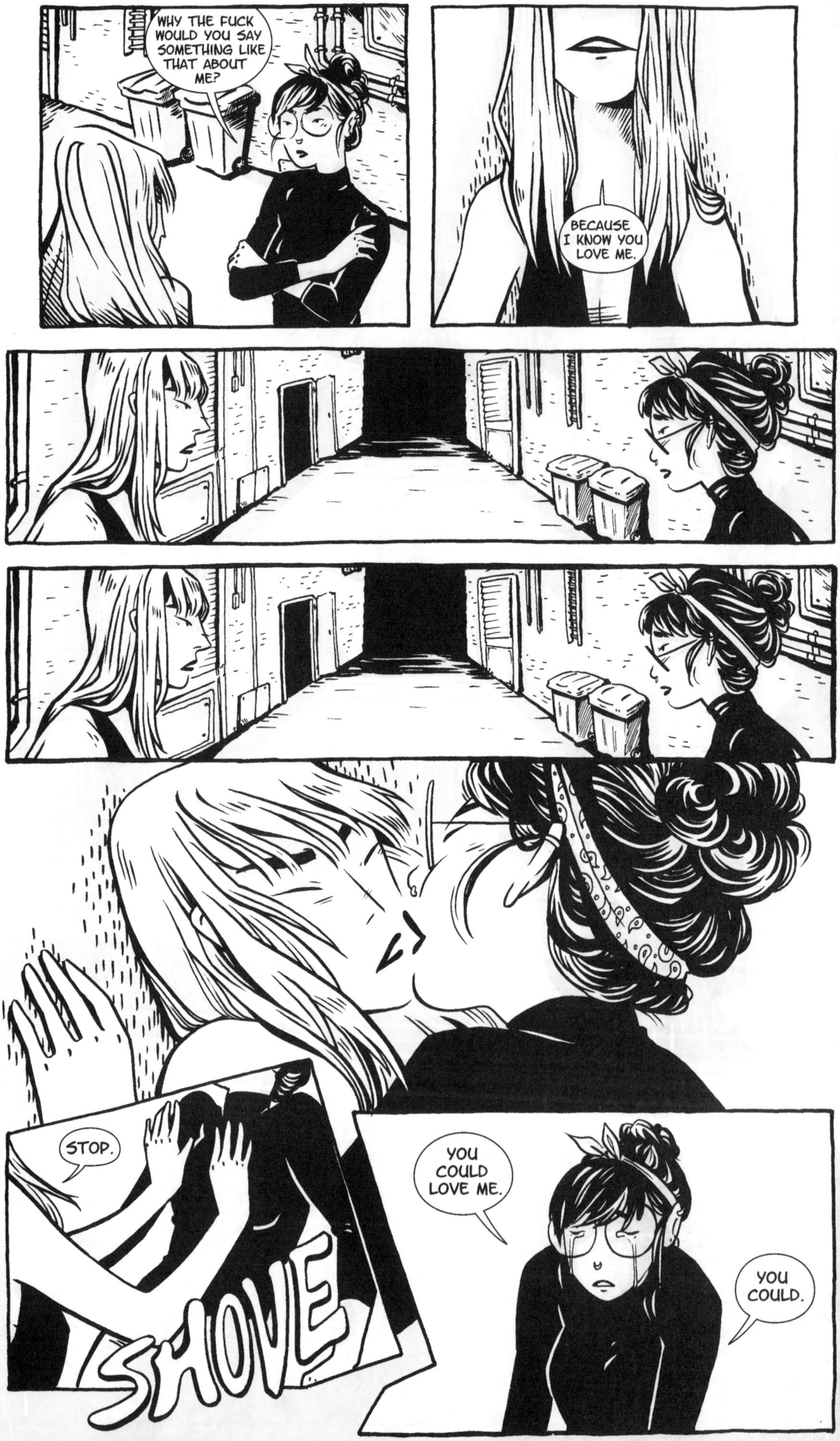
WHY THE FUCK WOULD YOU SAY SOMETHING LIKE THAT ABOUT ME?
BECAUSE I KNOW YOU LOVE ME.
STOP.
SHOVE
YOU COULD LOVE ME.
YOU COULD.

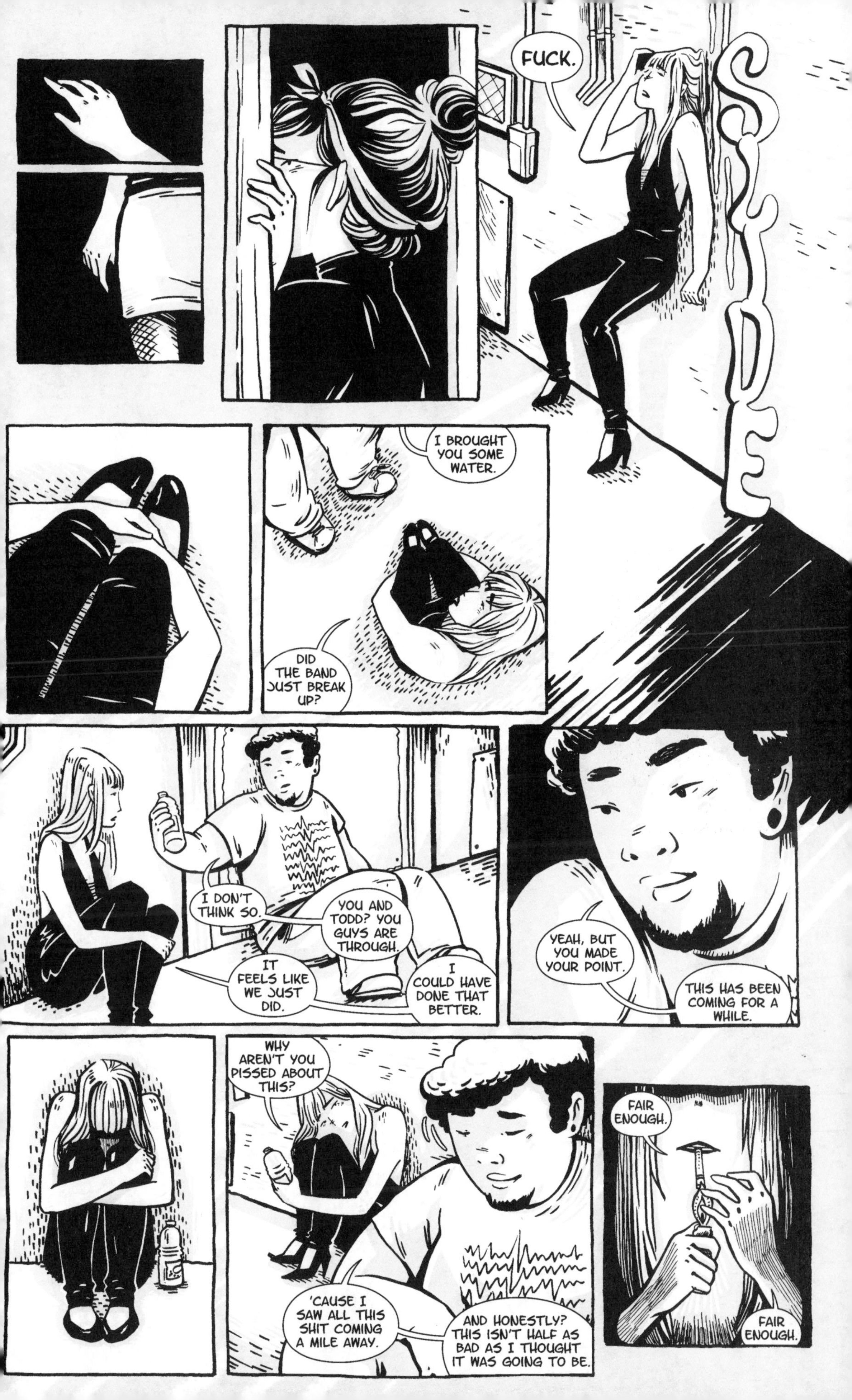
FUCK.
SLIDE
I BROUGHT YOU SOME WATER.
DID THE BAND JUST BREAK UP?
I DON'T THINK SO.
YOU AND TODD? YOU GUYS ARE THROUGH.
IT FEELS LIKE WE JUST DID.
I COULD HAVE DONE THAT BETTER.
YEAH, BUT YOU MADE YOUR POINT.
THIS HAS BEEN COMING FOR A WHILE.
WHY AREN'T YOU PISSED ABOUT THIS?
'CAUSE I SAW ALL THIS SHIT COMING A MILE AWAY.
AND HONESTLY? THIS ISN'T HALF AS BAD AS I THOUGHT IT WAS GOING TO BE.
FAIR ENOUGH.
FAIR ENOUGH.

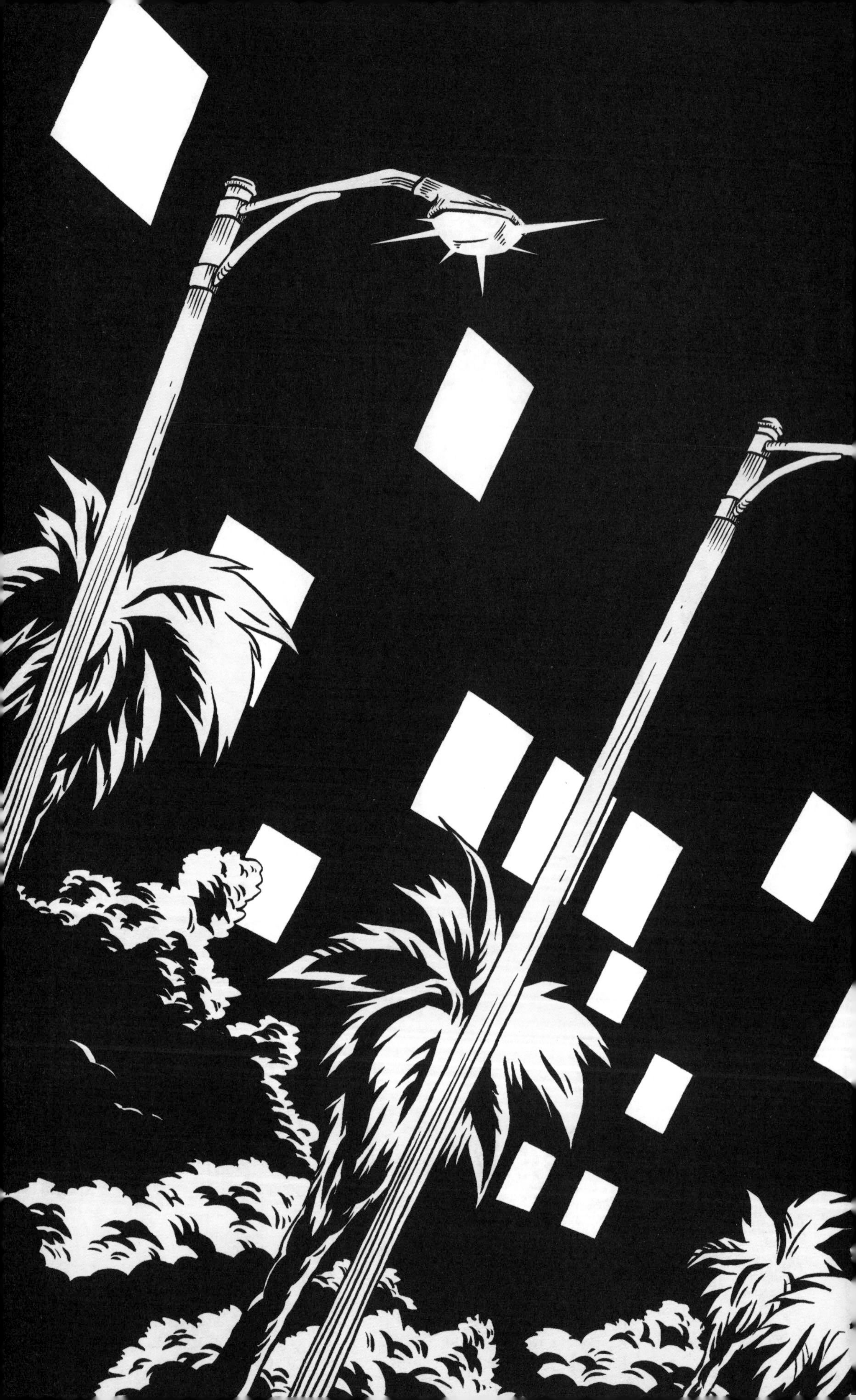

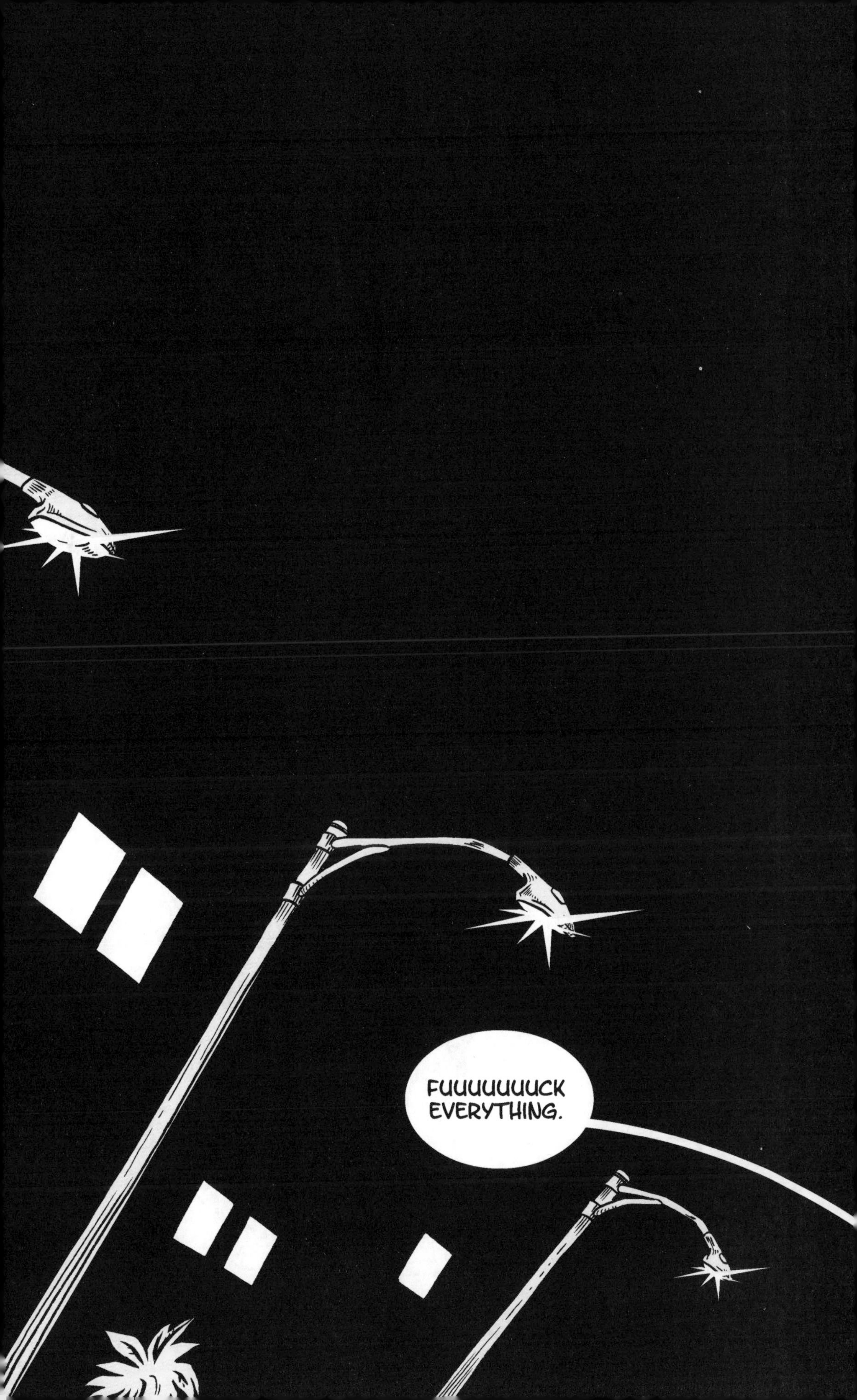
FUUUUUUUCK EVERYTHING.

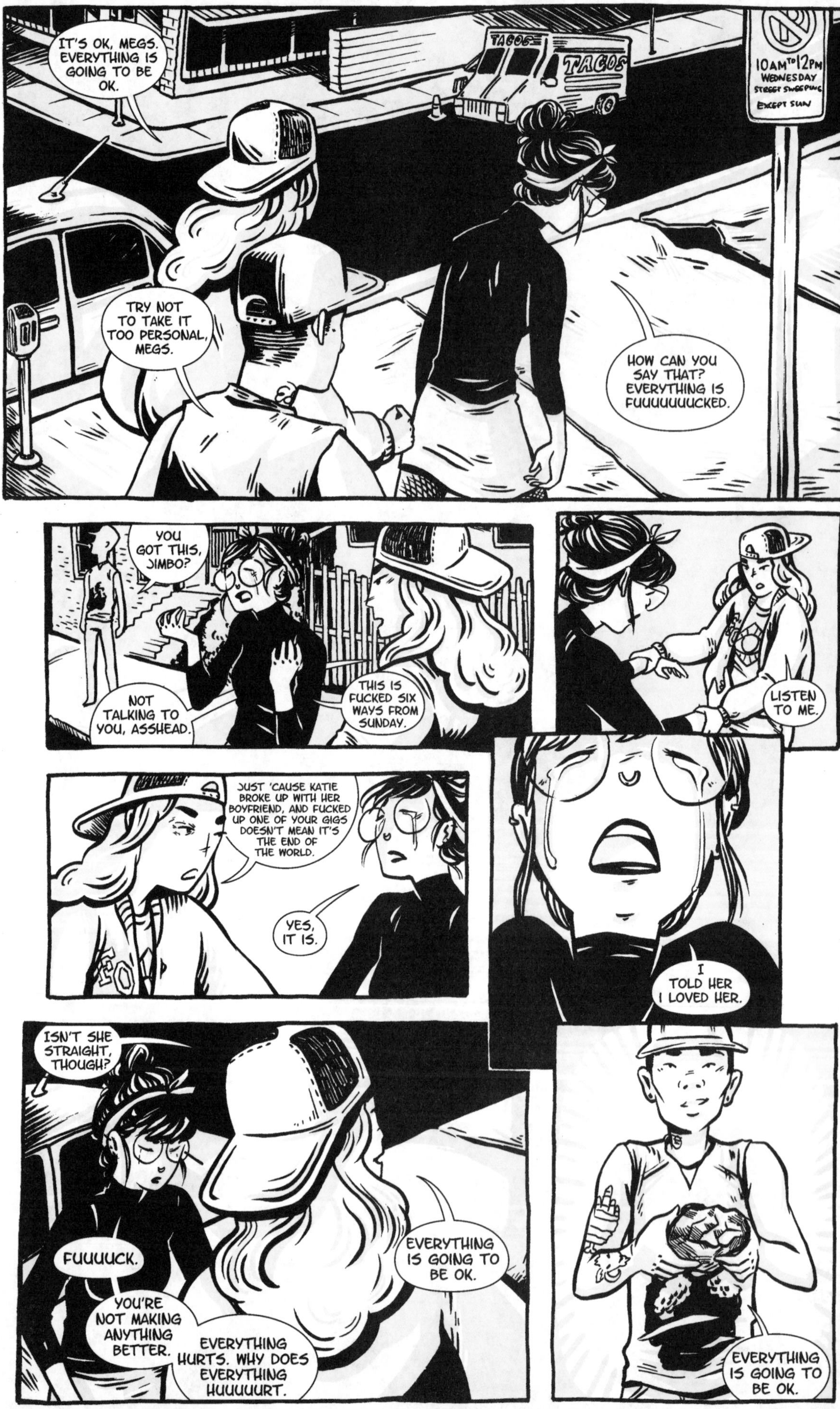

IT'S OK, MEGS. EVERYTHING IS GOING TO BE OK.
TACOS
TACOS
10AM TO 12PM WEDNESDAY STREET SWEEPING EXCEPT SUN
TRY NOT TO TAKE IT TOO PERSONAL, MEGS.
HOW CAN YOU SAY THAT? EVERYTHING IS FUUUUUUUCKED.
YOU GOT THIS, JIMBO?
NOT TALKING TO YOU, ASSHEAD.
THIS IS FUCKED SIX WAYS FROM SUNDAY.
LISTEN TO ME.
JUST 'CAUSE KATIE BROKE UP WITH HER BOYFRIEND, AND FUCKED UP ONE OF YOUR GIGS DOESN'T MEAN IT'S THE END OF THE WORLD.
YES, IT IS.
I TOLD HER I LOVED HER.
ISN'T SHE STRAIGHT, THOUGH?
FUUUUCK.
YOU'RE NOT MAKING ANYTHING BETTER.
EVERYTHING HURTS. WHY DOES EVERYTHING HUUUUURT.
EVERYTHING IS GOING TO BE OK.
EVERYTHING IS GOING TO BE OK.

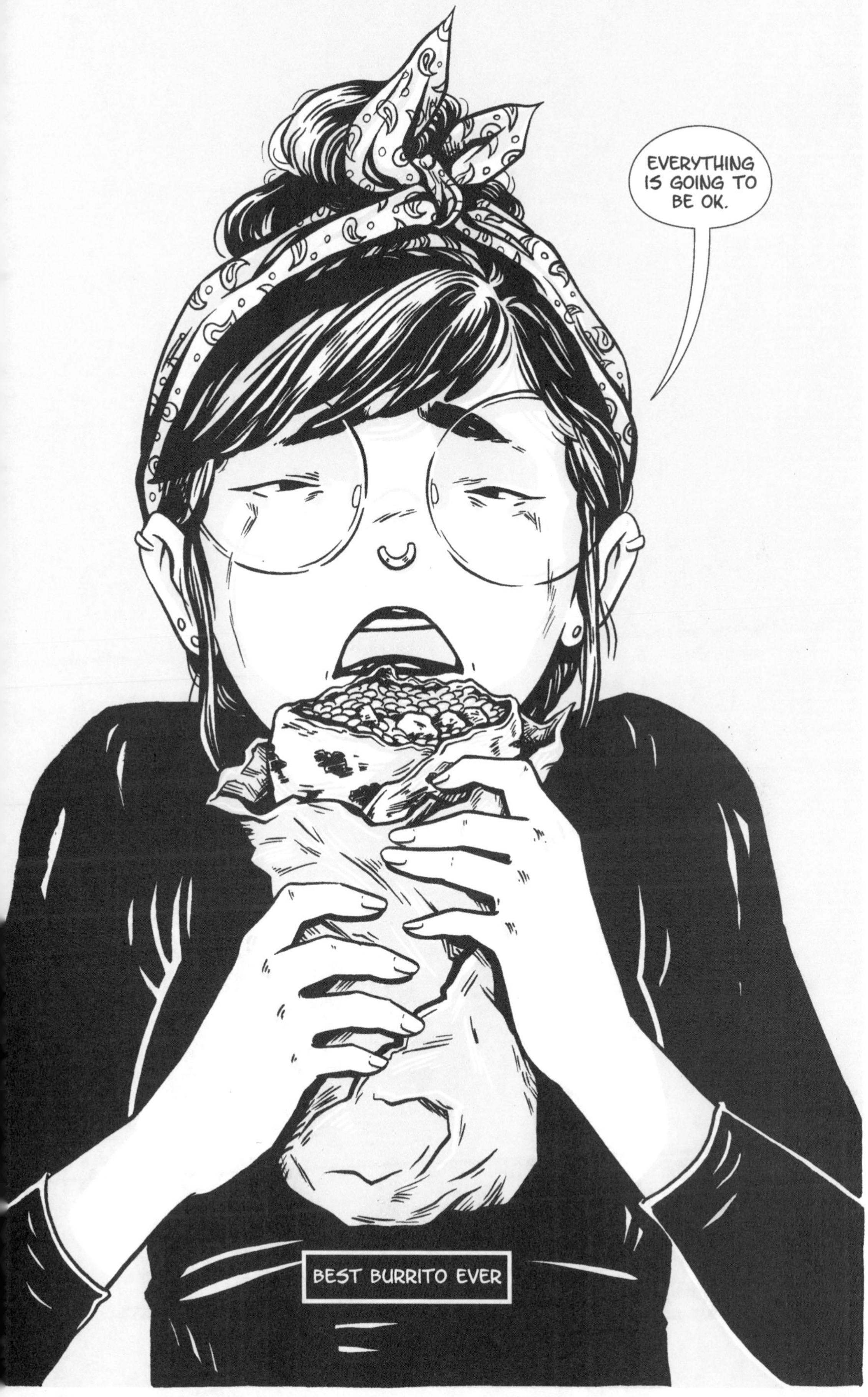
EVERYTHING IS GOING TO BE OK.
BEST BURRITO EVER

FEVER COAST

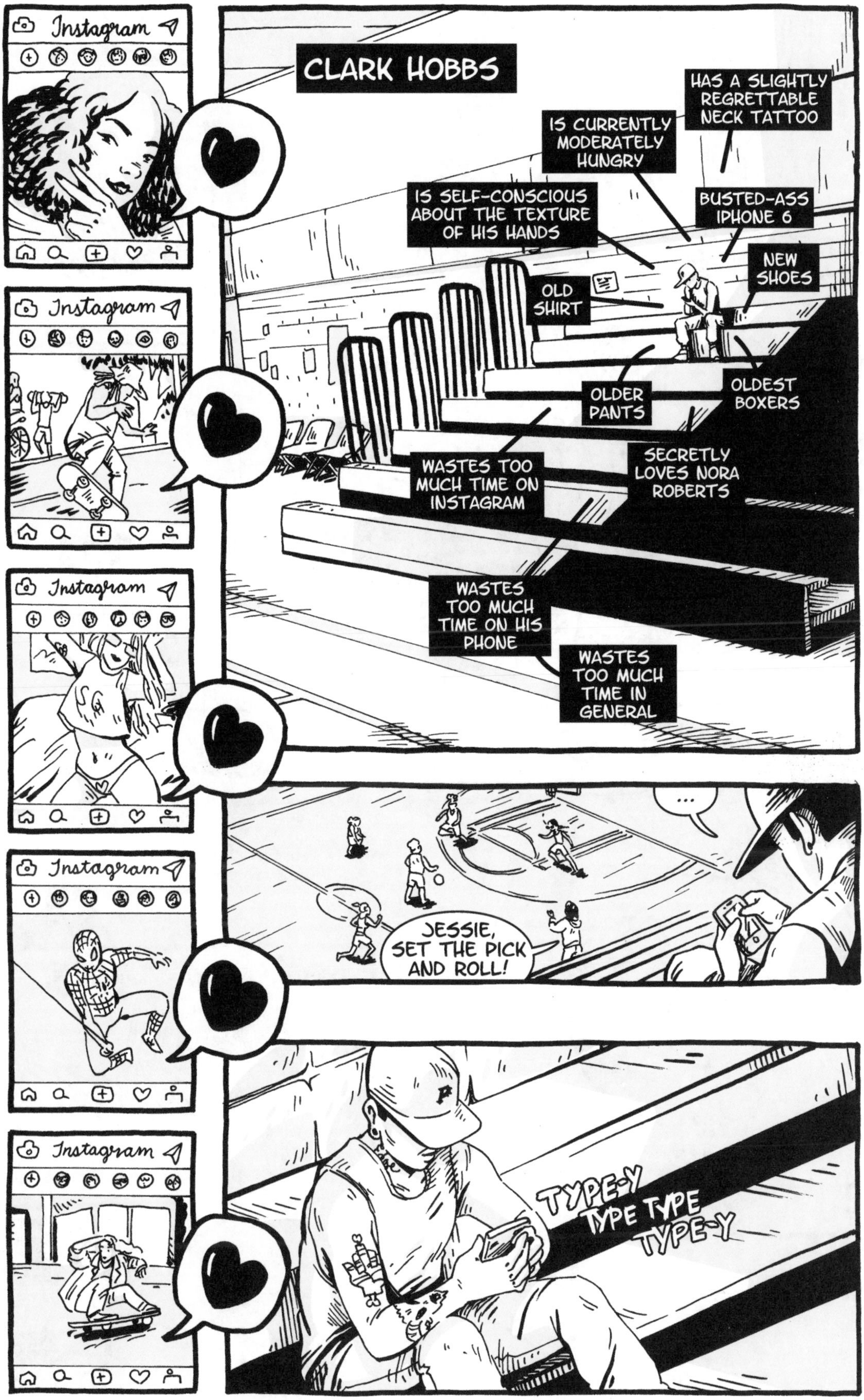
Instagram
Instagram
Instagram
Instagram
Instagram
CLARK HOBBS
HAS A SLIGHTLY REGRETTABLE NECK TATTOO
IS CURRENTLY MODERATELY HUNGRY
IS SELF-CONSCIOUS ABOUT THE TEXTURE OF HIS HANDS
BUSTED-ASS IPHONE 6
NEW SHOES
OLD SHIRT
OLDER PANTS
OLDEST BOXERS
WASTES TOO MUCH TIME ON INSTAGRAM
SECRETLY LOVES NORA ROBERTS
WASTES TOO MUCH TIME ON HIS PHONE
WASTES TOO MUCH TIME IN GENERAL
...
JESSIE, SET THE PICK AND ROLL!
TYPE-Y TYPE TYPE TYPE-Y

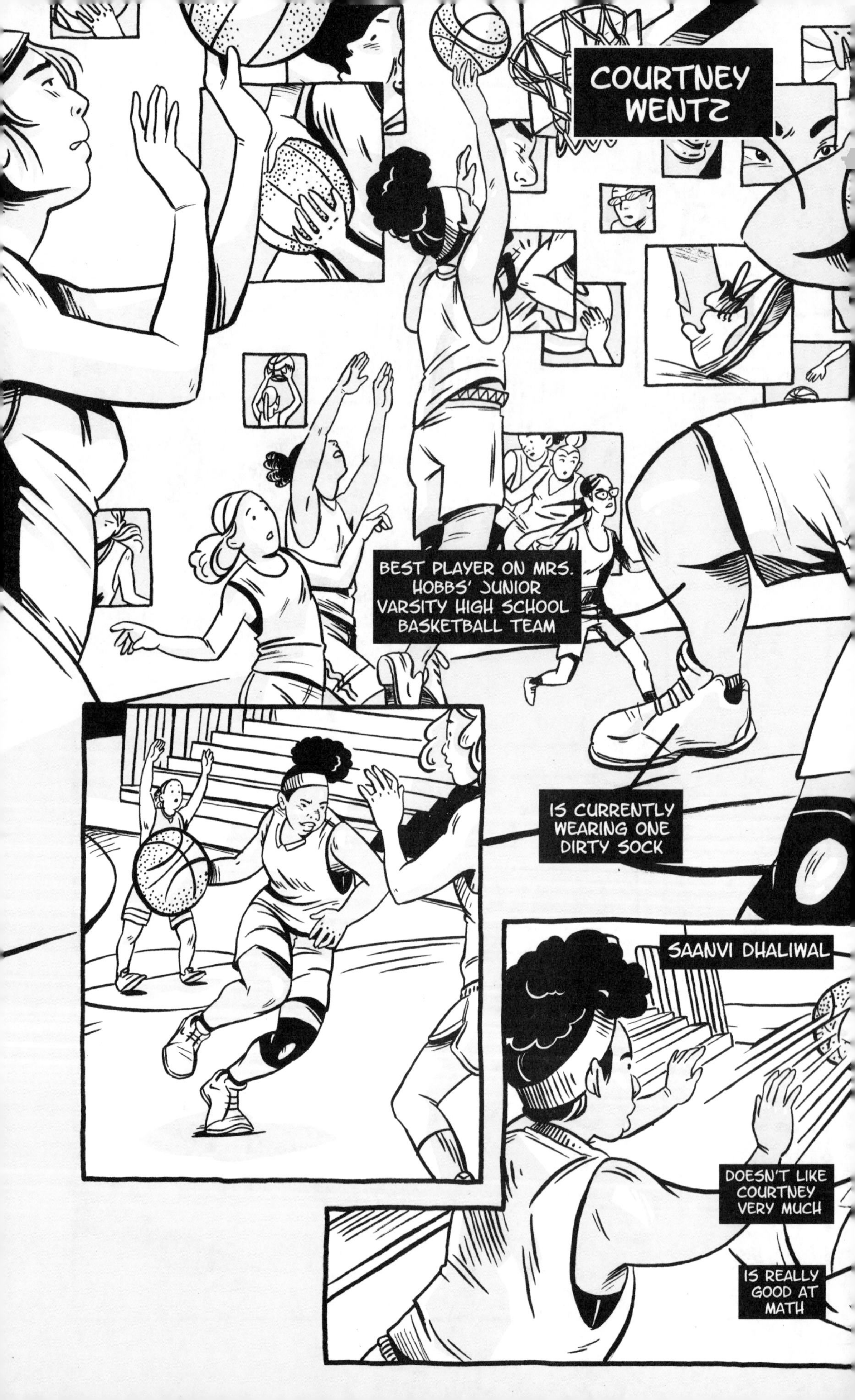
COURTNEY WENTZ
BEST PLAYER ON MRS. HOBBS' JUNIOR VARSITY HIGH SCHOOL BASKETBALL TEAM
IS CURRENTLY WEARING ONE DIRTY SOCK
SAANVI DHALIWAL
DOESN'T LIKE COURTNEY VERY MUCH
IS REALLY GOOD AT MATH

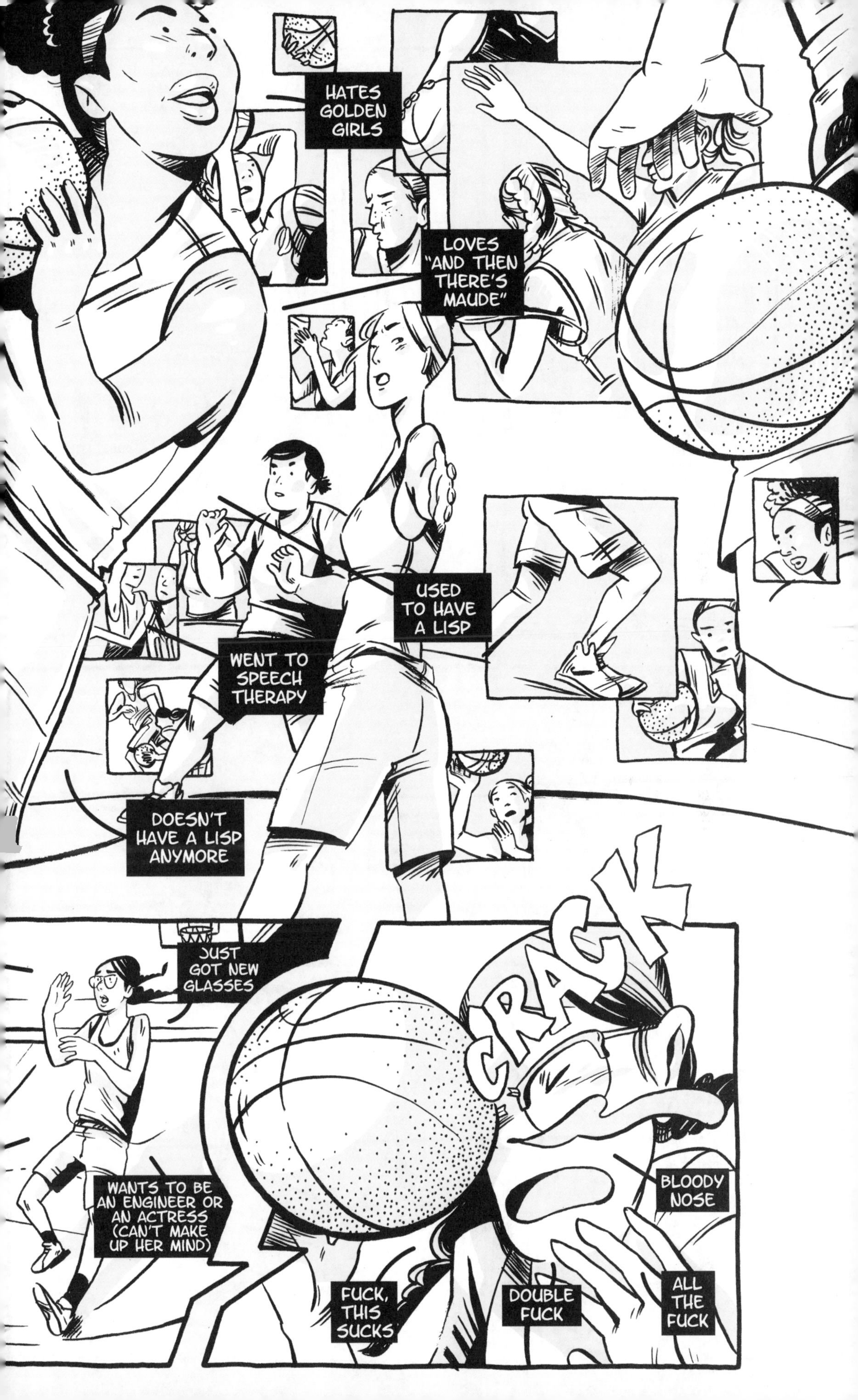
HATES GOLDEN GIRLS
LOVES "AND THEN THERE'S MAUDE"
USED TO HAVE A LISP
WENT TO SPEECH THERAPY
DOESN'T HAVE A LISP ANYMORE
JUST GOT NEW GLASSES
CRACK
WANTS TO BE AN ENGINEER OR AN ACTRESS (CAN'T MAKE UP HER MIND)
BLOODY NOSE
FUCK, THIS SUCKS
DOUBLE FUCK
ALL THE FUCK

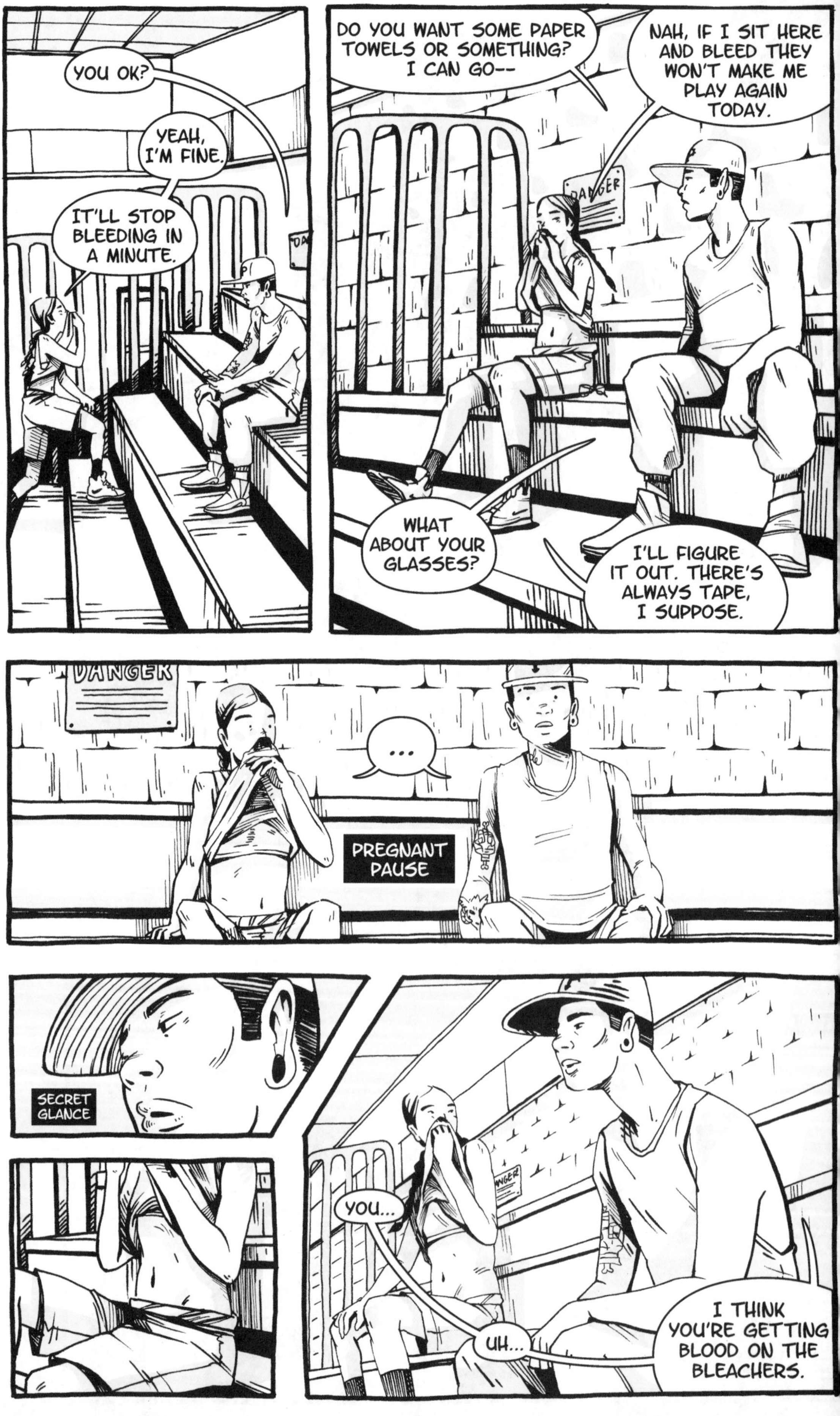
YOU OK?
YEAH, I'M FINE.
IT'LL STOP BLEEDING IN A MINUTE.
DANGER
DO YOU WANT SOME PAPER TOWELS OR SOMETHING? I CAN GO--
NAH, IF I SIT HERE AND BLEED THEY WON'T MAKE ME PLAY AGAIN TODAY.
WHAT ABOUT YOUR GLASSES?
I'LL FIGURE IT OUT. THERE'S ALWAYS TAPE, I SUPPOSE.
DANGER
...
PREGNANT PAUSE
SECRET GLANCE
YOU...
UH...
I THINK YOU'RE GETTING BLOOD ON THE BLEACHERS.

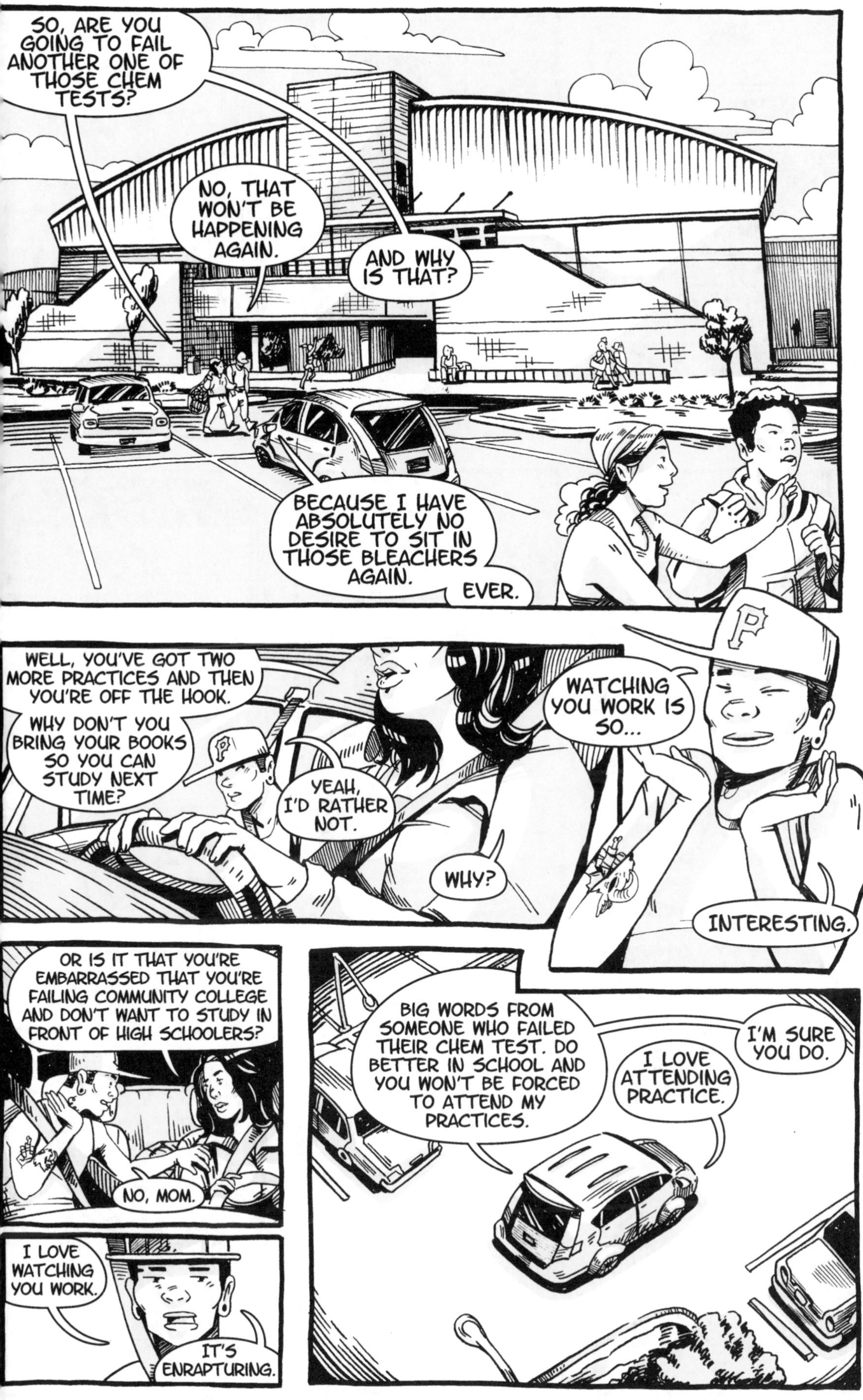
SO, ARE YOU GOING TO FAIL ANOTHER ONE OF THOSE CHEM TESTS?
NO, THAT WON'T BE HAPPENING AGAIN.
AND WHY IS THAT?
BECAUSE I HAVE ABSOLUTELY NO DESIRE TO SIT IN THOSE BLEACHERS AGAIN.
EVER.
WELL, YOU'VE GOT TWO MORE PRACTICES AND THEN YOU'RE OFF THE HOOK.
WHY DON'T YOU BRING YOUR BOOKS SO YOU CAN STUDY NEXT TIME?
YEAH, I'D RATHER NOT.
WHY?
WATCHING YOU WORK IS SO...
INTERESTING.
OR IS IT THAT YOU'RE EMBARRASSED THAT YOU'RE FAILING COMMUNITY COLLEGE AND DON'T WANT TO STUDY IN FRONT OF HIGH SCHOOLERS?
NO, MOM.
I LOVE WATCHING YOU WORK.
IT'S ENRAPTURING.
BIG WORDS FROM SOMEONE WHO FAILED THEIR CHEM TEST. DO BETTER IN SCHOOL AND YOU WON'T BE FORCED TO ATTEND MY PRACTICES.
I LOVE ATTENDING PRACTICE.
I'M SURE YOU DO.

TYPE-Y TYPE TYPE TYPE-Y
4:11 PM
Dad
When are you getting home tonight?
Not sure
-Dad
Might go out with coworkers.
-Dad
Ok.
-Dad

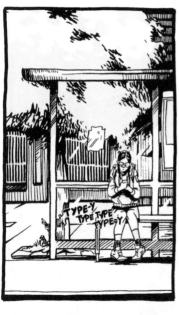

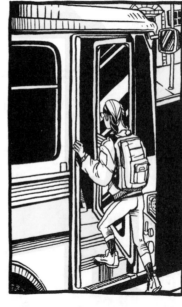

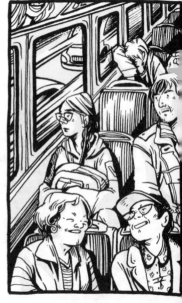

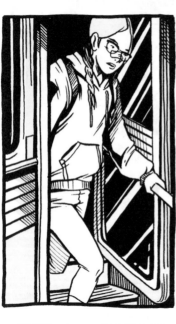

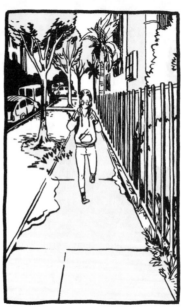

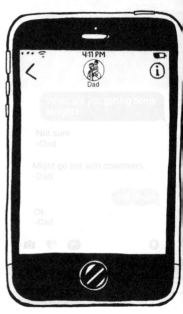

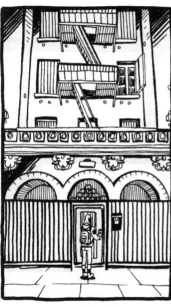

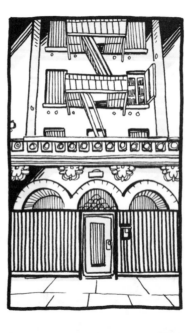

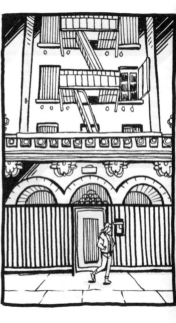

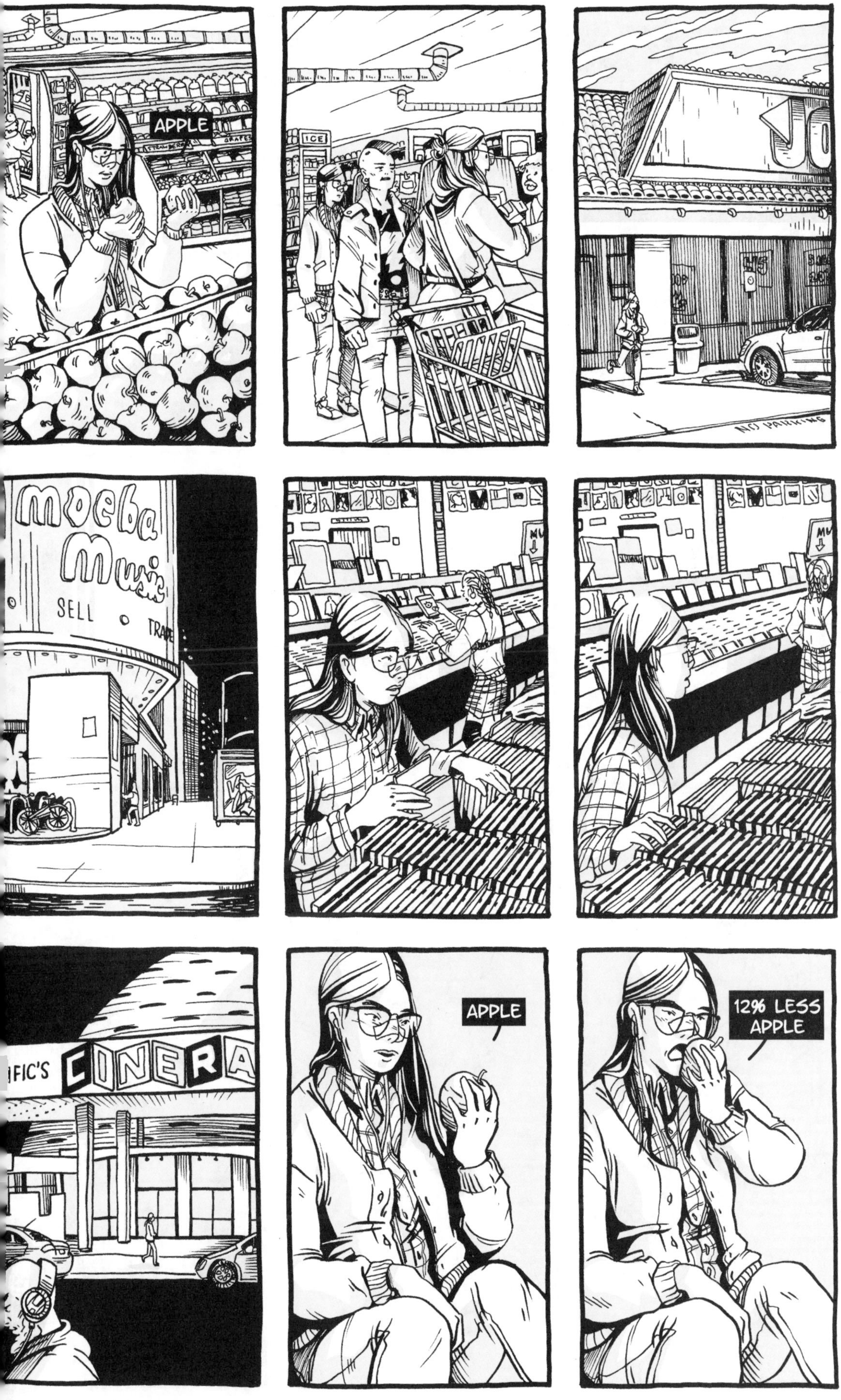
APPLE
ICE
NO PARKING
moeba
Music
SELL
TRADE
IFIC'S
CINERA
APPLE
12% LESS
APPLE

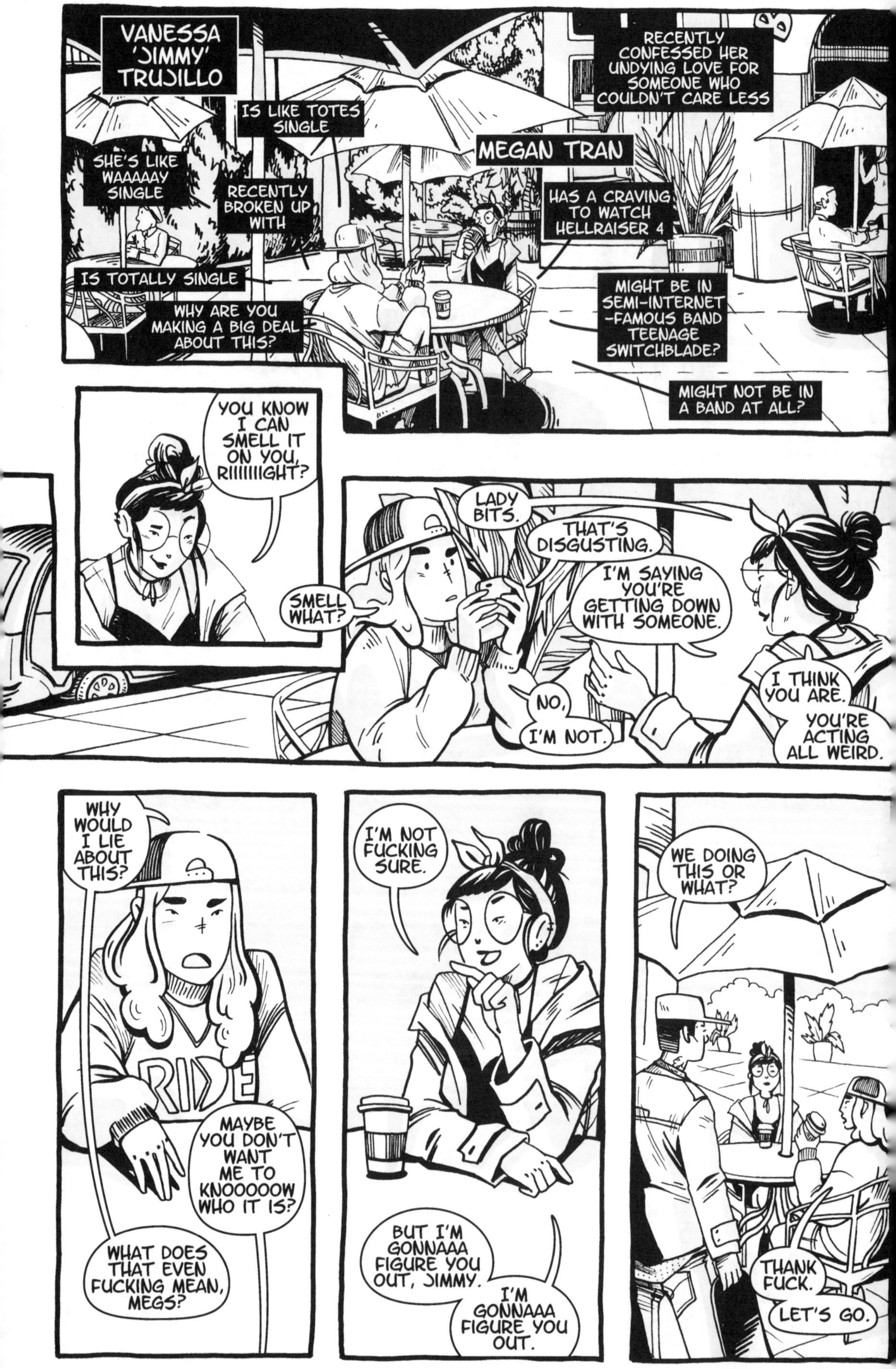
VANESSA 'JIMMY' TRUJILLO
IS LIKE TOTES SINGLE
SHE'S LIKE WAAAAAY SINGLE
RECENTLY BROKEN UP WITH
IS TOTALLY SINGLE
WHY ARE YOU MAKING A BIG DEAL ABOUT THIS?
RECENTLY CONFESSED HER UNDYING LOVE FOR SOMEONE WHO COULDN'T CARE LESS
MEGAN TRAN
HAS A CRAVING TO WATCH HELLRAISER 4
MIGHT BE IN SEMI-INTERNET-FAMOUS BAND TEENAGE SWITCHBLADE?
MIGHT NOT BE IN A BAND AT ALL?
YOU KNOW I CAN SMELL IT ON YOU, RIIIIIIIGHT?
SMELL WHAT?
LADY BITS.
THAT'S DISGUSTING.
I'M SAYING YOU'RE GETTING DOWN WITH SOMEONE.
NO,
I'M NOT.
I THINK YOU ARE.
YOU'RE ACTING ALL WEIRD.
WHY WOULD I LIE ABOUT THIS?
RIDE
MAYBE YOU DON'T WANT ME TO KNOOOOOW WHO IT IS?
WHAT DOES THAT EVEN FUCKING MEAN, MEGS?
I'M NOT FUCKING SURE.
BUT I'M GONNAAA FIGURE YOU OUT, JIMMY.
I'M GONNAAA FIGURE YOU OUT.
WE DOING THIS OR WHAT?
THANK FUCK.
LET'S GO.

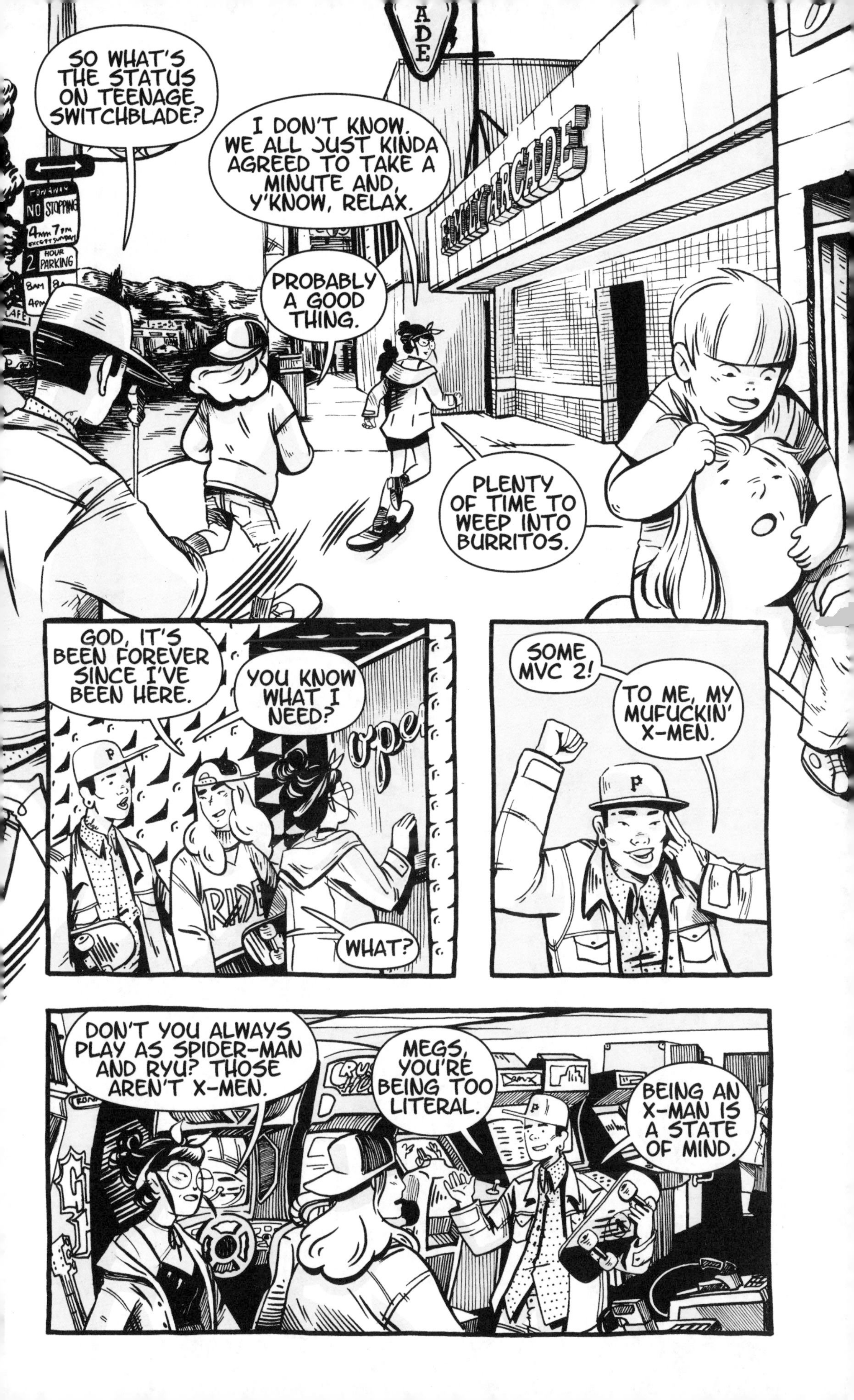
SO WHAT'S THE STATUS ON TEENAGE SWITCHBLADE?
I DON'T KNOW. WE ALL JUST KINDA AGREED TO TAKE A MINUTE AND, Y'KNOW, RELAX.
PROBABLY A GOOD THING.
PLENTY OF TIME TO WEEP INTO BURRITOS.
NO STOPPING
2 HOUR PARKING
GOD, IT'S BEEN FOREVER SINCE I'VE BEEN HERE.
YOU KNOW WHAT I NEED?
WHAT?
SOME MVC 2!
TO ME, MY MUFUCKIN' X-MEN.
DON'T YOU ALWAYS PLAY AS SPIDER-MAN AND RYU? THOSE AREN'T X-MEN.
MEGS, YOU'RE BEING TOO LITERAL.
BEING AN X-MAN IS A STATE OF MIND.

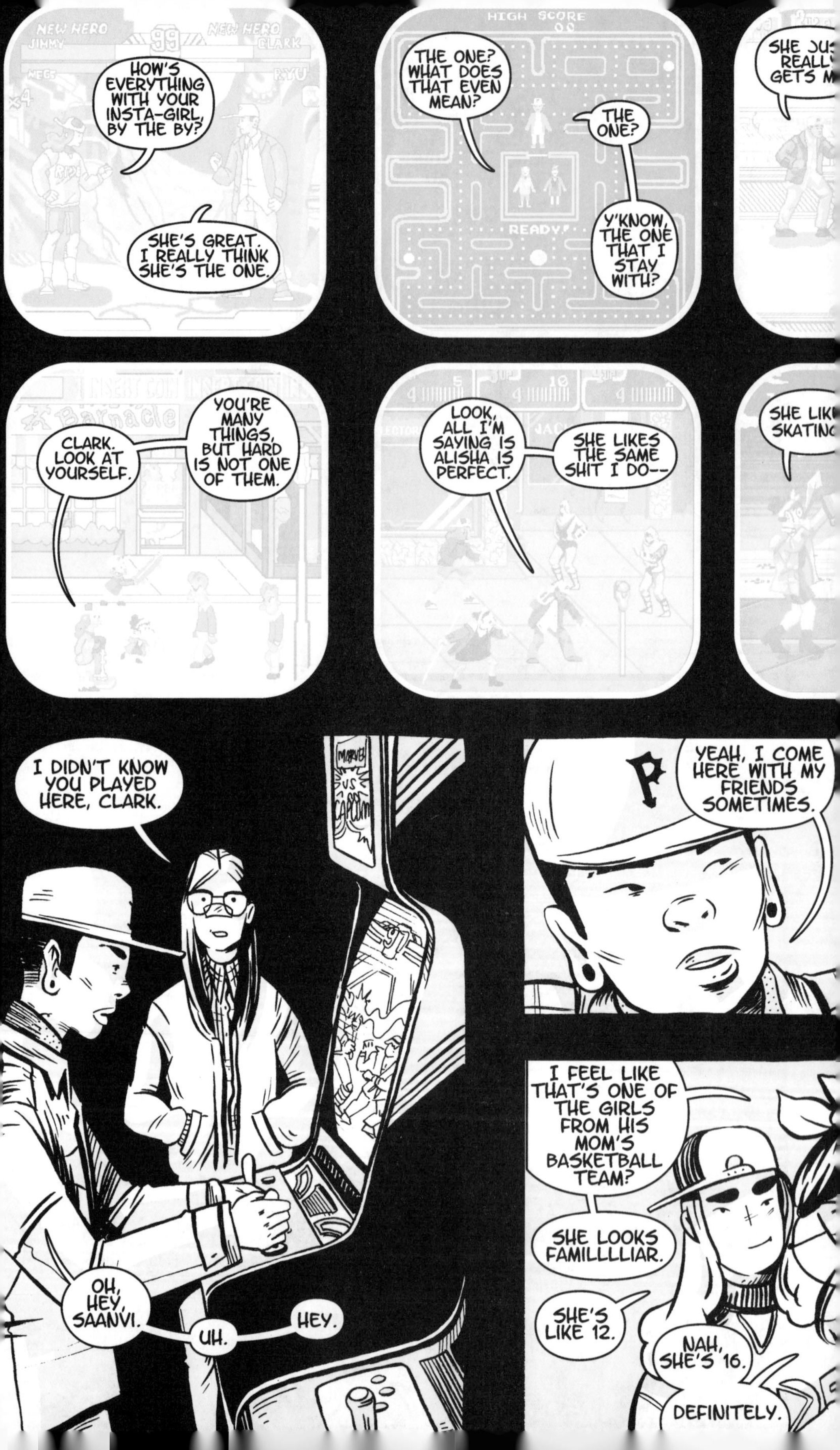
NEW HERO
JIMMY
99
NEW HERO
CLARK
HOW'S EVERYTHING WITH YOUR INSTA-GIRL, BY THE BY?
SHE'S GREAT. I REALLY THINK SHE'S THE ONE.
HIGH SCORE
THE ONE?
THE ONE? WHAT DOES THAT EVEN MEAN?
Y'KNOW, THE ONE THAT I STAY WITH?
READY!
CLARK. LOOK AT YOURSELF.
YOU'RE MANY THINGS, BUT HARD IS NOT ONE OF THEM.
LOOK, ALL I'M SAYING IS ALISHA IS PERFECT.
SHE LIKES THE SAME SHIT I DO--
I DIDN'T KNOW YOU PLAYED HERE, CLARK.
OH, HEY, SAANVI.
UH.
HEY.
YEAH, I COME HERE WITH MY FRIENDS SOMETIMES.
I FEEL LIKE THAT'S ONE OF THE GIRLS FROM HIS MOM'S BASKETBALL TEAM?
SHE LOOKS FAMILLLLIAR.
SHE'S LIKE 12.
NAH, SHE'S 16.
DEFINITELY.

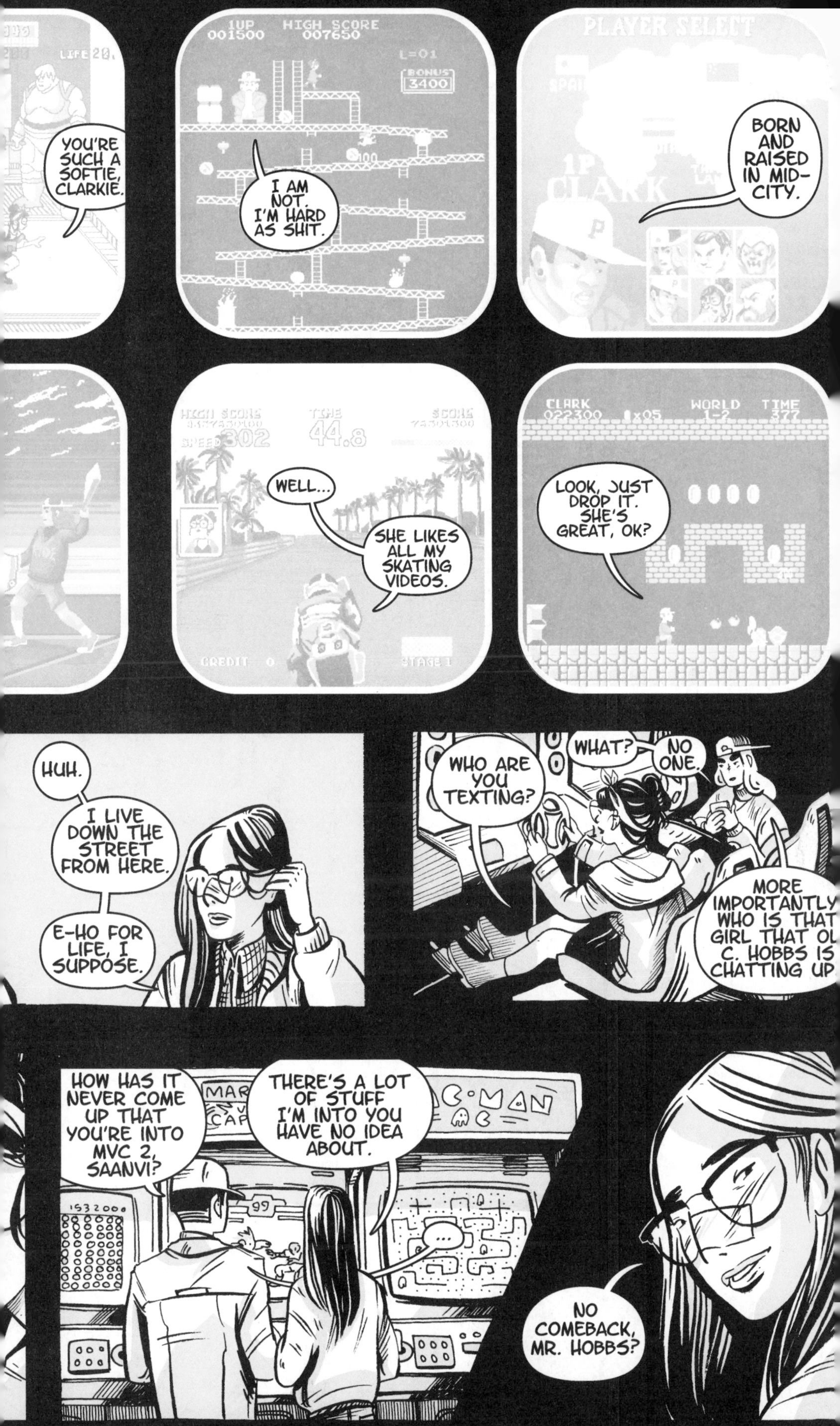

LIFE 20
YOU'RE SUCH A SOFTIE, CLARKIE.
1UP 001500 HIGH SCORE 007650
L=01
BONUS 3400
I AM NOT. I'M HARD AS SHIT.
PLAYER SELECT
1P CLARK
BORN AND RAISED IN MID-CITY.
HIGH SCORE
TIME 44.8
SCORE
SPEED 302
WELL...
SHE LIKES ALL MY SKATING VIDEOS.
CREDIT 0
STAGE 1
CLARK 022300 x05 WORLD 1-2 TIME 377
LOOK, JUST DROP IT. SHE'S GREAT, OK?
HUH.
I LIVE DOWN THE STREET FROM HERE.
E-HO FOR LIFE, I SUPPOSE.
WHO ARE YOU TEXTING?
WHAT?
NO ONE.
MORE IMPORTANTLY WHO IS THAT GIRL THAT OL C. HOBBS IS CHATTING UP
HOW HAS IT NEVER COME UP THAT YOU'RE INTO MVC 2, SAANVI?
THERE'S A LOT OF STUFF I'M INTO YOU HAVE NO IDEA ABOUT.
...
NO COMEBACK, MR. HOBBS?

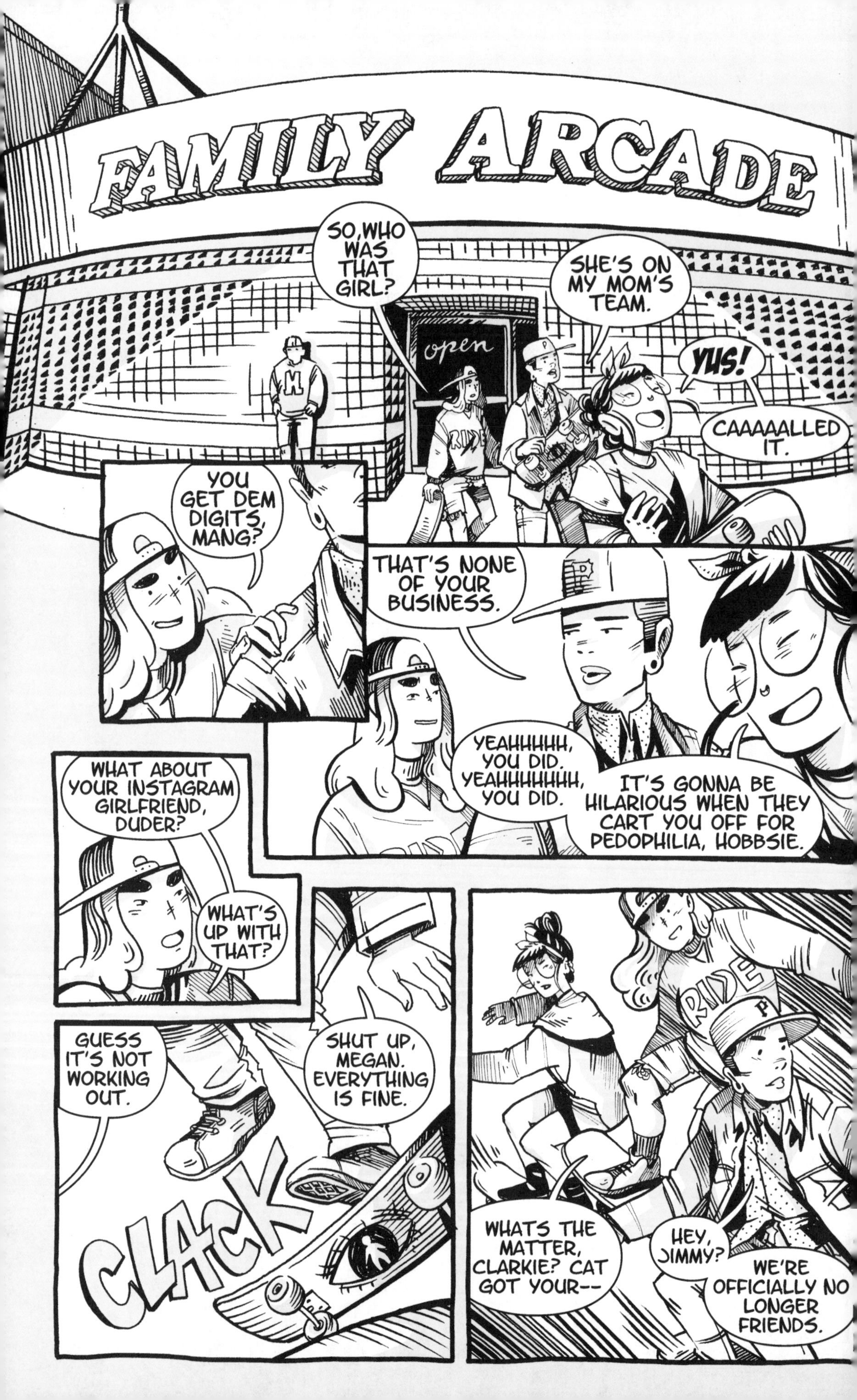
FAMILY ARCADE
open
SO, WHO WAS THAT GIRL?
SHE'S ON MY MOM'S TEAM.
YUS!
CAAAAALLED IT.
YOU GET DEM DIGITS, MANG?
THAT'S NONE OF YOUR BUSINESS.
YEAHHHHH, YOU DID. YEAHHHHHHH, YOU DID.
IT'S GONNA BE HILARIOUS WHEN THEY CART YOU OFF FOR PEDOPHILIA, HOBBSIE.
WHAT ABOUT YOUR INSTAGRAM GIRLFRIEND, DUDER?
WHAT'S UP WITH THAT?
GUESS IT'S NOT WORKING OUT.
SHUT UP, MEGAN. EVERYTHING IS FINE.
CLACK
WHATS THE MATTER, CLARKIE? CAT GOT YOUR--
HEY, JIMMY?
WE'RE OFFICIALLY NO LONGER FRIENDS.

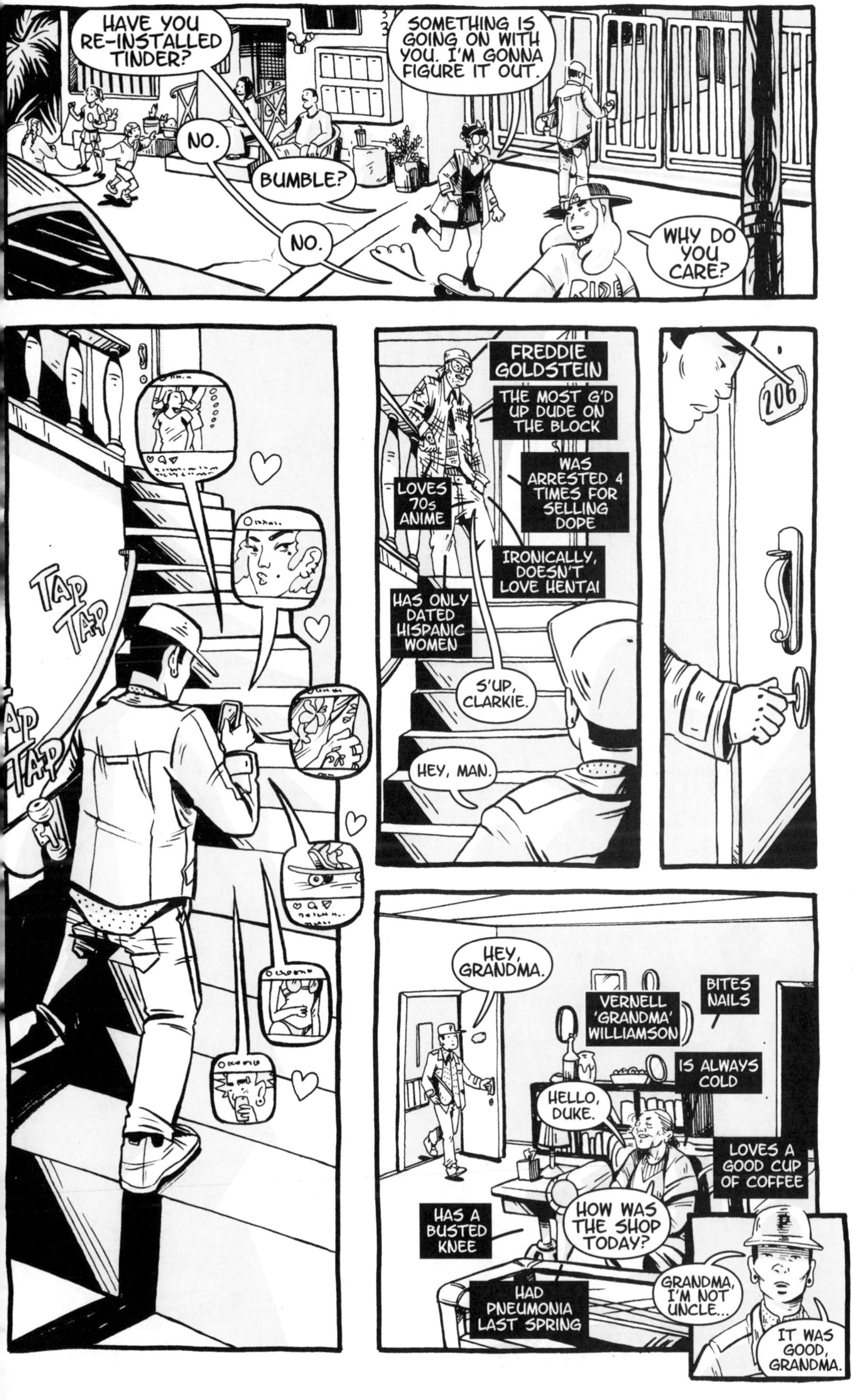
HAVE YOU RE-INSTALLED TINDER?
NO.
BUMBLE?
NO.
SOMETHING IS GOING ON WITH YOU. I'M GONNA FIGURE IT OUT.
WHY DO YOU CARE?
TAP TAP
TAP TAP
FREDDIE GOLDSTEIN
THE MOST G'D UP DUDE ON THE BLOCK
WAS ARRESTED 4 TIMES FOR SELLING DOPE
LOVES 70s ANIME
IRONICALLY, DOESN'T LOVE HENTAI
HAS ONLY DATED HISPANIC WOMEN
S'UP, CLARKIE.
HEY, MAN.
206
HEY, GRANDMA.
VERNELL 'GRANDMA' WILLIAMSON
BITES NAILS
IS ALWAYS COLD
HELLO, DUKE.
LOVES A GOOD CUP OF COFFEE
HAS A BUSTED KNEE
HOW WAS THE SHOP TODAY?
HAD PNEUMONIA LAST SPRING
GRANDMA, I'M NOT UNCLE...
IT WAS GOOD, GRANDMA.

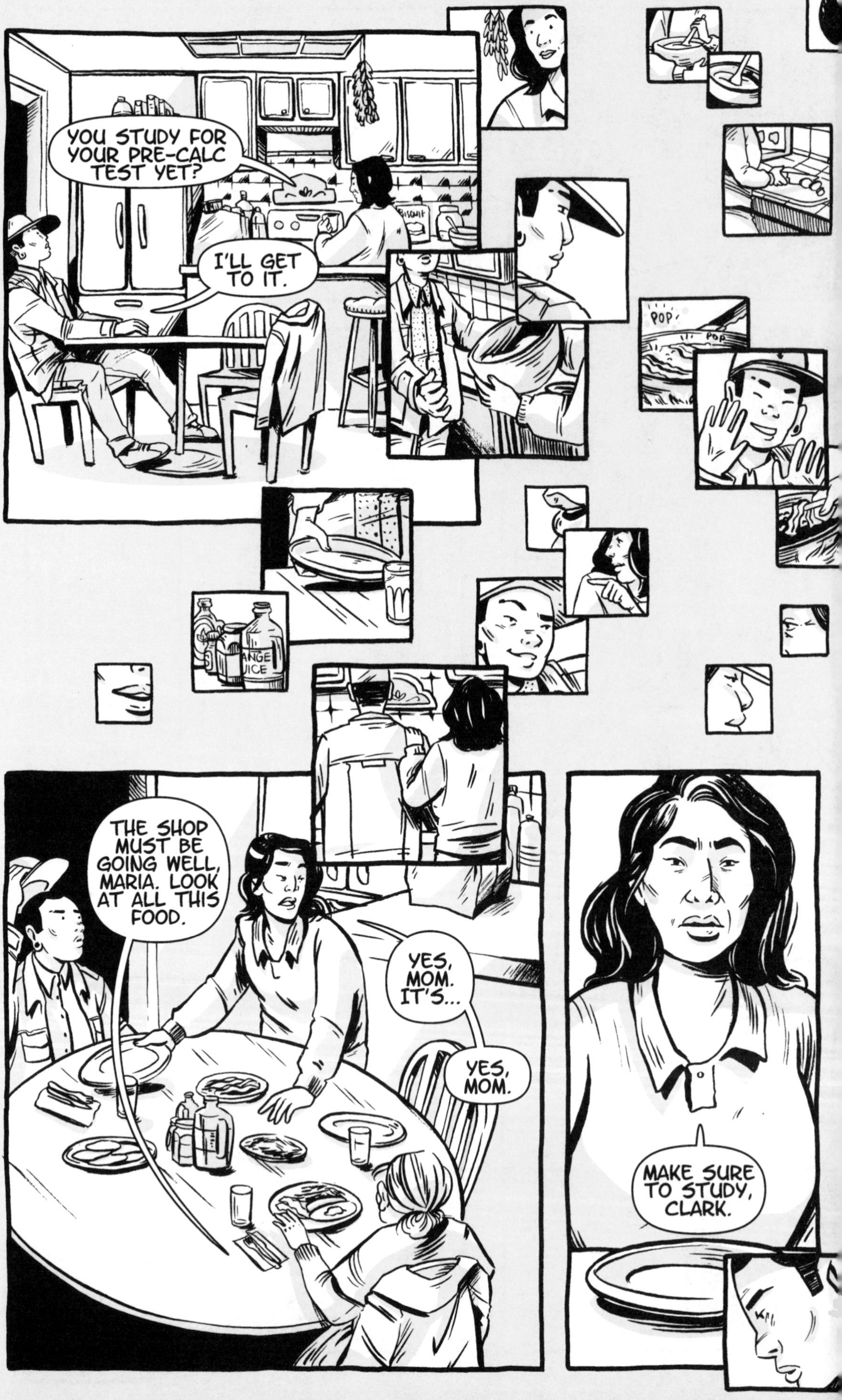

YOU STUDY FOR YOUR PRE-CALC TEST YET?
I'LL GET TO IT.
POP
POP
THE SHOP MUST BE GOING WELL, MARIA. LOOK AT ALL THIS FOOD.
YES, MOM. IT'S...
YES, MOM.
MAKE SURE TO STUDY, CLARK.

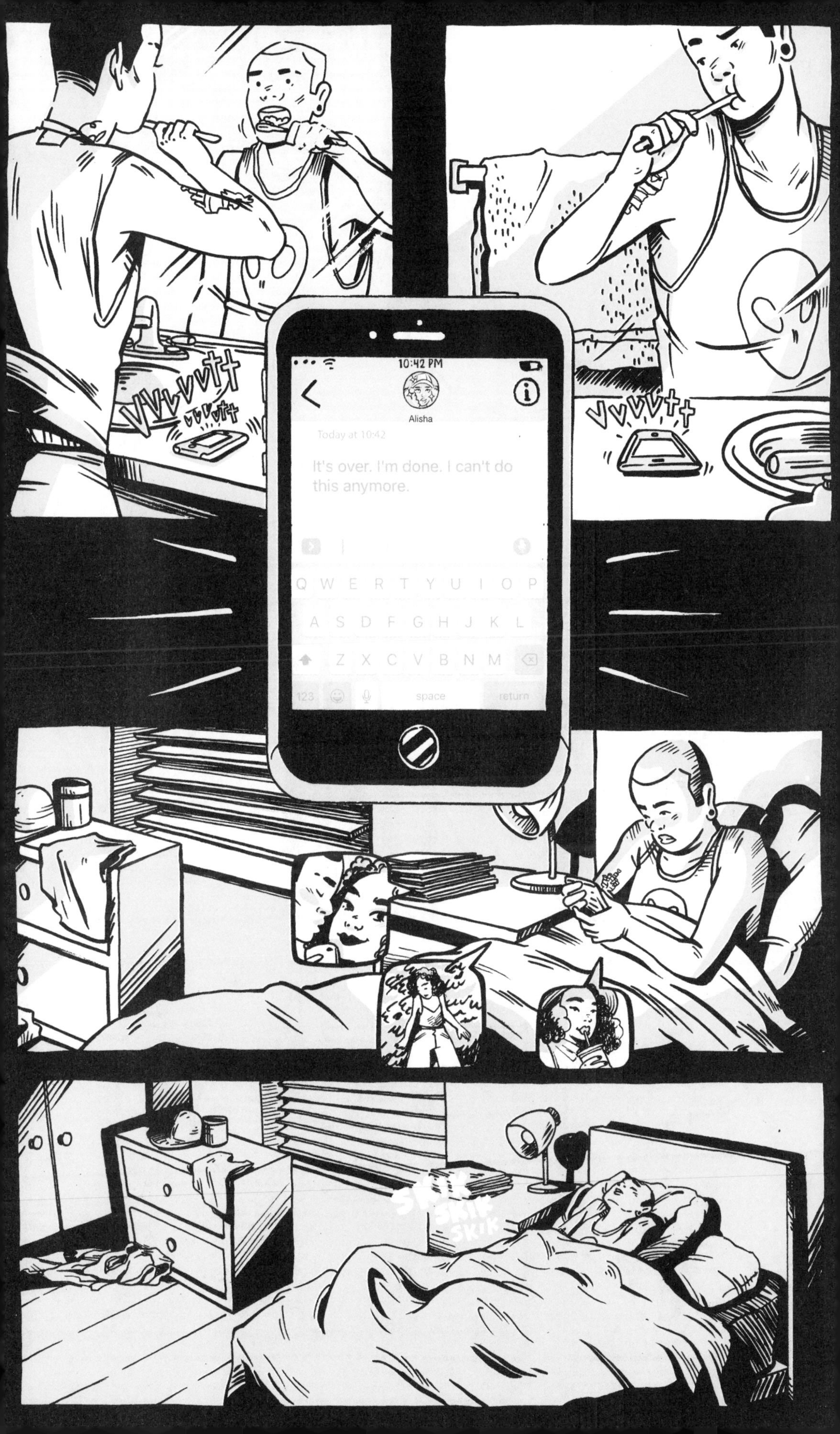

VVVVVTT
VVVVTT
VVVVTT
10:42 PM
Alisha
Today at 10:42
It's over. I'm done. I can't do this anymore.
SKIK
SKIK
SKIK

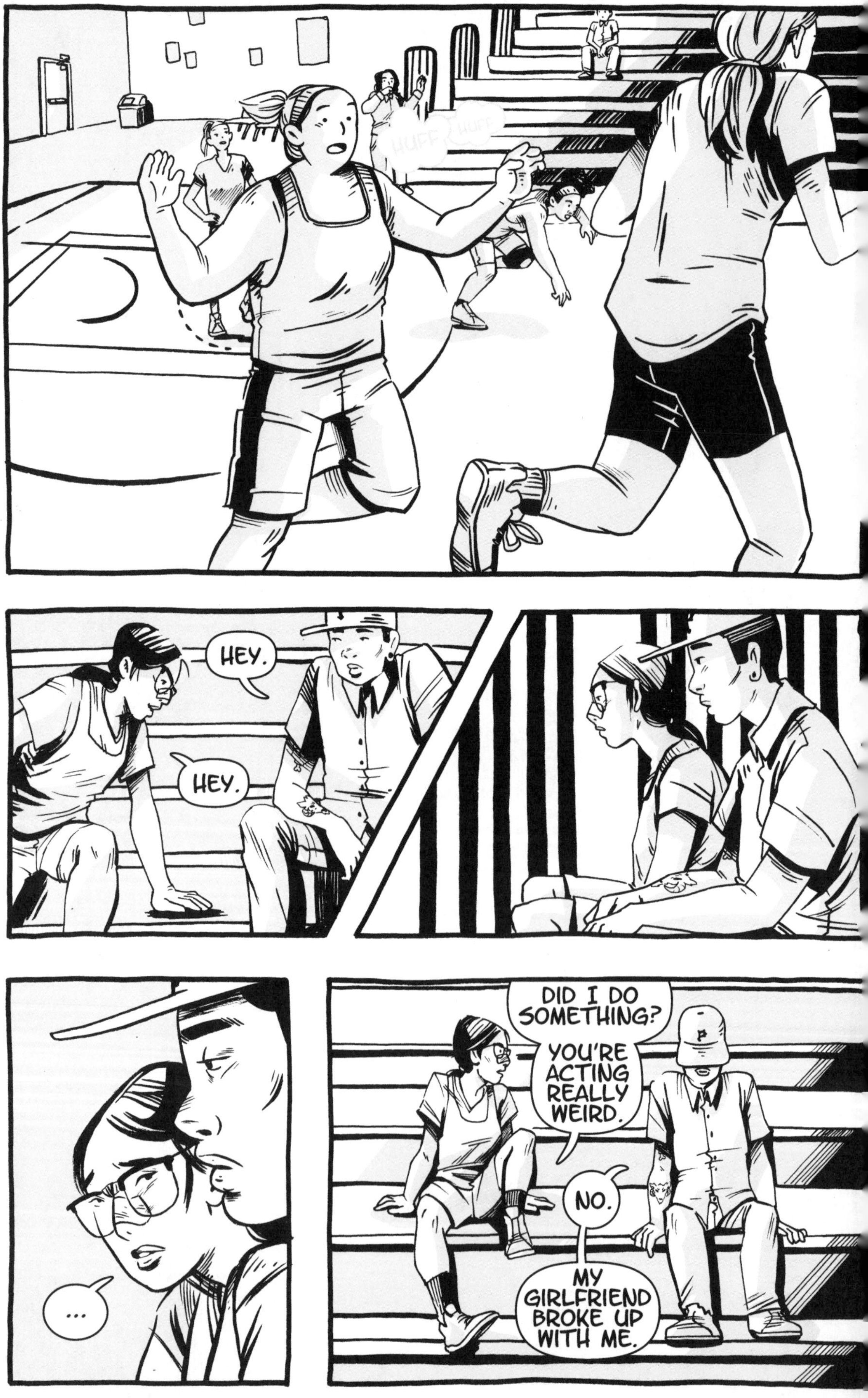
HUFF
HUFF
HEY.
HEY.
...
DID I DO SOMETHING?
YOU'RE ACTING REALLY WEIRD.
NO.
MY GIRLFRIEND BROKE UP WITH ME.

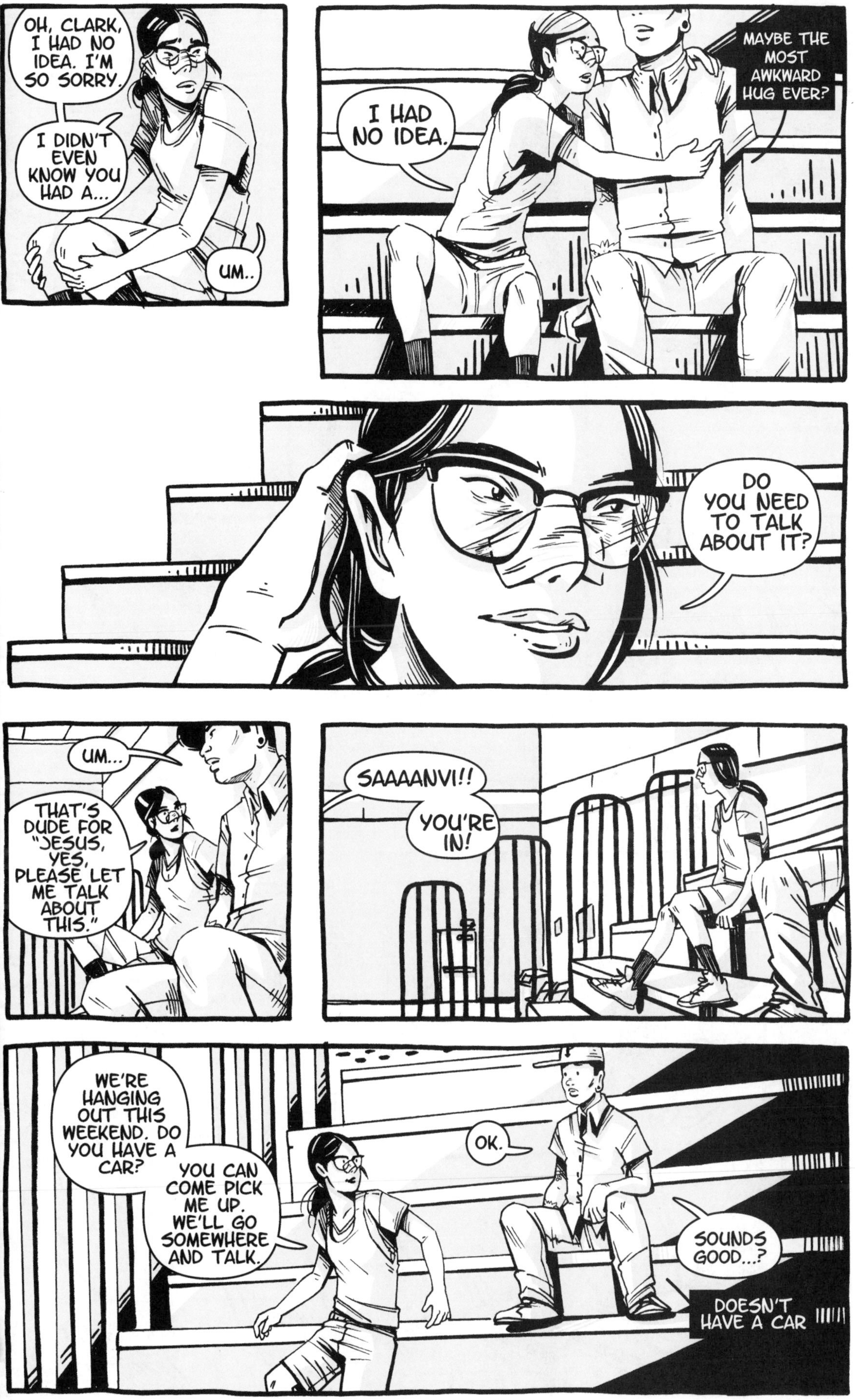
OH, CLARK, I HAD NO IDEA. I'M SO SORRY.
I DIDN'T EVEN KNOW YOU HAD A...
UM..
I HAD NO IDEA.
MAYBE THE MOST AWKWARD HUG EVER?
DO YOU NEED TO TALK ABOUT IT?
UM...
THAT'S DUDE FOR "JESUS, YES, PLEASE LET ME TALK ABOUT THIS."
SAAAANVI!!
YOU'RE IN!
WE'RE HANGING OUT THIS WEEKEND. DO YOU HAVE A CAR?
YOU CAN COME PICK ME UP. WE'LL GO SOMEWHERE AND TALK.
OK.
SOUNDS GOOD...?
DOESN'T HAVE A CAR

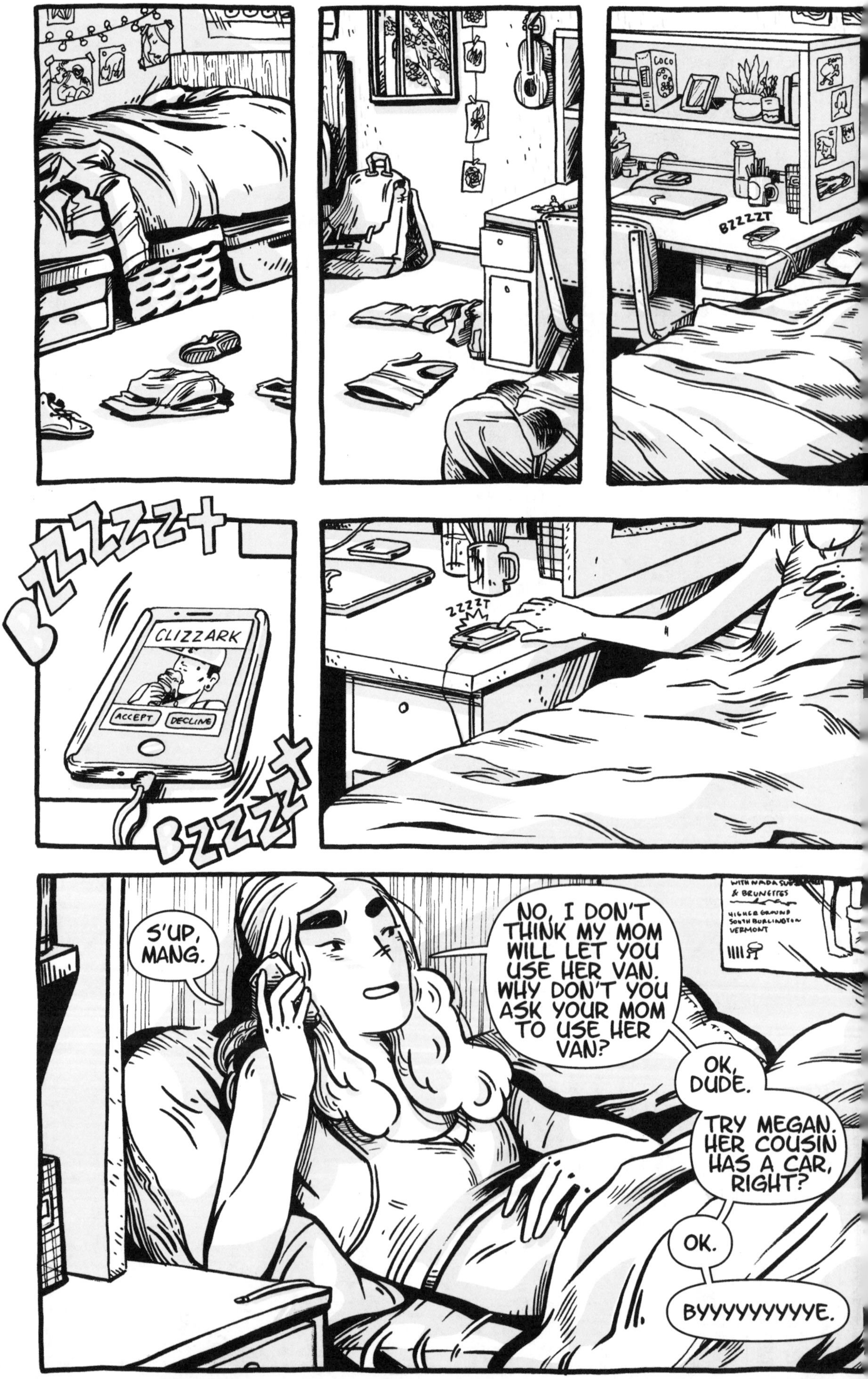
COCO
BZZZZT
BZZZZZT
CLIZZARK
ACCEPT
DECLINE
BZZZZT
ZZZZT
S'UP, MANG.
NO, I DON'T THINK MY MOM WILL LET YOU USE HER VAN. WHY DON'T YOU ASK YOUR MOM TO USE HER VAN?
OK, DUDE.
TRY MEGAN. HER COUSIN HAS A CAR, RIGHT?
OK.
BYYYYYYYYYE.
& BRUNETTES
HIGHER GROUND
SOUTH BURLINGTON
VERMONT

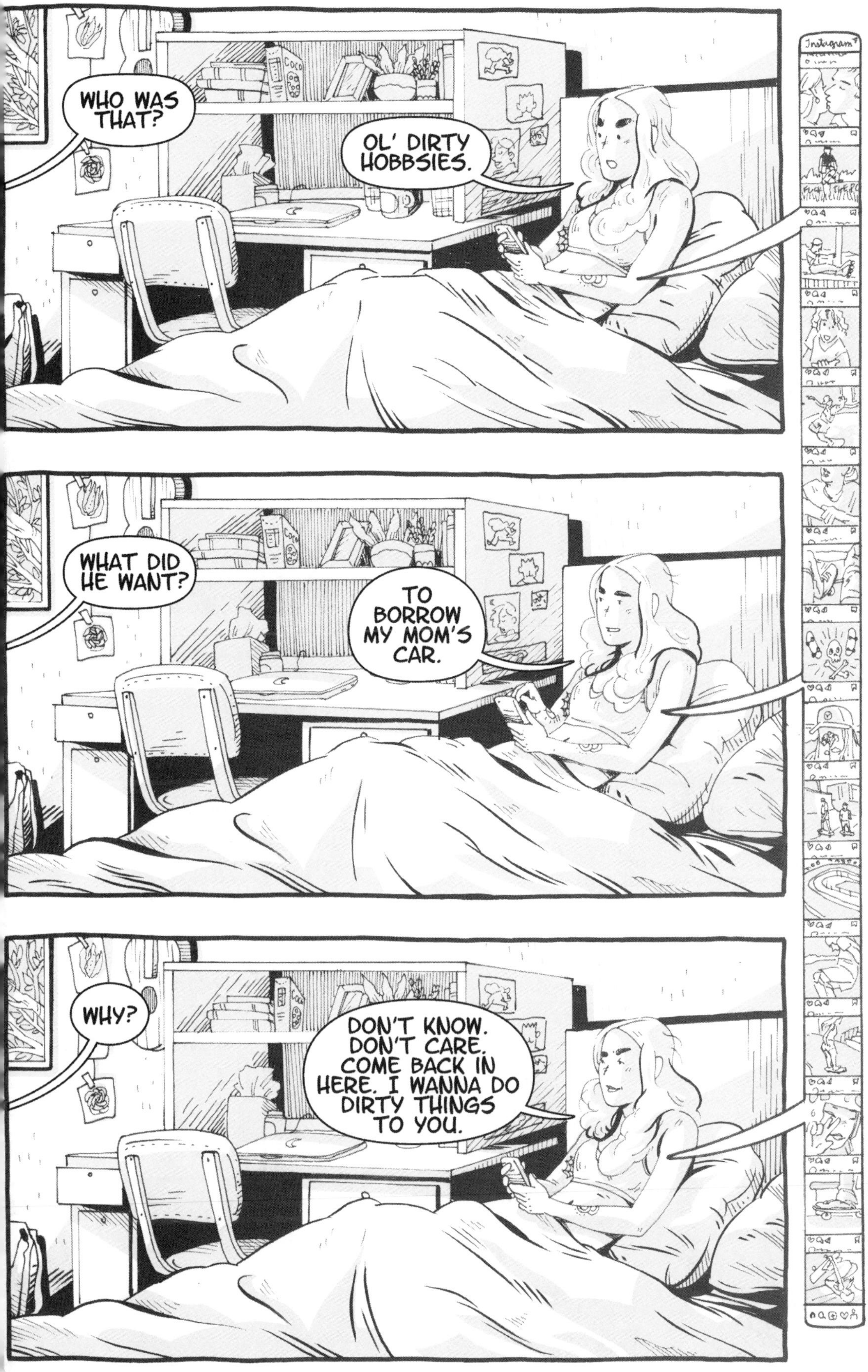
WHO WAS THAT?
OL' DIRTY HOBBSIES.
Instagram
WHAT DID HE WANT?
TO BORROW MY MOM'S CAR.
WHY?
DON'T KNOW. DON'T CARE. COME BACK IN HERE. I WANNA DO DIRTY THINGS TO YOU.

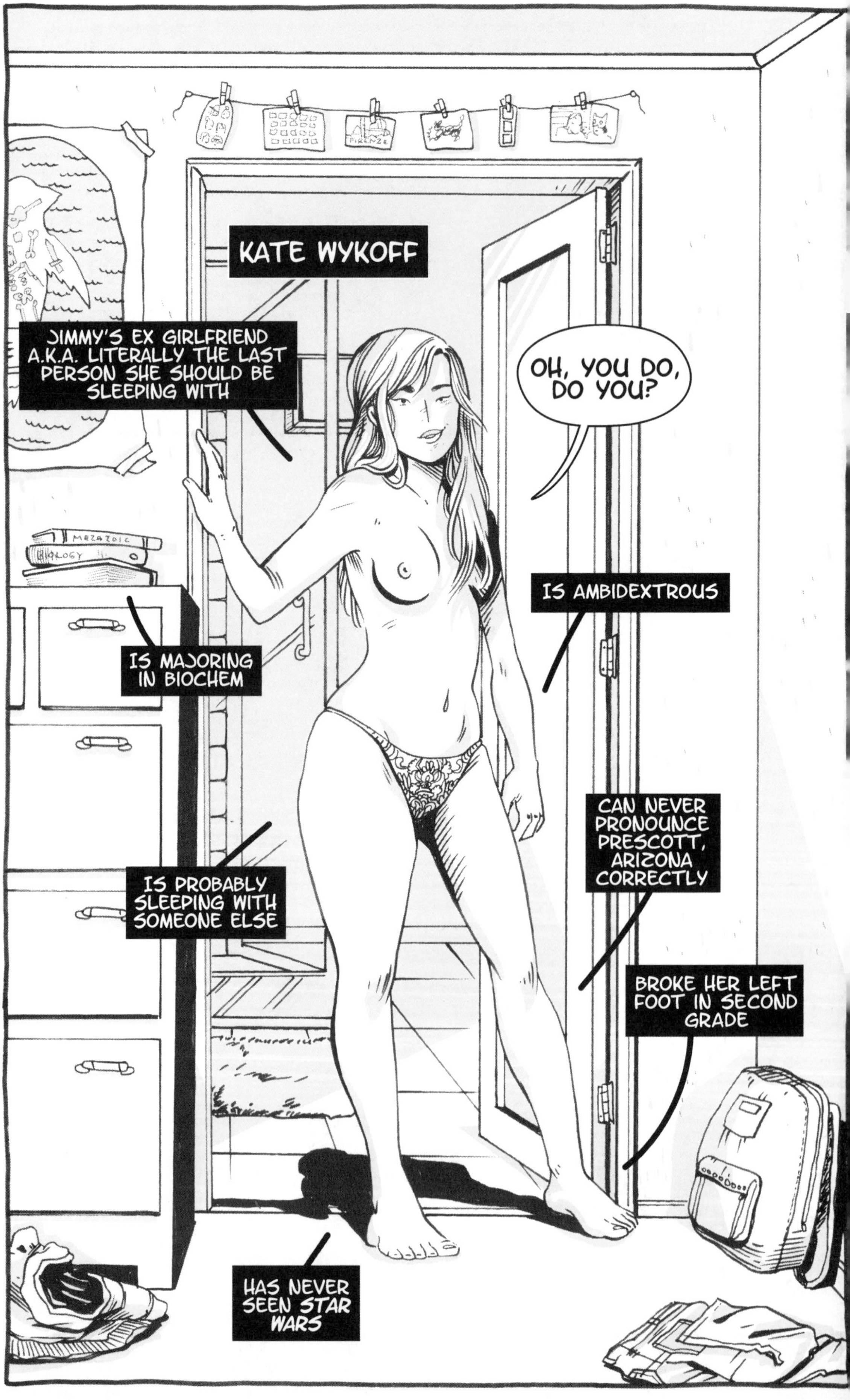
KATE WYKOFF
JIMMY'S EX GIRLFRIEND A.K.A. LITERALLY THE LAST PERSON SHE SHOULD BE SLEEPING WITH
OH, YOU DO, DO YOU?
IS AMBIDEXTROUS
IS MAJORING IN BIOCHEM
CAN NEVER PRONOUNCE PRESCOTT, ARIZONA CORRECTLY
IS PROBABLY SLEEPING WITH SOMEONE ELSE
BROKE HER LEFT FOOT IN SECOND GRADE
HAS NEVER SEEN STAR WARS

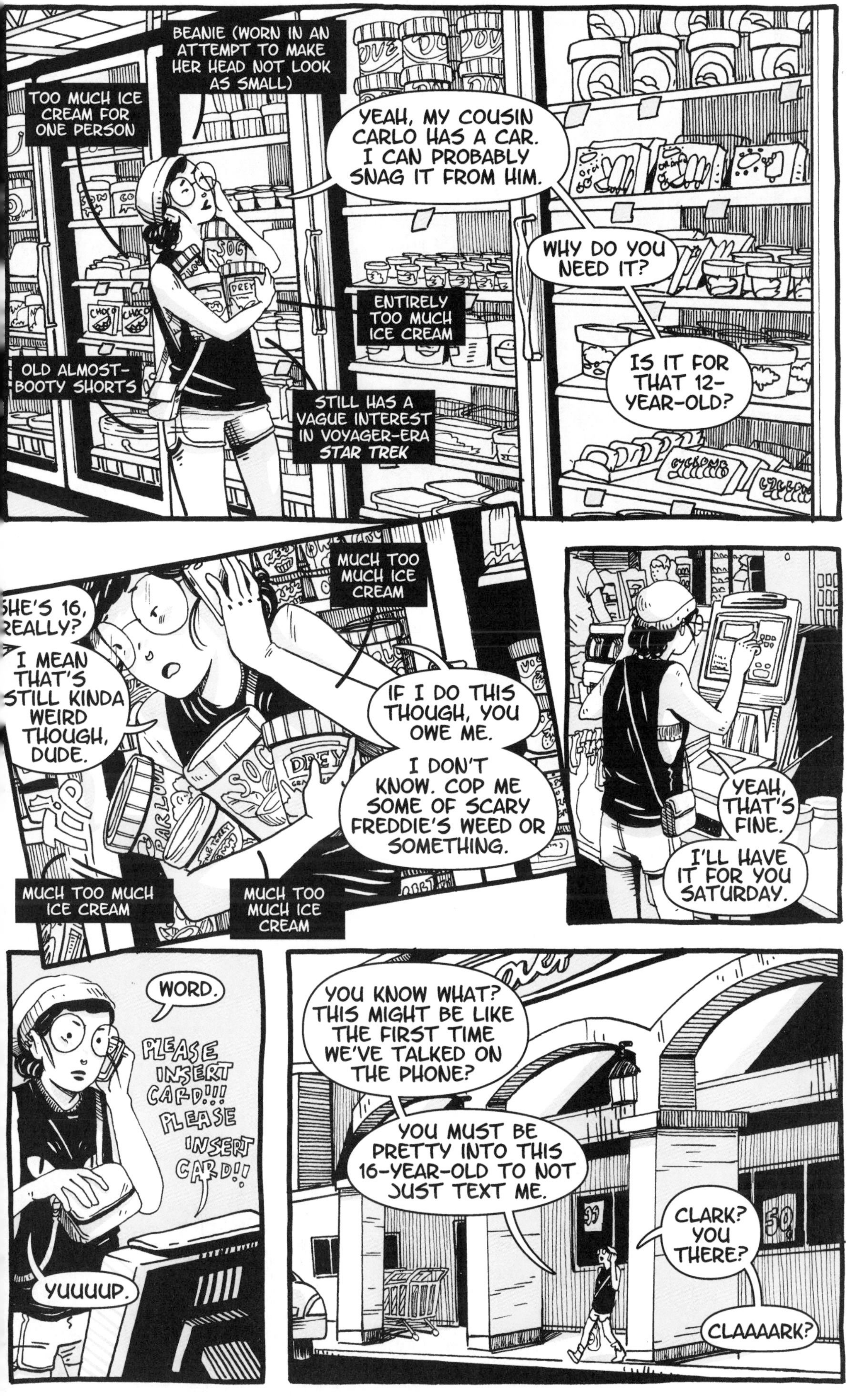

BEANIE (WORN IN AN ATTEMPT TO MAKE HER HEAD NOT LOOK AS SMALL)
TOO MUCH ICE CREAM FOR ONE PERSON
YEAH, MY COUSIN CARLO HAS A CAR. I CAN PROBABLY SNAG IT FROM HIM.
WHY DO YOU NEED IT?
ENTIRELY TOO MUCH ICE CREAM
OLD ALMOST-BOOTY SHORTS
STILL HAS A VAGUE INTEREST IN VOYAGER-ERA STAR TREK
IS IT FOR THAT 12-YEAR-OLD?
MUCH TOO MUCH ICE CREAM
HE'S 16, REALLY?
I MEAN THAT'S STILL KINDA WEIRD THOUGH, DUDE.
IF I DO THIS THOUGH, YOU OWE ME.
I DON'T KNOW. COP ME SOME OF SCARY FREDDIE'S WEED OR SOMETHING.
MUCH TOO MUCH ICE CREAM
MUCH TOO MUCH ICE CREAM
YEAH, THAT'S FINE.
I'LL HAVE IT FOR YOU SATURDAY.
WORD.
PLEASE INSERT CARD!!! PLEASE INSERT CARD!!
YUUUUP.
YOU KNOW WHAT? THIS MIGHT BE LIKE THE FIRST TIME WE'VE TALKED ON THE PHONE?
YOU MUST BE PRETTY INTO THIS 16-YEAR-OLD TO NOT JUST TEXT ME.
CLARK? YOU THERE?
CLAAAARK?

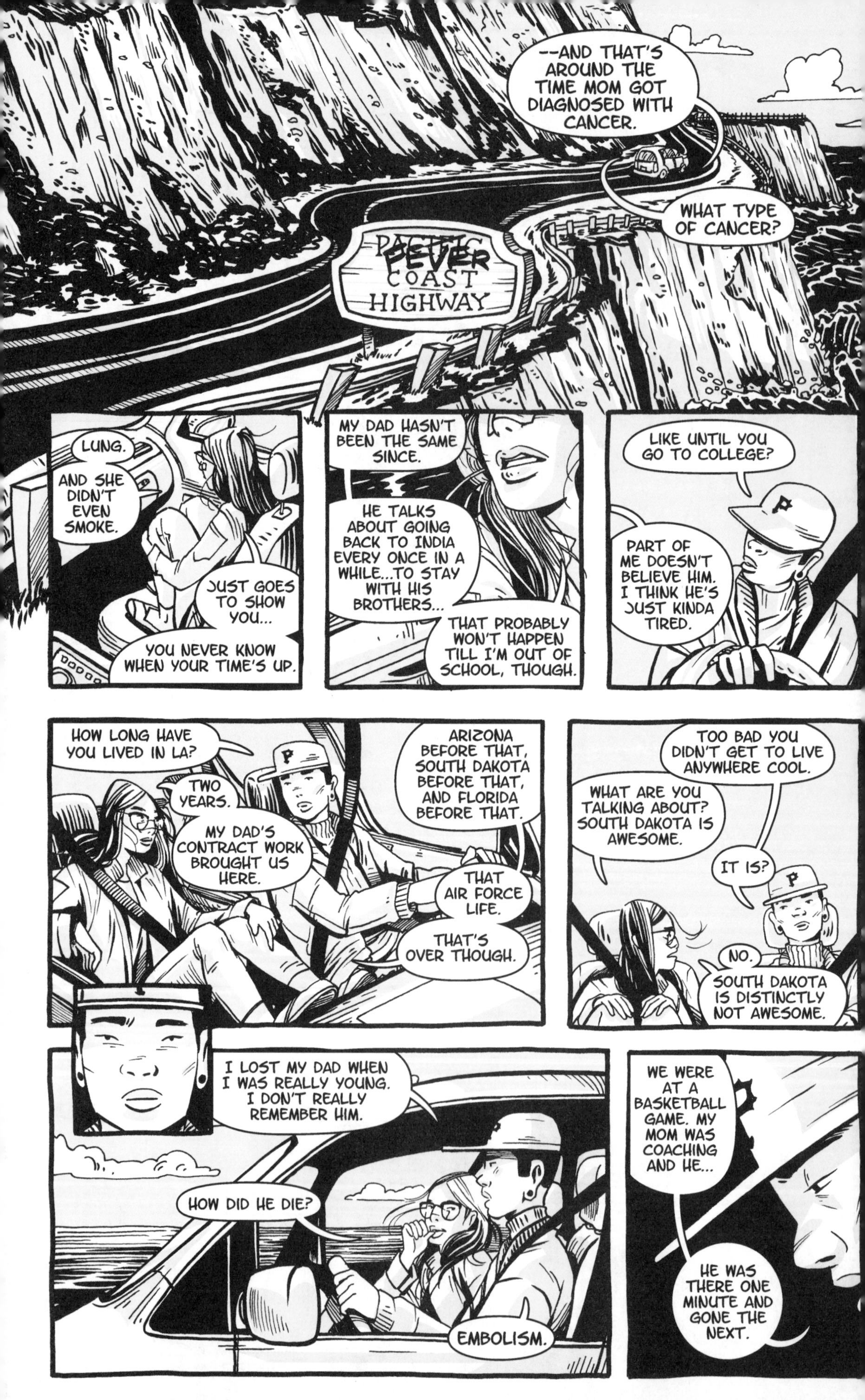
--AND THAT'S AROUND THE TIME MOM GOT DIAGNOSED WITH CANCER.
PACIFIC FEVER COAST HIGHWAY
WHAT TYPE OF CANCER?
LUNG.
AND SHE DIDN'T EVEN SMOKE.
JUST GOES TO SHOW YOU...
YOU NEVER KNOW WHEN YOUR TIME'S UP.
MY DAD HASN'T BEEN THE SAME SINCE.
HE TALKS ABOUT GOING BACK TO INDIA EVERY ONCE IN A WHILE...TO STAY WITH HIS BROTHERS...
THAT PROBABLY WON'T HAPPEN TILL I'M OUT OF SCHOOL, THOUGH.
LIKE UNTIL YOU GO TO COLLEGE?
PART OF ME DOESN'T BELIEVE HIM. I THINK HE'S JUST KINDA TIRED.
HOW LONG HAVE YOU LIVED IN LA?
TWO YEARS.
MY DAD'S CONTRACT WORK BROUGHT US HERE.
ARIZONA BEFORE THAT, SOUTH DAKOTA BEFORE THAT, AND FLORIDA BEFORE THAT.
THAT AIR FORCE LIFE.
THAT'S OVER THOUGH.
TOO BAD YOU DIDN'T GET TO LIVE ANYWHERE COOL.
WHAT ARE YOU TALKING ABOUT? SOUTH DAKOTA IS AWESOME.
IT IS?
NO.
SOUTH DAKOTA IS DISTINCTLY NOT AWESOME.
I LOST MY DAD WHEN I WAS REALLY YOUNG. I DON'T REALLY REMEMBER HIM.
HOW DID HE DIE?
EMBOLISM.
WE WERE AT A BASKETBALL GAME. MY MOM WAS COACHING AND HE...
HE WAS THERE ONE MINUTE AND GONE THE NEXT.

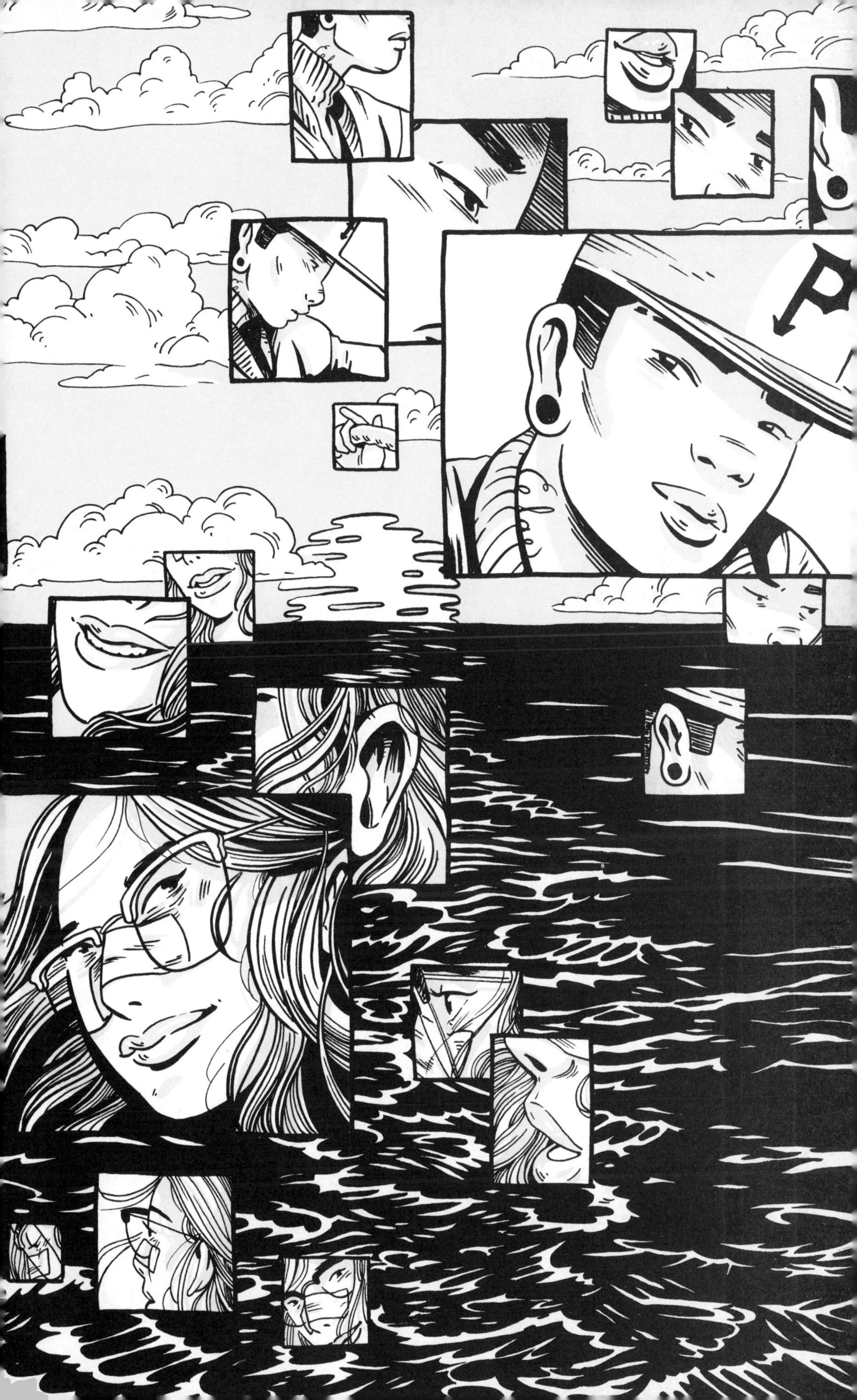

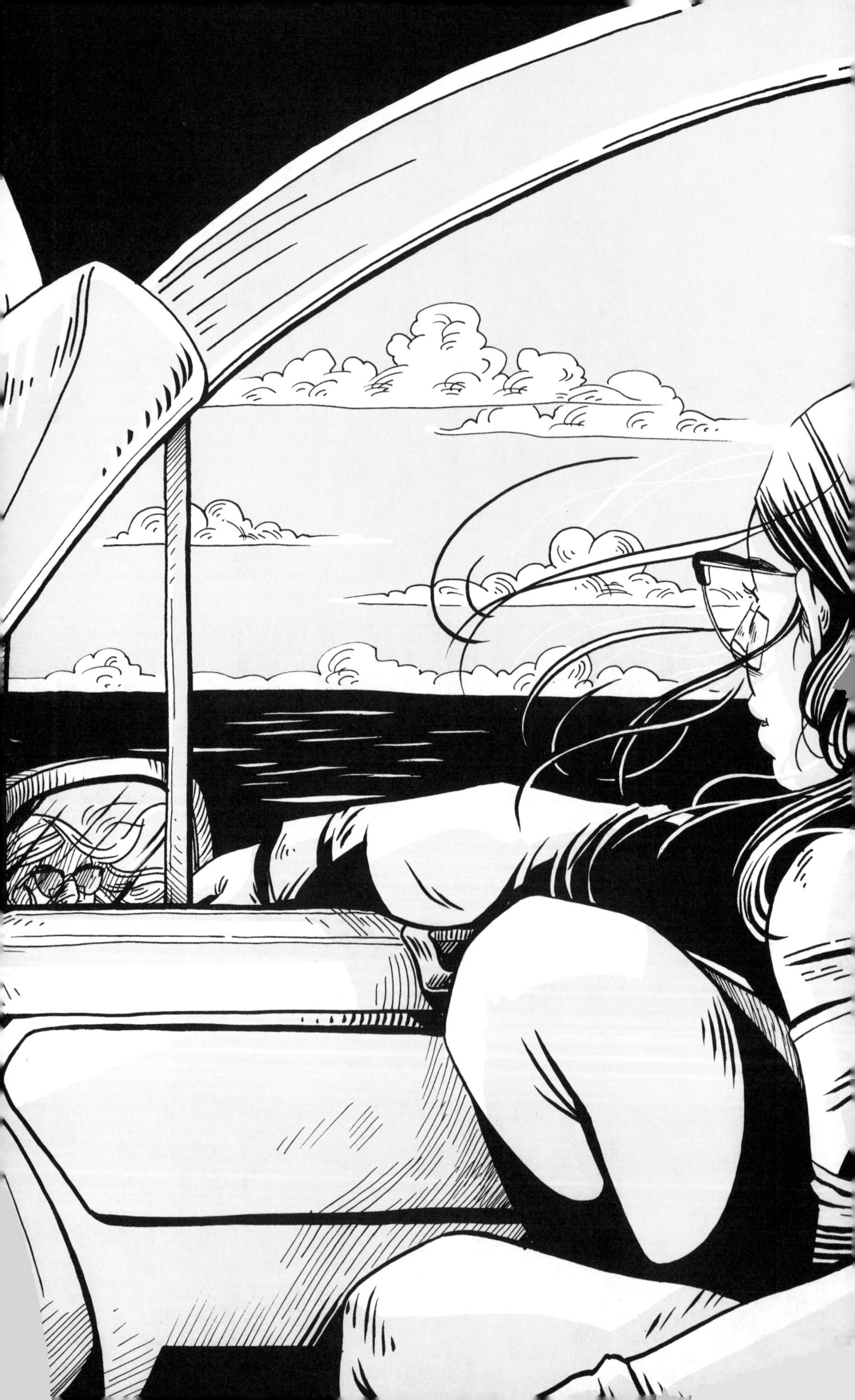

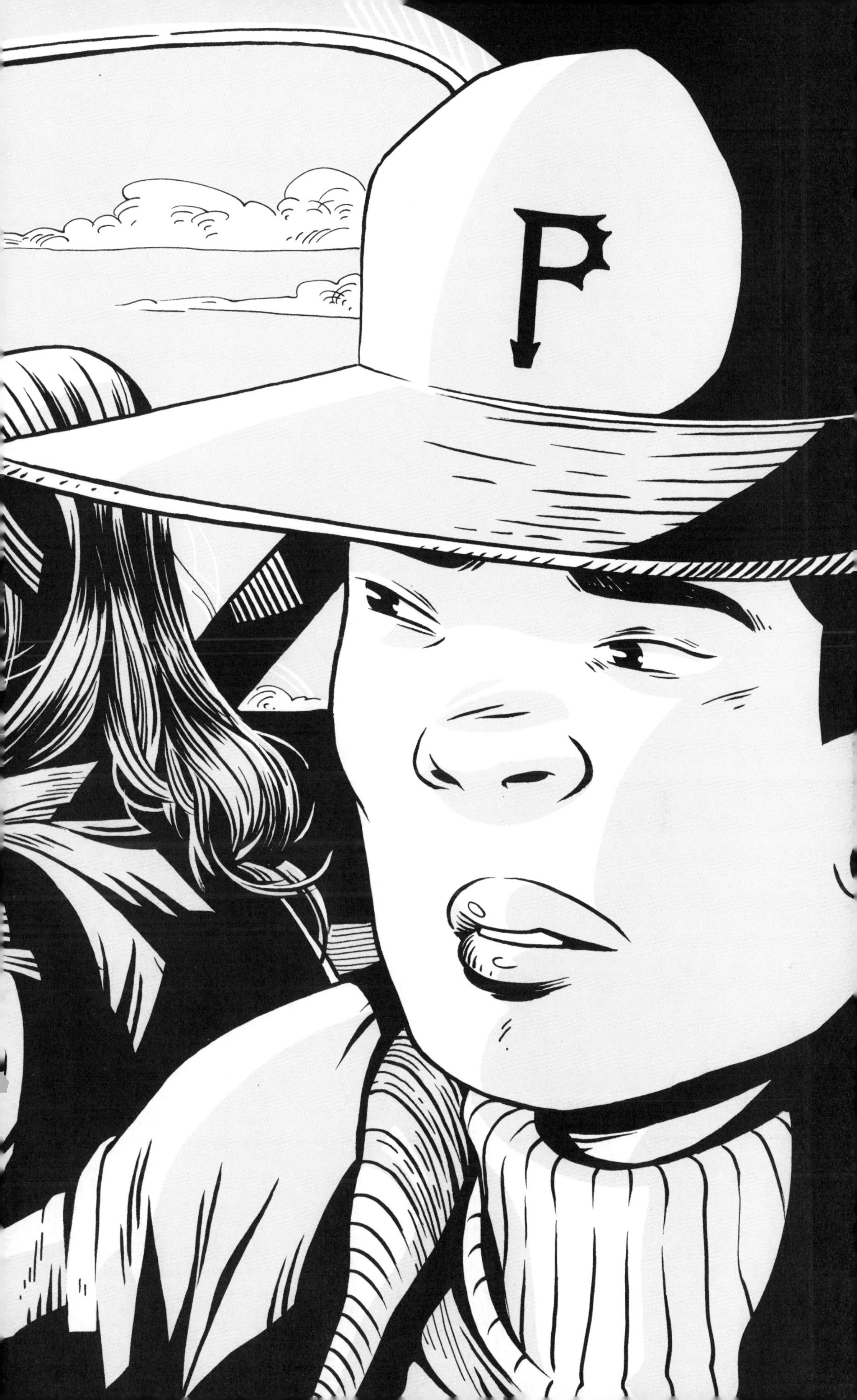

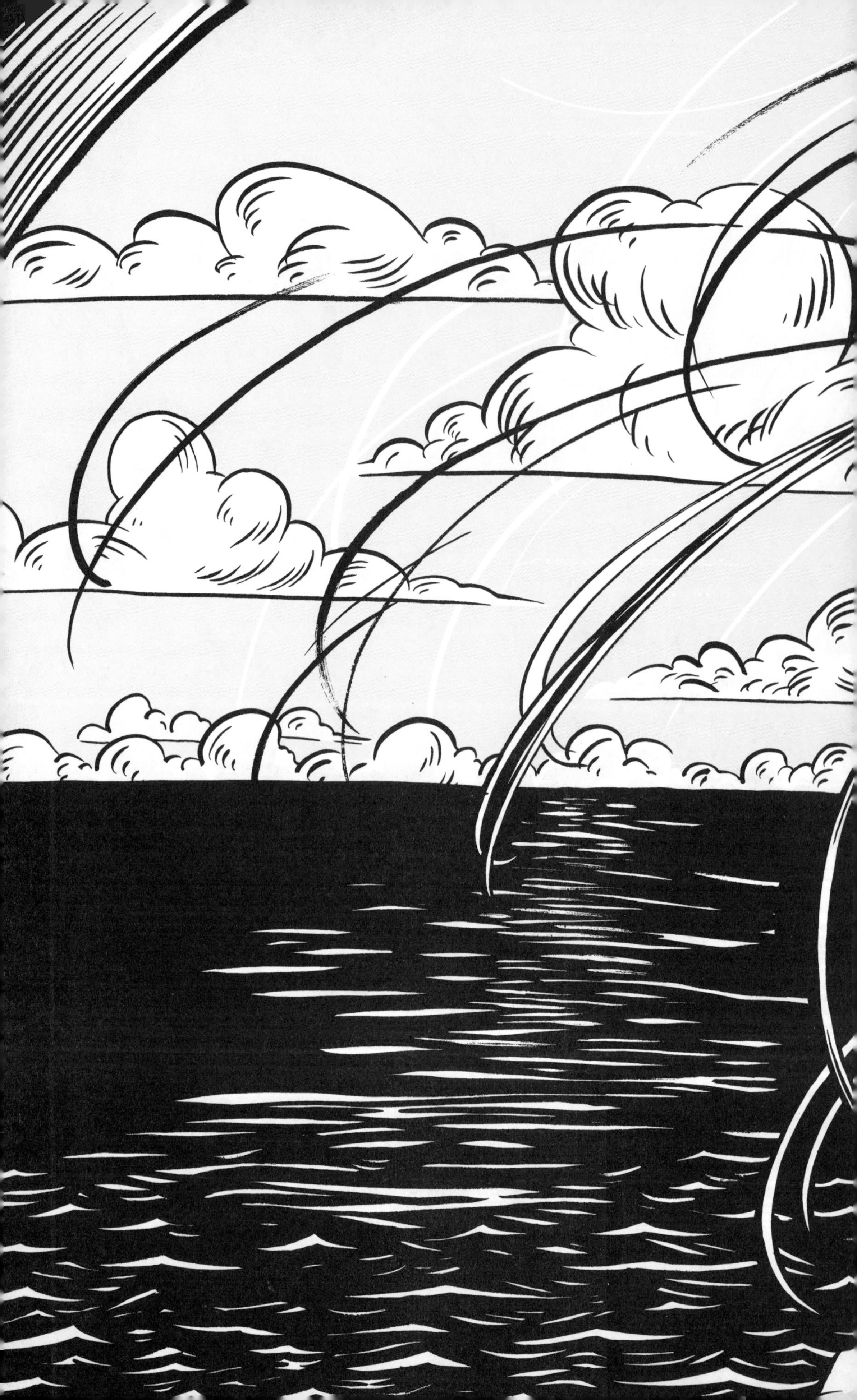

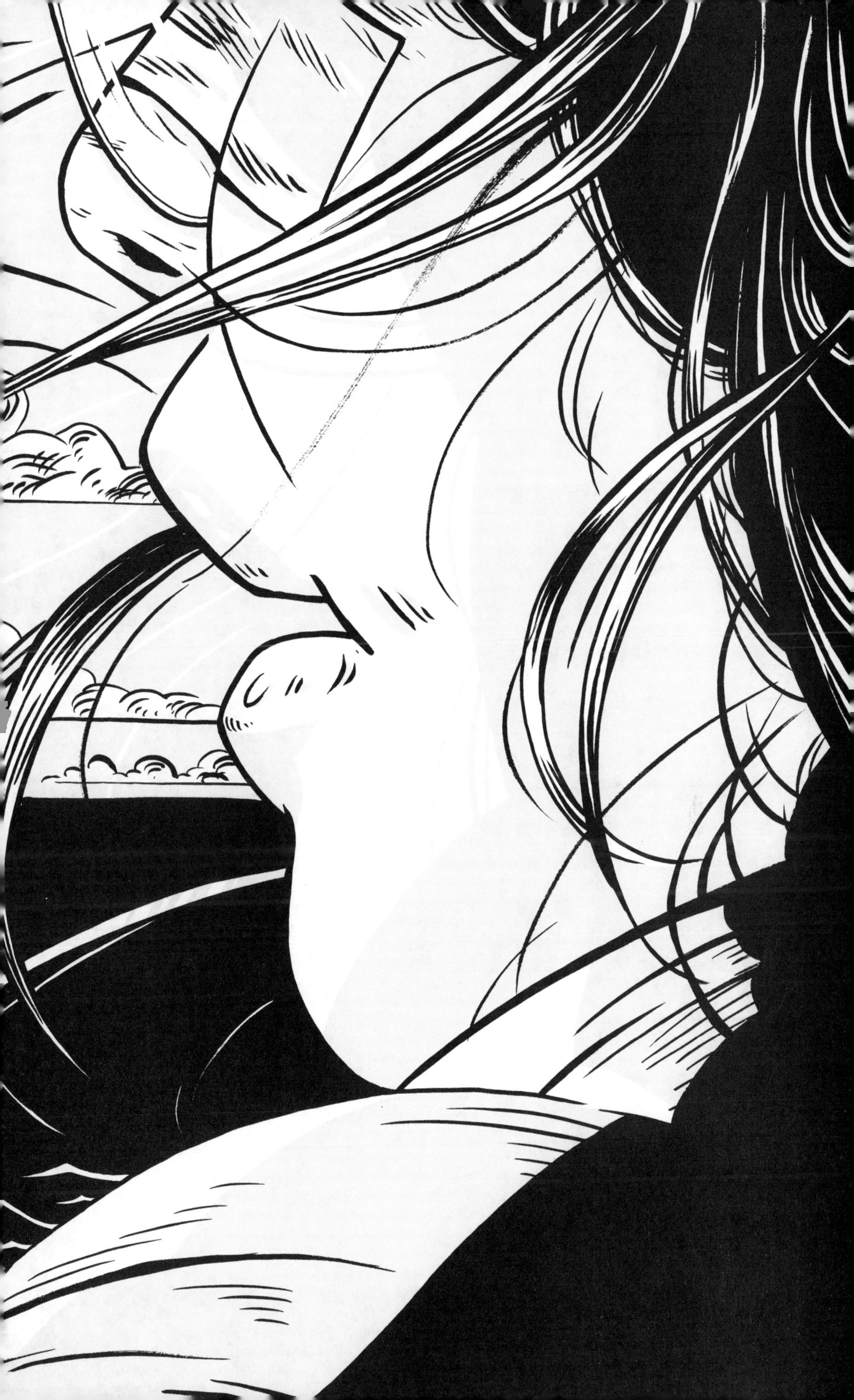

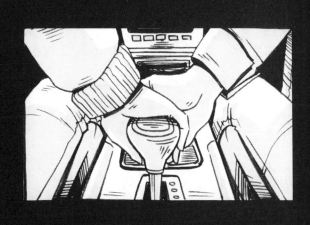

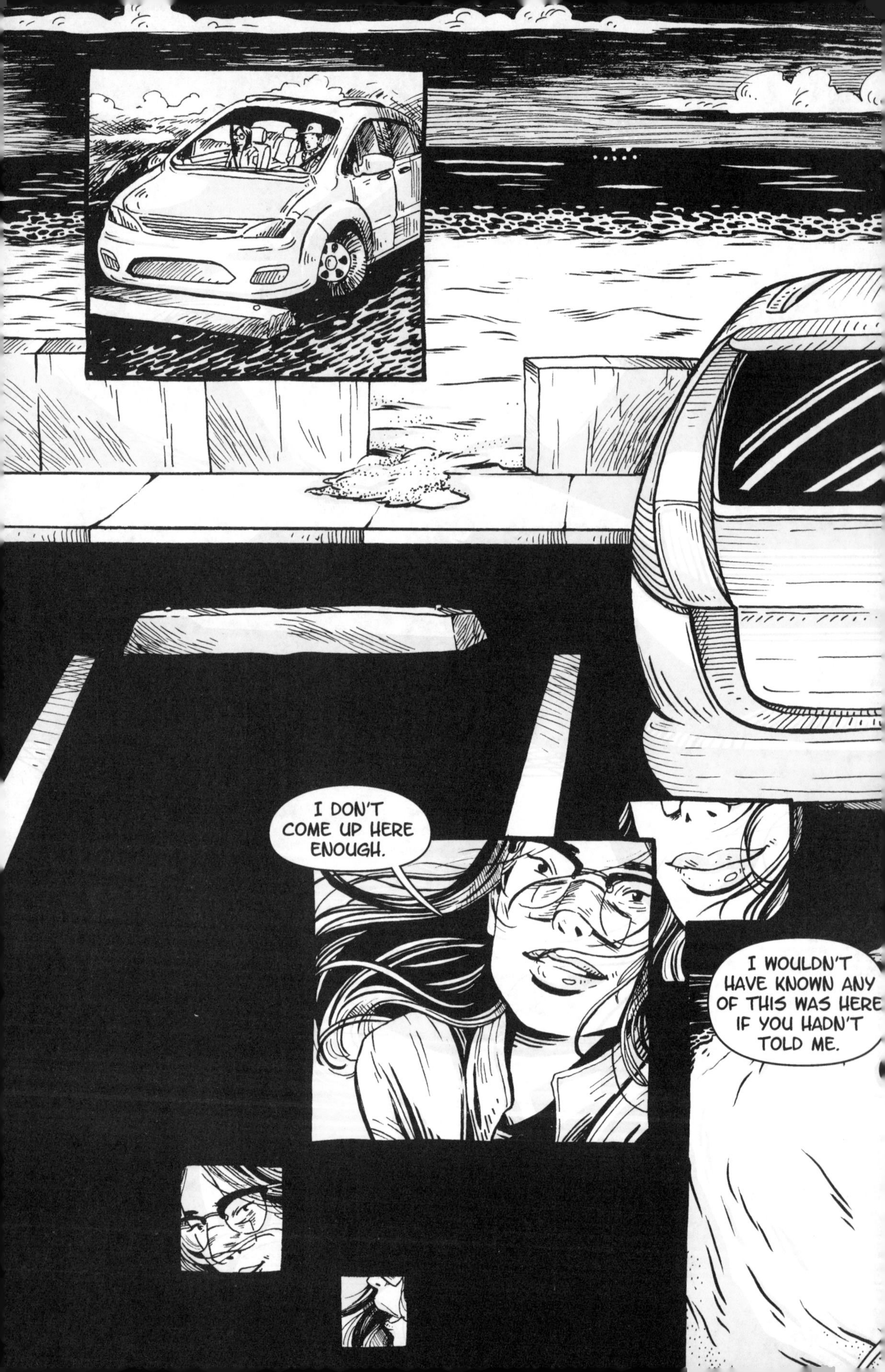
I DON'T COME UP HERE ENOUGH.
I WOULDN'T HAVE KNOWN ANY OF THIS WAS HERE IF YOU HADN'T TOLD ME.

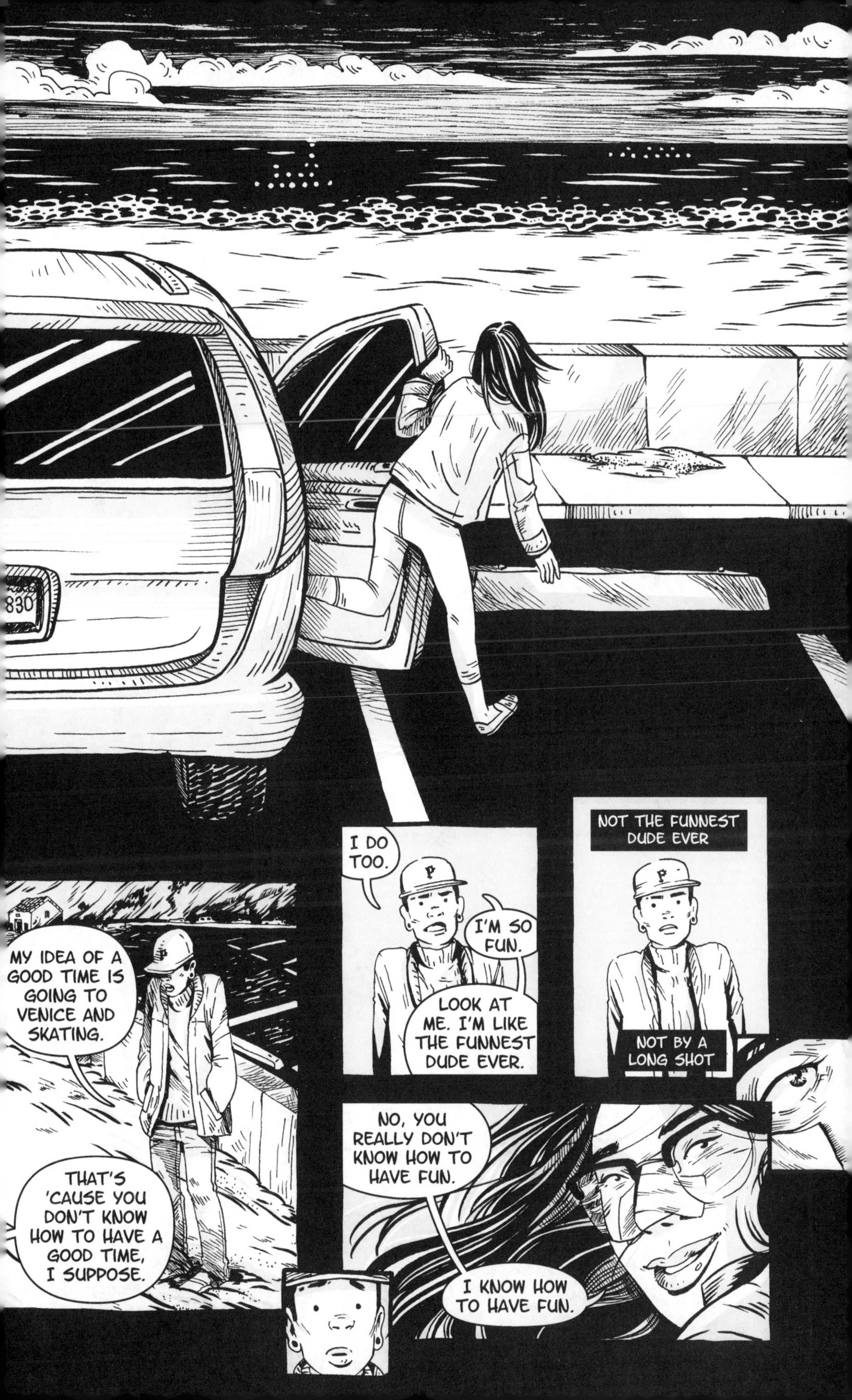
MY IDEA OF A GOOD TIME IS GOING TO VENICE AND SKATING.
THAT'S 'CAUSE YOU DON'T KNOW HOW TO HAVE A GOOD TIME, I SUPPOSE.
I DO TOO.
I'M SO FUN.
LOOK AT ME. I'M LIKE THE FUNNEST DUDE EVER.
NOT THE FUNNEST DUDE EVER
NOT BY A LONG SHOT
NO, YOU REALLY DON'T KNOW HOW TO HAVE FUN.
I KNOW HOW TO HAVE FUN.

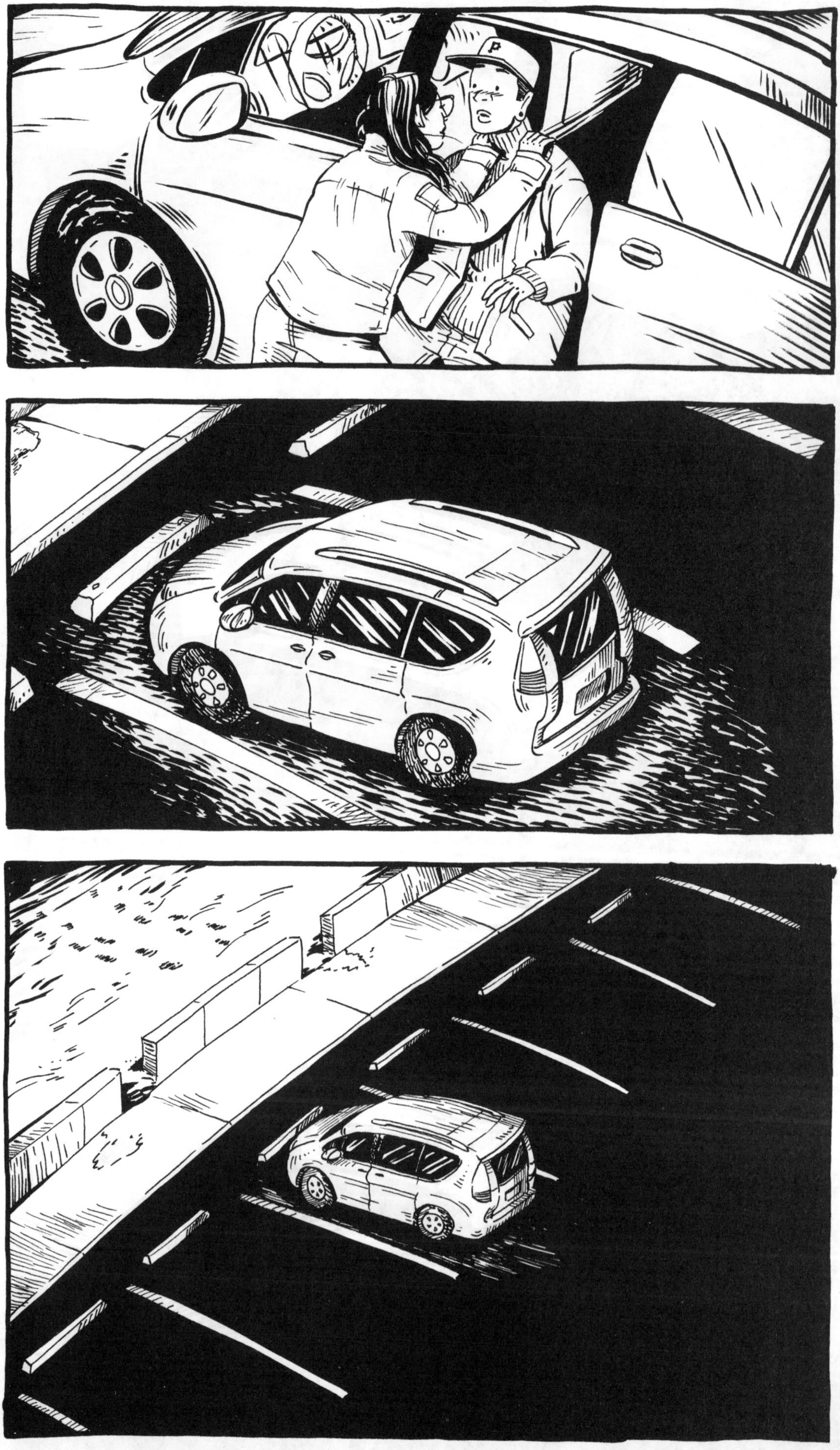

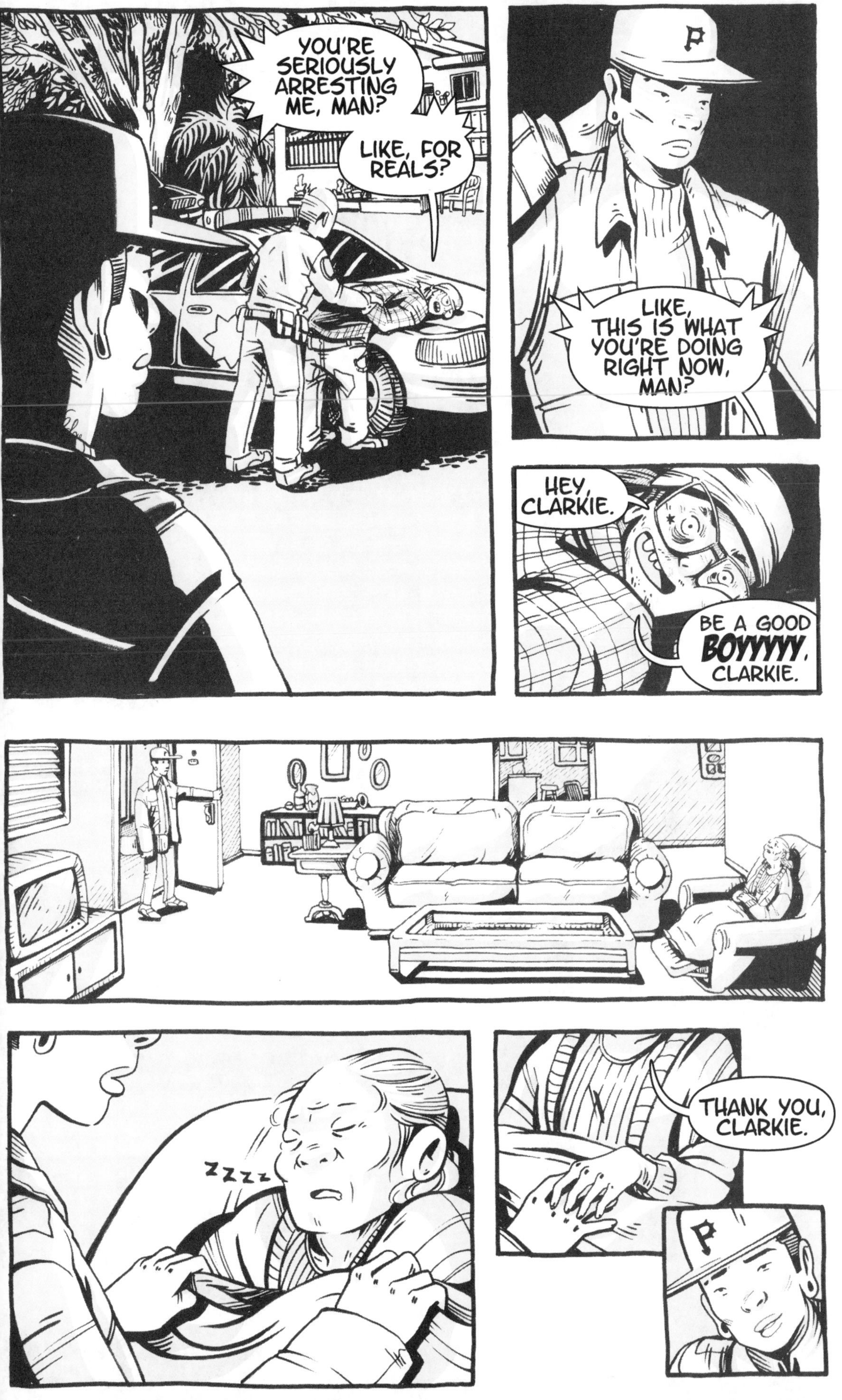
YOU'RE SERIOUSLY ARRESTING ME, MAN?
LIKE, FOR REALS?
LIKE, THIS IS WHAT YOU'RE DOING RIGHT NOW, MAN?
HEY, CLARKIE.
BE A GOOD BOYYYYY, CLARKIE.
ZZZZ
THANK YOU, CLARKIE.

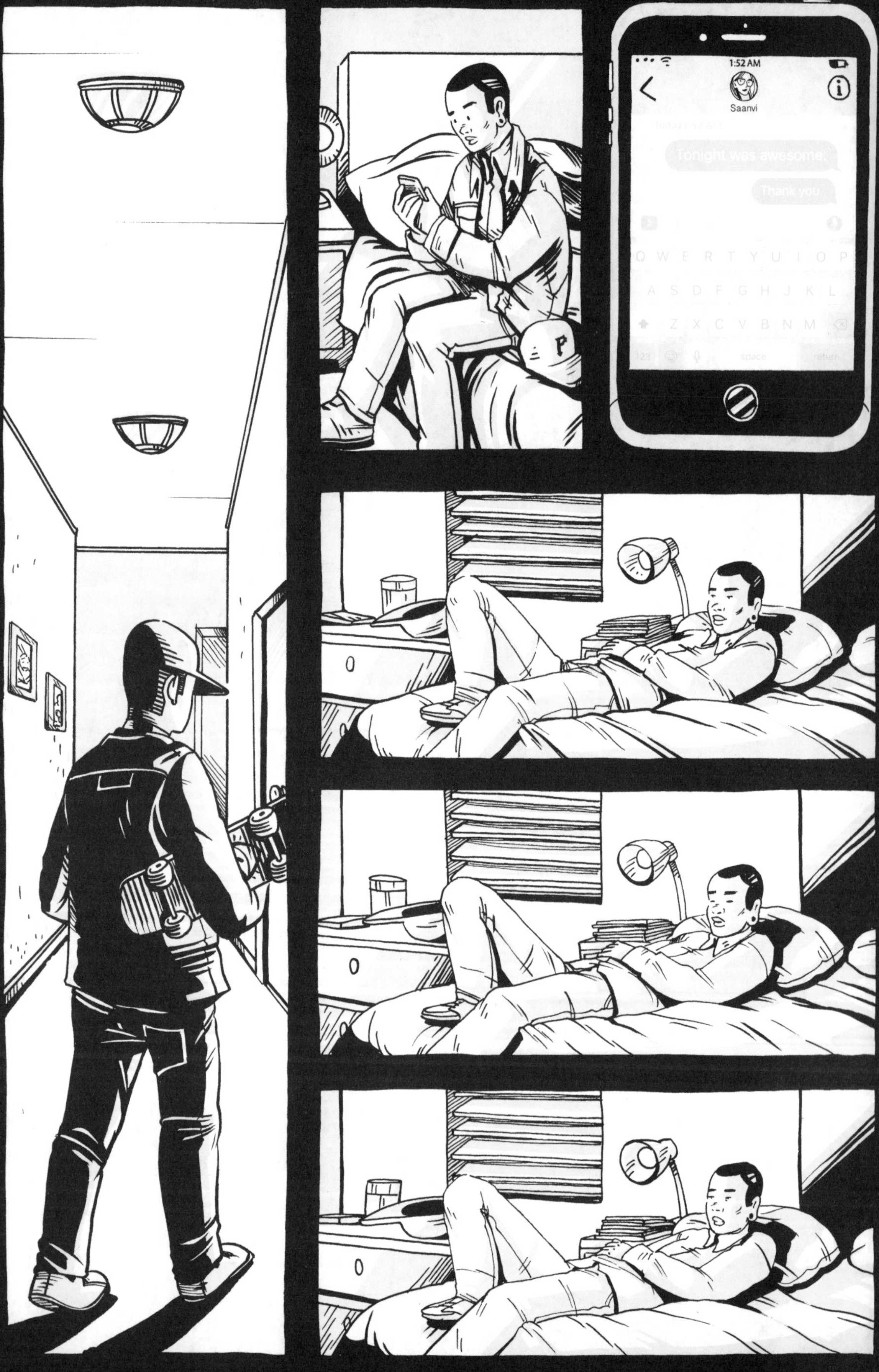
1:52 AM
Saanvi
Tonight was awesome.
Thank you.

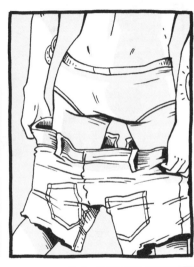

YOU'RE
JUST GONNA
LEAVE?

NO
GOODBYE?

HAVE YOU
SEEN MY
MANIAC COP
SHIRT?

YEAH,
IT'S ON
THE CHAIR.

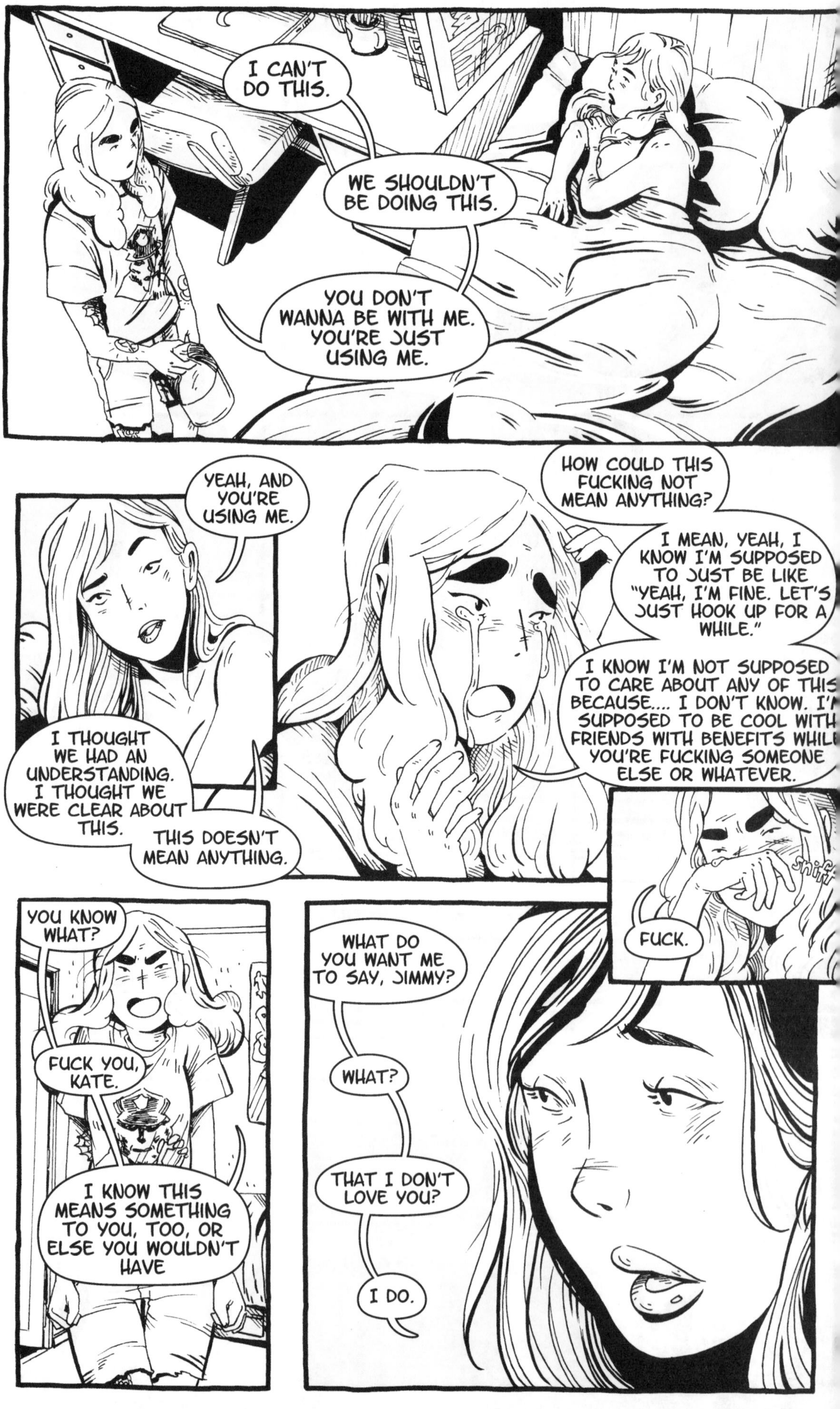
I CAN'T DO THIS.
WE SHOULDN'T BE DOING THIS.
YOU DON'T WANNA BE WITH ME. YOU'RE JUST USING ME.
YEAH, AND YOU'RE USING ME.
I THOUGHT WE HAD AN UNDERSTANDING. I THOUGHT WE WERE CLEAR ABOUT THIS.
THIS DOESN'T MEAN ANYTHING.
HOW COULD THIS FUCKING NOT MEAN ANYTHING?
I MEAN, YEAH, I KNOW I'M SUPPOSED TO JUST BE LIKE "YEAH, I'M FINE. LET'S JUST HOOK UP FOR A WHILE."
I KNOW I'M NOT SUPPOSED TO CARE ABOUT ANY OF THIS BECAUSE.... I DON'T KNOW. I'M SUPPOSED TO BE COOL WITH FRIENDS WITH BENEFITS WHILE YOU'RE FUCKING SOMEONE ELSE OR WHATEVER.
sniff
FUCK.
YOU KNOW WHAT?
FUCK YOU, KATE.
I KNOW THIS MEANS SOMETHING TO YOU, TOO, OR ELSE YOU WOULDN'T HAVE
WHAT DO YOU WANT ME TO SAY, JIMMY?
WHAT?
THAT I DON'T LOVE YOU?
I DO.

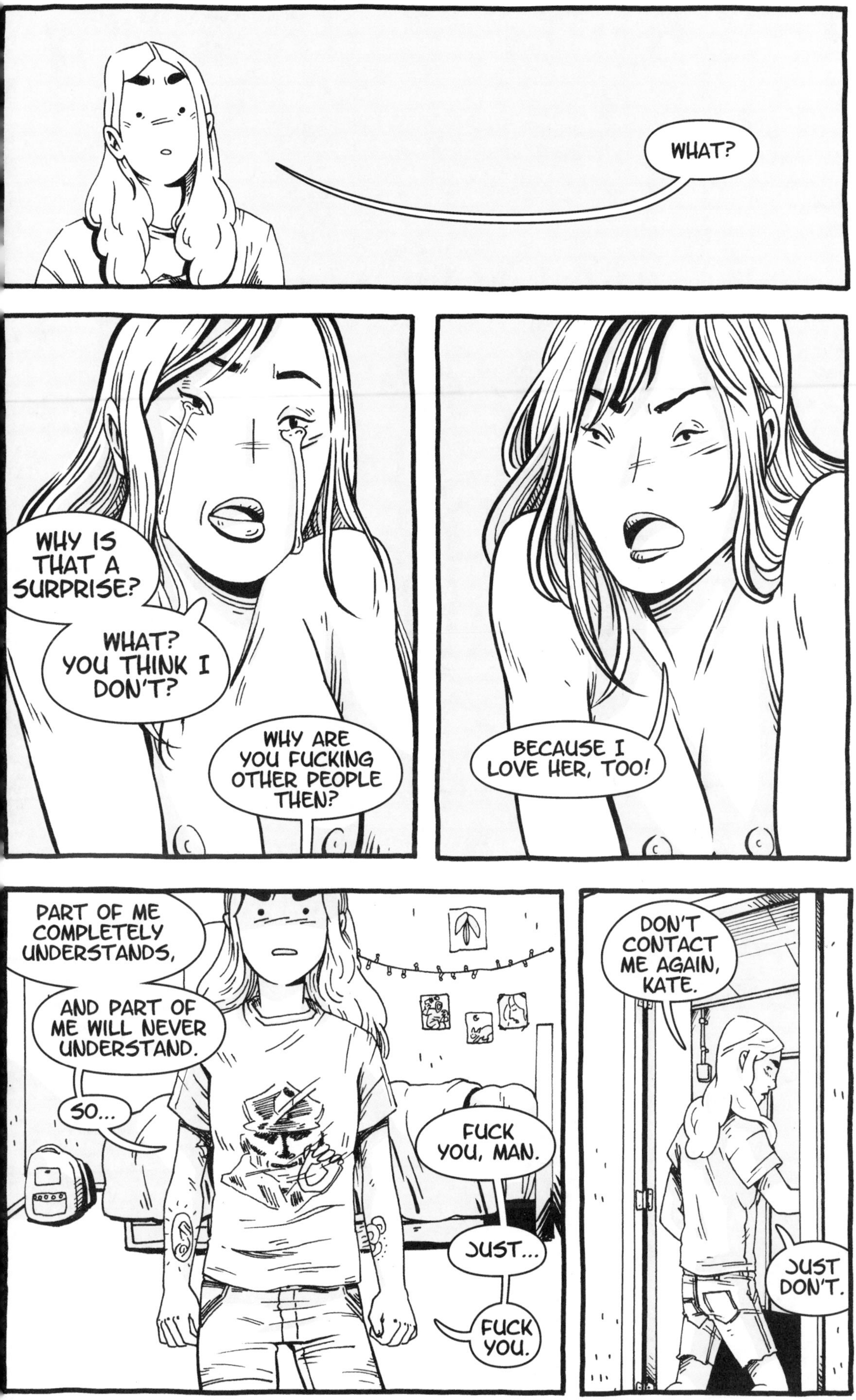
WHAT?
WHY IS THAT A SURPRISE?
WHAT? YOU THINK I DON'T?
WHY ARE YOU FUCKING OTHER PEOPLE THEN?
BECAUSE I LOVE HER, TOO!
PART OF ME COMPLETELY UNDERSTANDS,
AND PART OF ME WILL NEVER UNDERSTAND.
SO...
FUCK YOU, MAN.
JUST...
FUCK YOU.
DON'T CONTACT ME AGAIN, KATE.
JUST DON'T.

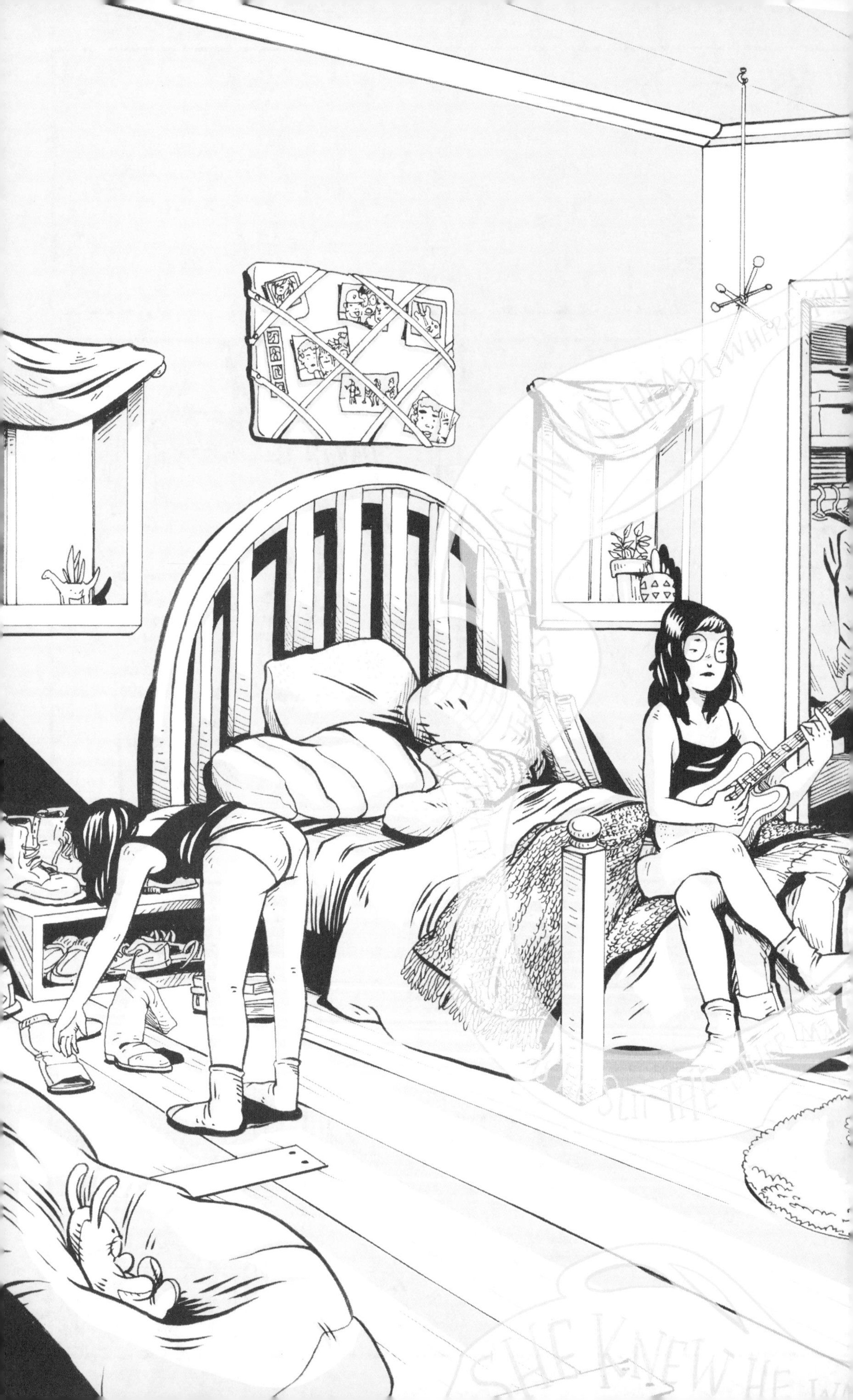

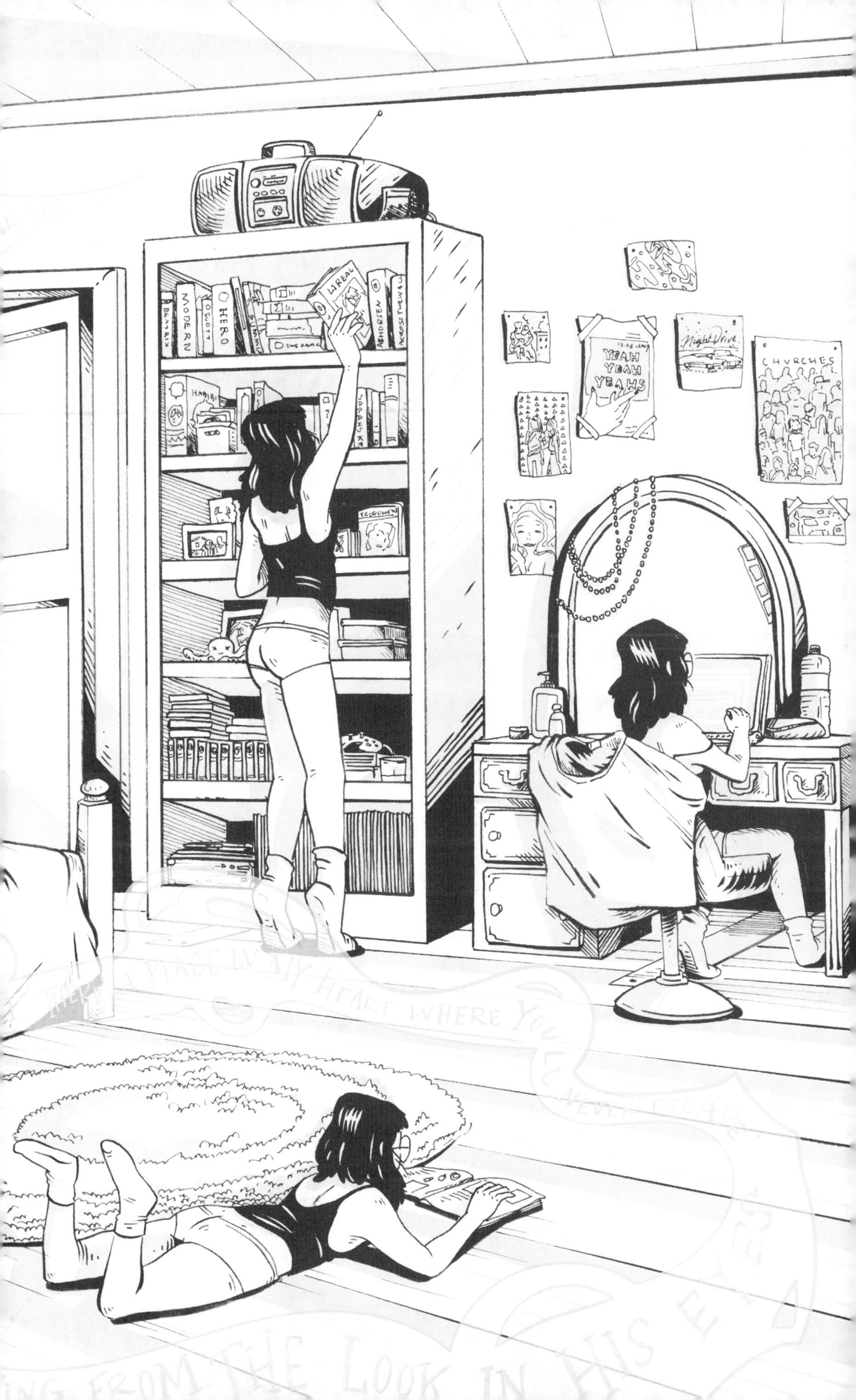
YEAH YEAH YEAHS
Night Drive
CHVRCHES
MODERN
HERO

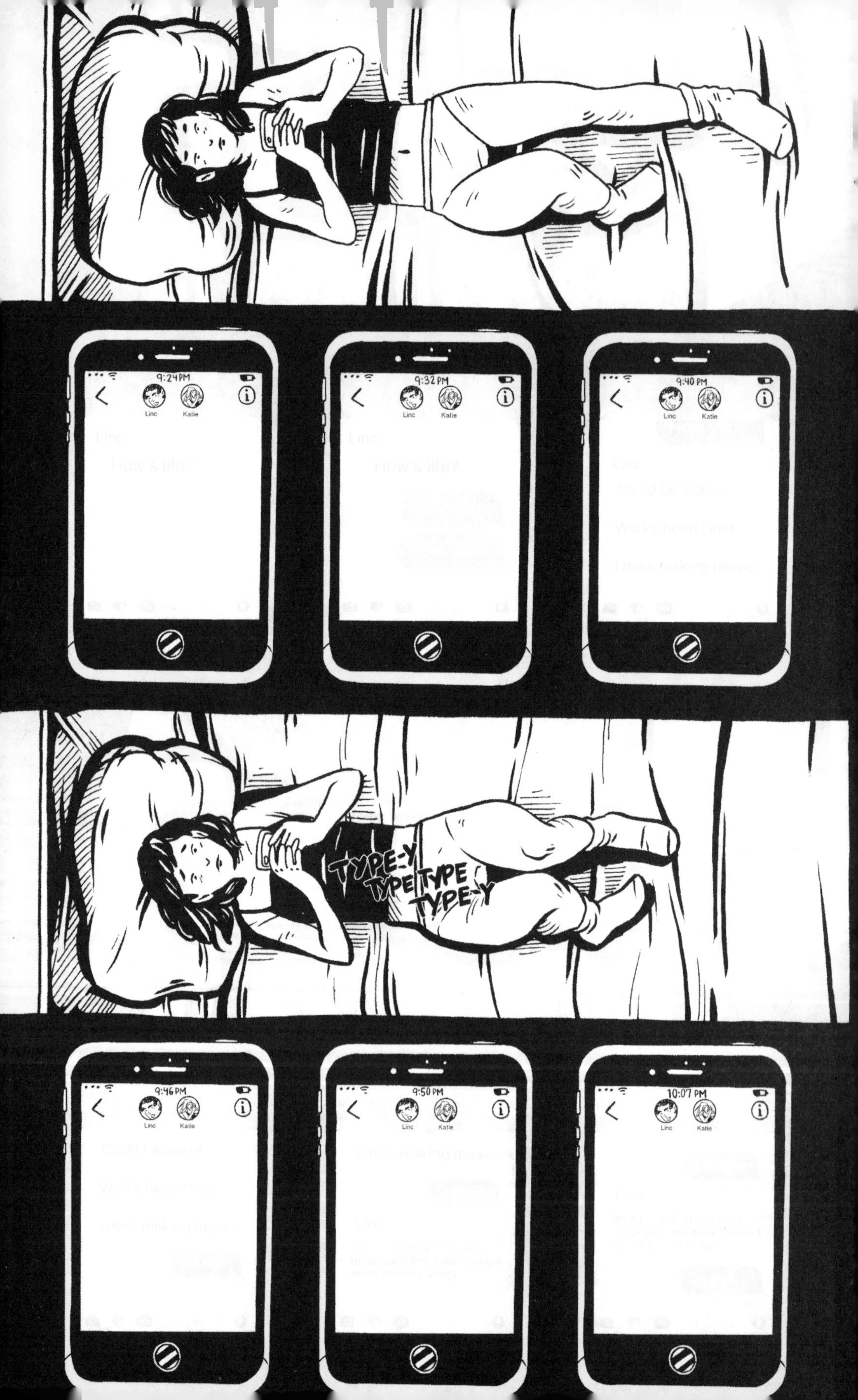
9:24 PM
Linc
Katie
Linc
How's life?
9:32 PM
Linc
Katie
Linc
How's life?
9:40 PM
Linc
Katie
Linc
Could be worse
Works been lame
I miss making music
TYPE-Y
TYPE TYPE
TYPE-Y
9:46 PM
Linc
Katie
Could be worse
I miss making music
9:50 PM
Linc
Katie
I miss making music
Linc
10:07 PM
Linc
Katie
Linc

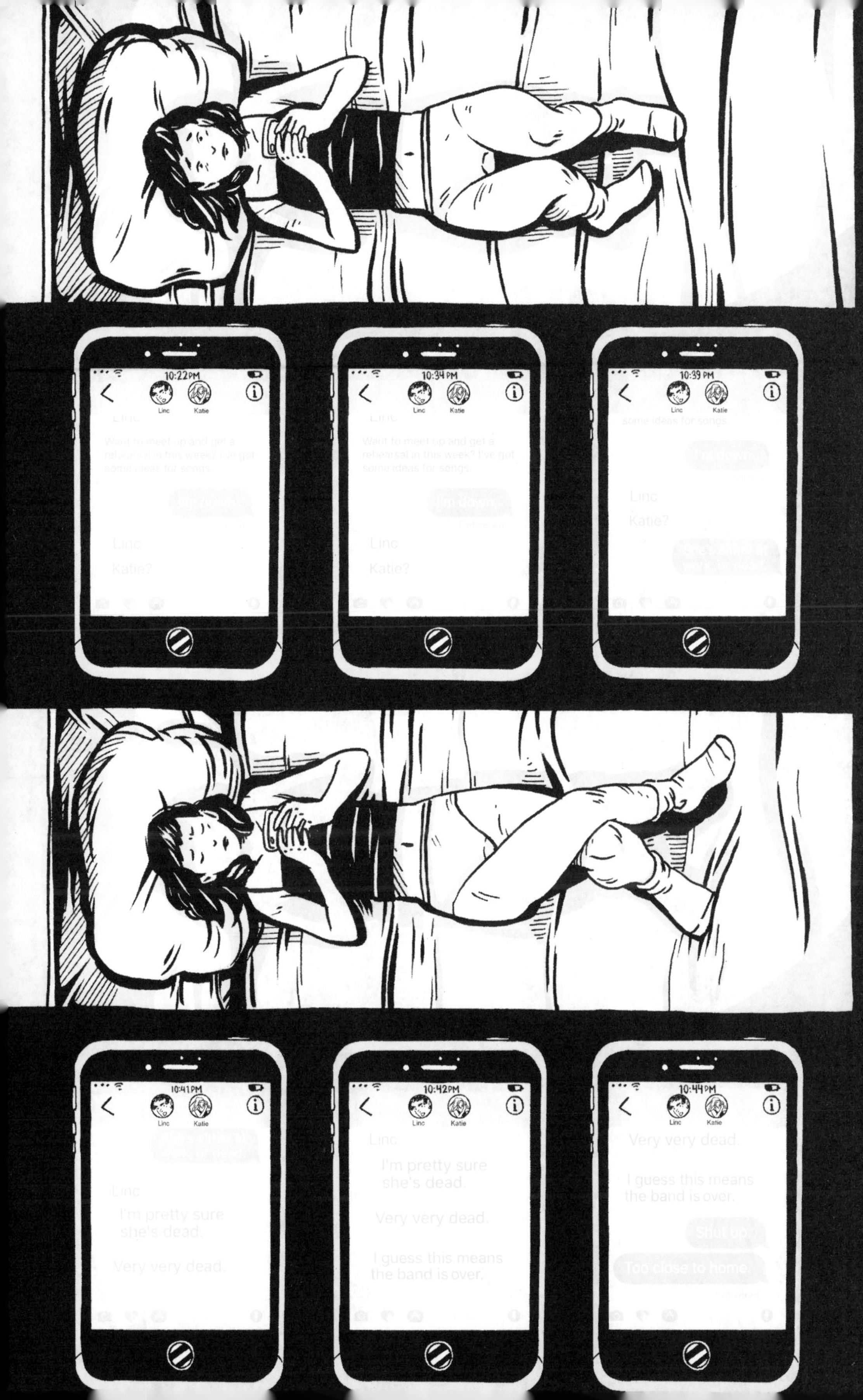

10:22PM
Linc
Katie
Want to meet up and get a rehearsal in this week? I've got some ideas for songs.
Linc
Katie?
10:34PM
Linc
Katie
Want to meet up and get a rehearsal in this week? I've got some ideas for songs.
Linc
Katie?
10:39PM
Linc
Katie
some ideas for songs.
Linc
Katie?
10:41PM
Linc
Katie
Linc
I'm pretty sure she's dead.
Very very dead.
10:42PM
Linc
Katie
Linc
I'm pretty sure she's dead.
Very very dead.
I guess this means the band is over.
10:44PM
Linc
Katie
Very very dead.
I guess this means the band is over.
Shut up.
Too close to home.

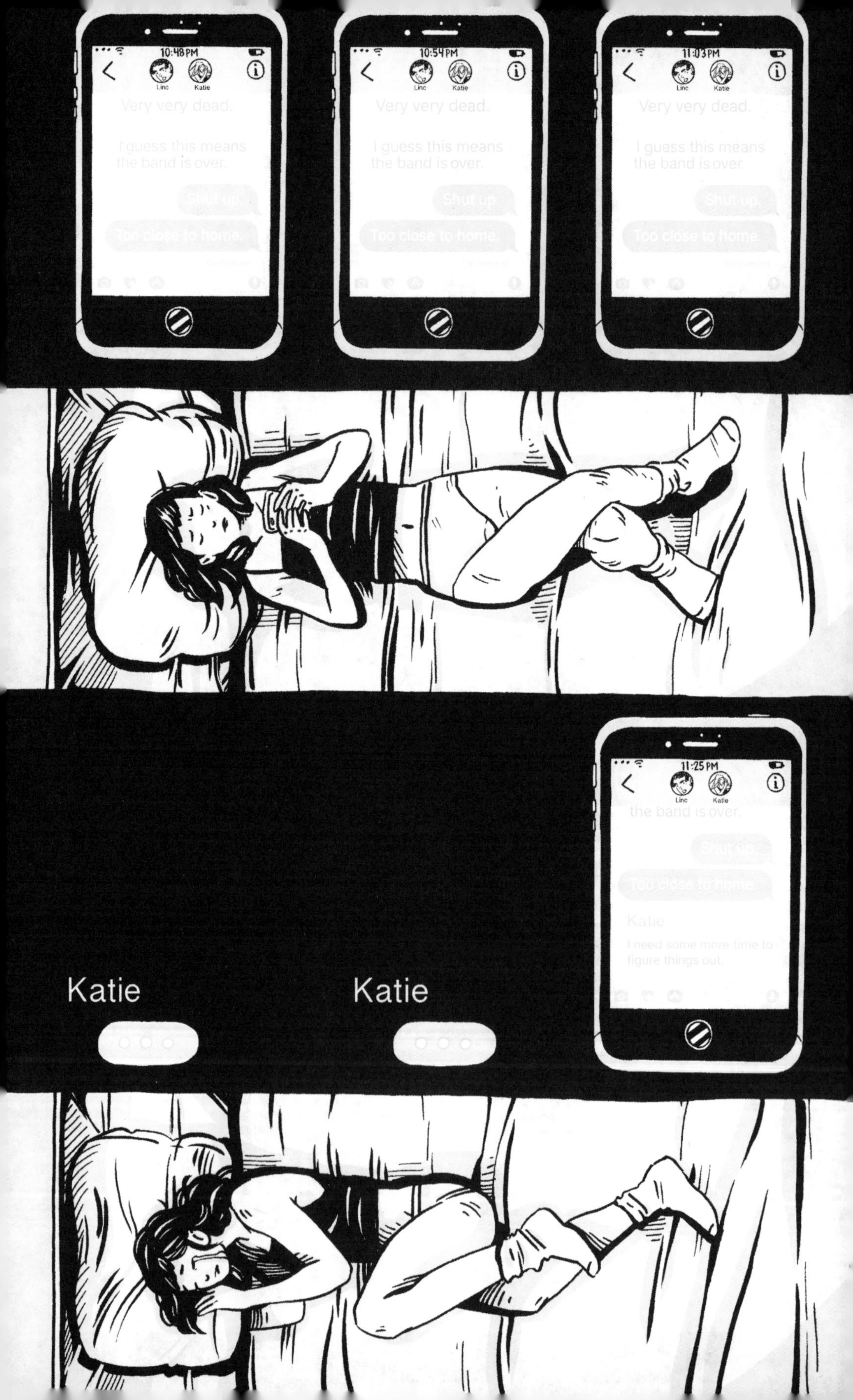
10:48 PM
Linc
Katie
Very very dead.
I guess this means the band is over.
Shut up.
Too close to home.
Delivered
10:54 PM
Linc
Katie
Very very dead.
I guess this means the band is over.
Shut up.
Too close to home.
Delivered
11:03 PM
Linc
Katie
Very very dead.
I guess this means the band is over.
Shut up.
Too close to home.
Delivered
Katie
Katie
11:25 PM
Linc
Katie
the band is over.
Shut up.
Too close to home.
Katie
I need some more time to figure things out.

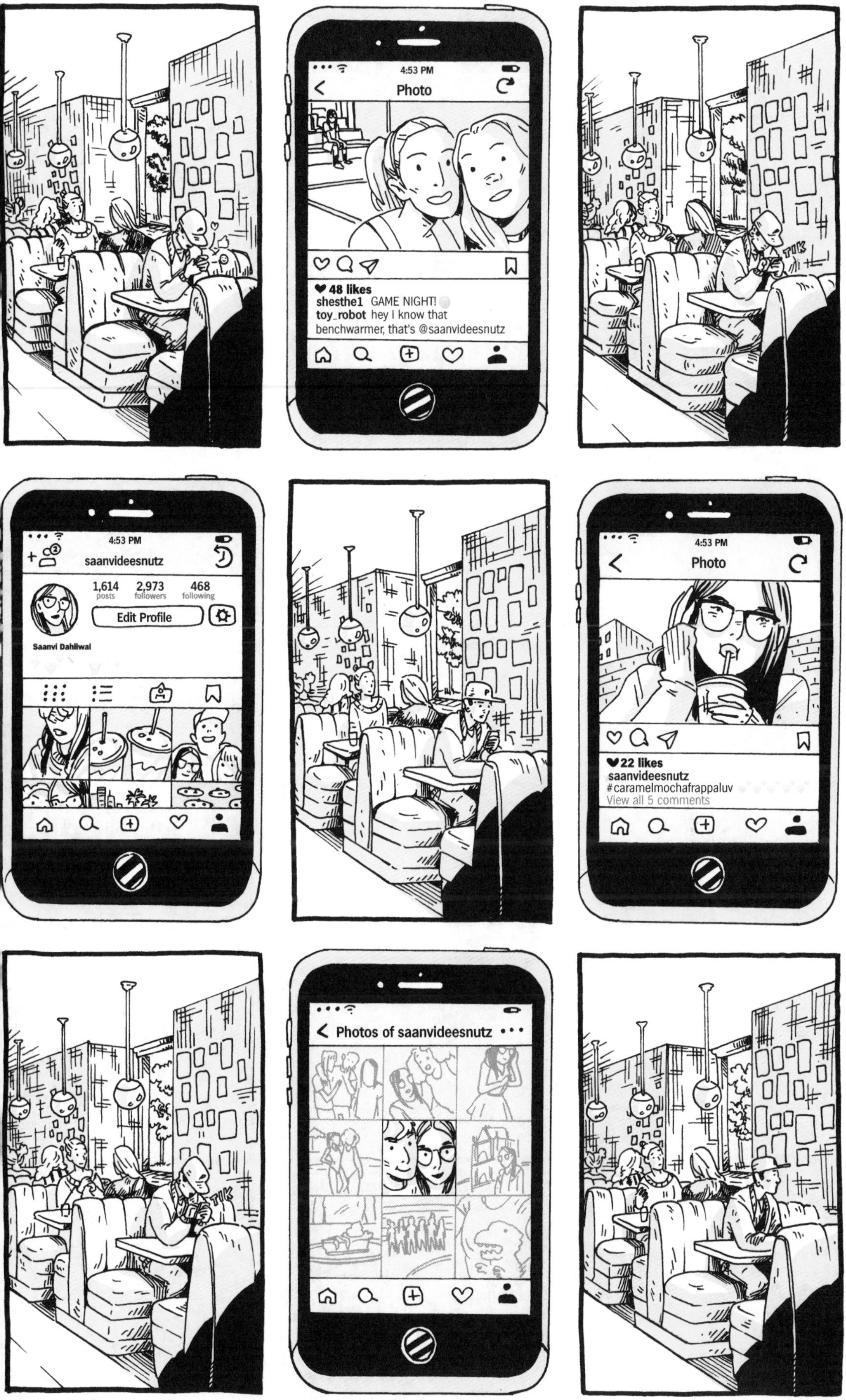
4:53 PM
Photo
48 likes
shesthe1 GAME NIGHT!
toy_robot hey i know that benchwarmer, that's @saanvideesnutz
TIK
4:53 PM
saanvideesnutz
1,614 posts
2,973 followers
468 following
Edit Profile
Saanvi Dahliwal
4:53 PM
Photo
22 likes
saanvideesnutz
#caramelmochafrappaluv
View all 5 comments
TIK
Photos of saanvideesnutz

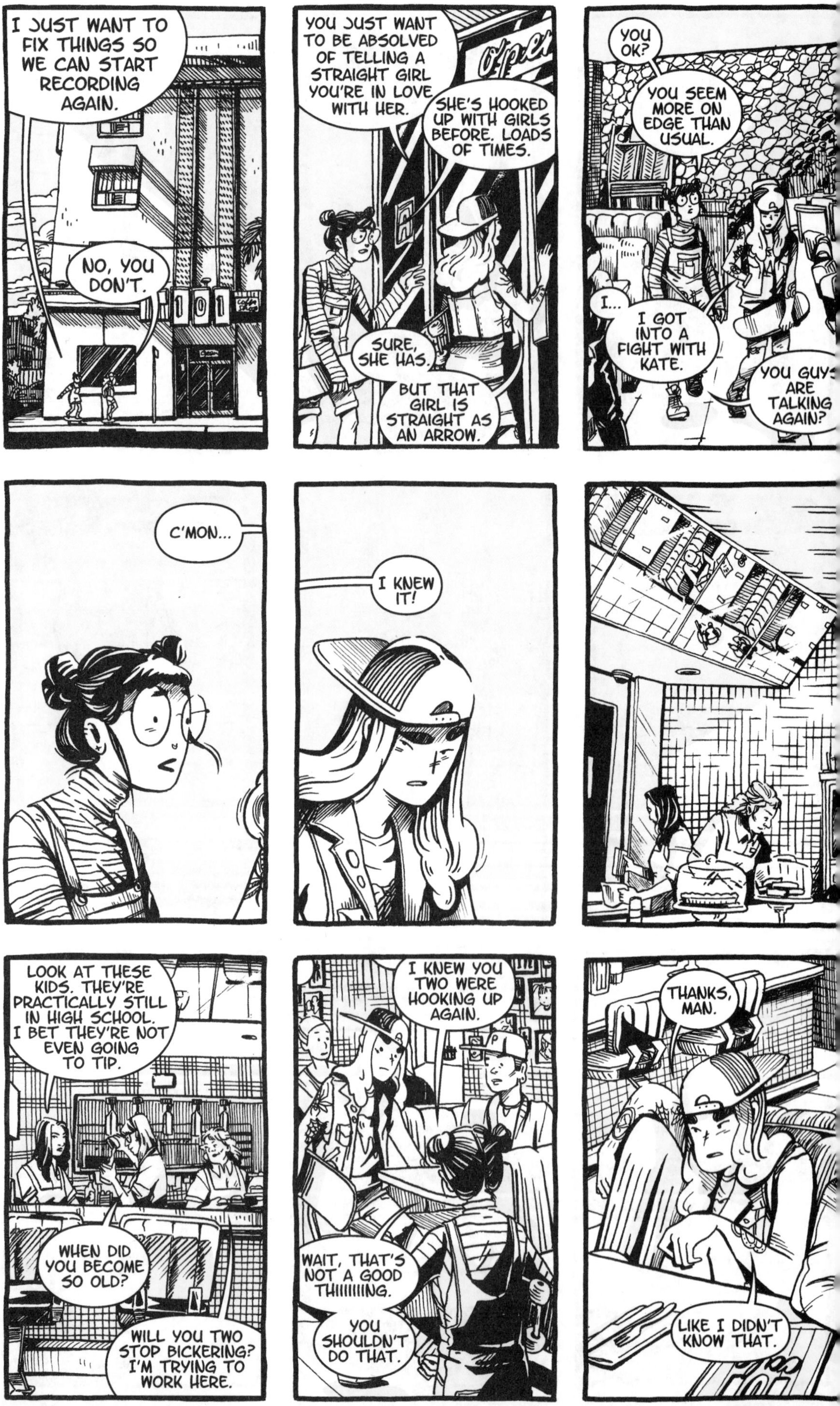

I JUST WANT TO FIX THINGS SO WE CAN START RECORDING AGAIN.
NO, YOU DON'T.
101
YOU JUST WANT TO BE ABSOLVED OF TELLING A STRAIGHT GIRL YOU'RE IN LOVE WITH HER.
SHE'S HOOKED UP WITH GIRLS BEFORE. LOADS OF TIMES.
SURE, SHE HAS.
BUT THAT GIRL IS STRAIGHT AS AN ARROW.
YOU OK?
YOU SEEM MORE ON EDGE THAN USUAL.
I...
I GOT INTO A FIGHT WITH KATE.
YOU GUYS ARE TALKING AGAIN?
C'MON...
I KNEW IT!
LOOK AT THESE KIDS. THEY'RE PRACTICALLY STILL IN HIGH SCHOOL. I BET THEY'RE NOT EVEN GOING TO TIP.
WHEN DID YOU BECOME SO OLD?
WILL YOU TWO STOP BICKERING? I'M TRYING TO WORK HERE.
I KNEW YOU TWO WERE HOOKING UP AGAIN.
WAIT, THAT'S NOT A GOOD THIIIIIIIING.
YOU SHOULDN'T DO THAT.
THANKS, MAN.
LIKE I DIDN'T KNOW THAT.

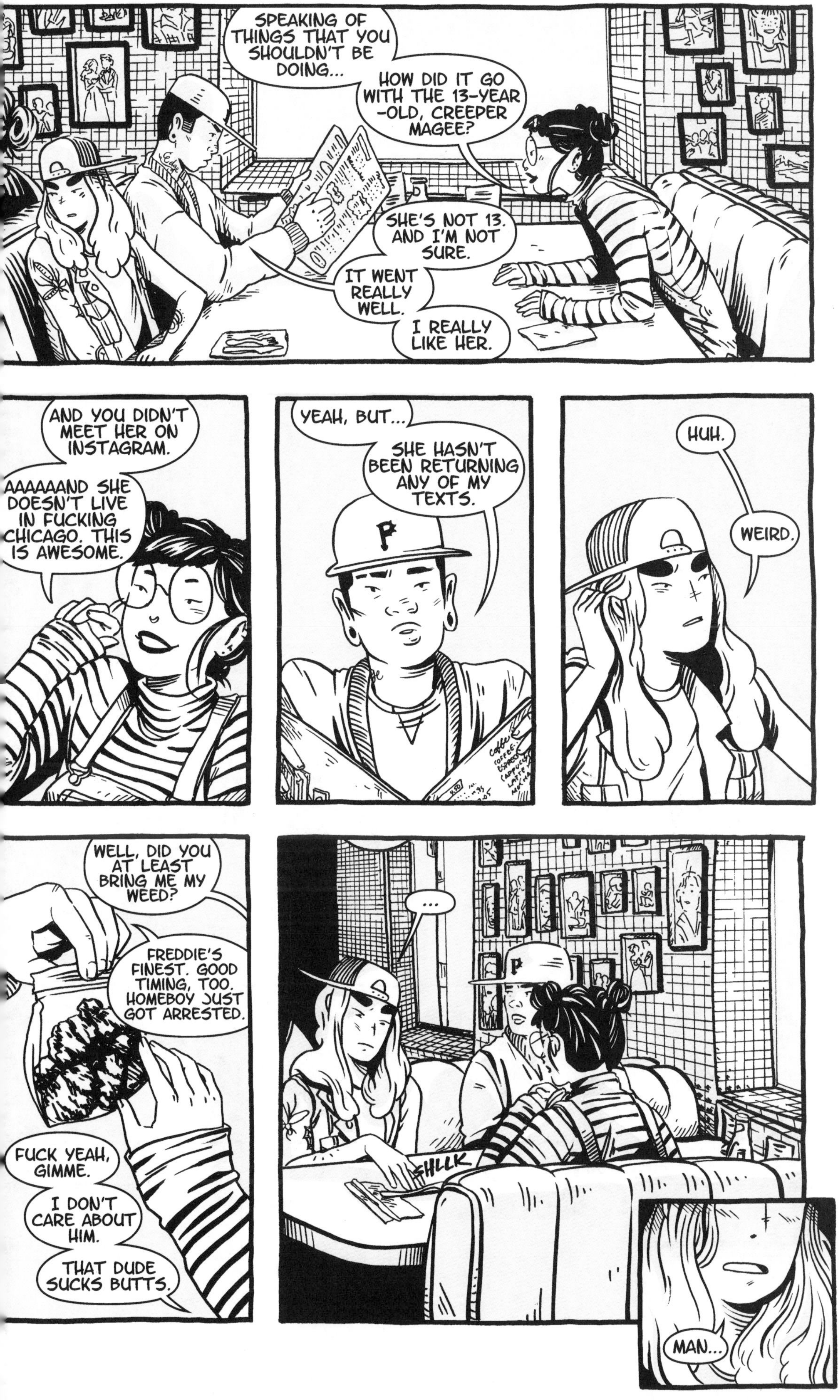
SPEAKING OF THINGS THAT YOU SHOULDN'T BE DOING...
HOW DID IT GO WITH THE 13-YEAR -OLD, CREEPER MAGEE?
SHE'S NOT 13. AND I'M NOT SURE.
IT WENT REALLY WELL.
I REALLY LIKE HER.
AND YOU DIDN'T MEET HER ON INSTAGRAM.
AAAAAAND SHE DOESN'T LIVE IN FUCKING CHICAGO. THIS IS AWESOME.
YEAH, BUT...
SHE HASN'T BEEN RETURNING ANY OF MY TEXTS.
HUH.
WEIRD.
WELL, DID YOU AT LEAST BRING ME MY WEED?
FREDDIE'S FINEST. GOOD TIMING, TOO. HOMEBOY JUST GOT ARRESTED.
FUCK YEAH, GIMME.
I DON'T CARE ABOUT HIM.
THAT DUDE SUCKS BUTTS.
...
SHLLK
MAN...

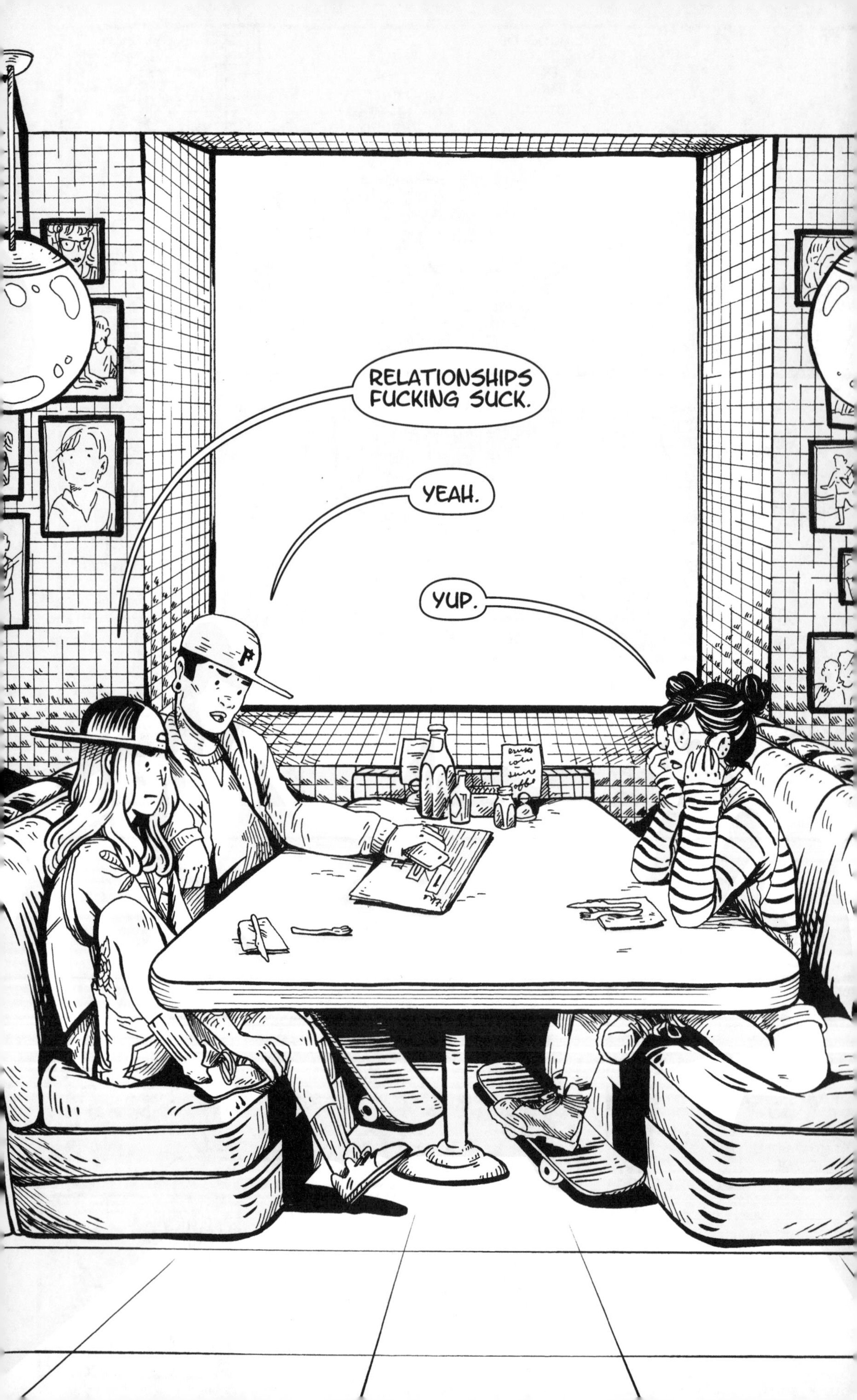
RELATIONSHIPS FUCKING SUCK.
YEAH.
YUP.

THE END

Let me start by saying that this is a completely surreal experience. The fact that this comic, that started out as a mini comic made in Nicole's kitchen, is now being read by people we don't know, in places we've never been is... well, it's just short of life-affirming. I've been making comics since I was 17, roughly. Nicole and I have been making comics together for about three years.

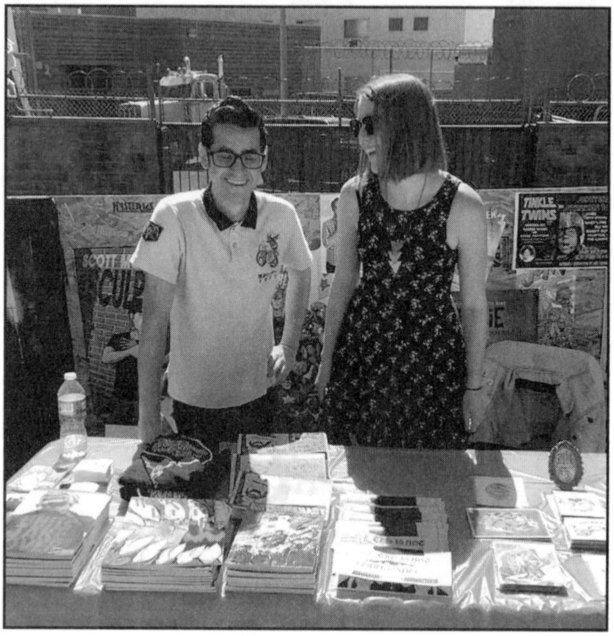
TINKLE TWINS

(See super cute photo of us at our first zinefest at Meltdown Comics in L.A.)

And now, after all the time and energy we've put into breathing life into them, I can't quite believe that Jimmy, Meg, and Clark are going to go out into the world and meet loads of new friends. I feel in some ways like a parent watching their child leave for college. You have a sense of excitement and exuberance for the achievement that your progeny has accomplished, but you're also terrified that they'll get hurt or people will be mean to them.

In a lot of ways the triumvirate known collectively as the Fuck Off Squad is a direct reflection of Nicole and me. There are parts of each of us in all three of them. However, they're also the reflections of the people I've met in Los Angeles and the people I knew growing up in Arizona. They're my slacker, stoner, and skater friends. They're that kid Max, who I went to high school with, who I'm pretty sure never showered the entire four years I knew him. They're the perennially lovelorn girl who awkwardly tried to ask me out sophomore year. They're the soft-eyed young woman from Montana that I befriended in a coffee shop, and who used to have a drug problem, but has now gone straight edge. They're the countless friends and loved ones who I've witnessed go through good times and bad.

If this is the first time you're reading one of the books that Nicole and I have made, hello. Welcome. I hope you enjoyed it. We worked diligently on it. We labored for an extended period of time, turned down more financially lucrative opportunities, and really attempted to craft a narrative that would be an honest reflection of the world around us. What we ended up making was a comic about sadness and skating and burritos.

This book, as you've noticed, is about queer people of color. I am not queer and I am not a person of color. I am supremely aware of the trope of white people telling stories about queer and POC characters instead of people who have actually lived the experiences. It's something that was on my mind when we initially started making this book. It's something that is still with me. Telling stories, especially stories starring people of color or queer people, is a huge responsibility. It's something I take very seriously.

I grew up in Arizona surrounded by people of all colors, from all walks of life. The experiences and narratives within *Fuck Off Squad* are based on the world I've seen. It's not always nice or easy or fun. Sometimes you just need to weep into a burrito. I think that's a fairly self-evident universal truth. I am highly aware that there are racist and homophobic structures within our society that keep writers and artists of color down. They keep queer writers and artists silenced. There are many ways in which I am not held back by those societal conventions.

I hope that it's readily apparent within the pages of this book that Nicole and I tried our damnedest to depict the awkward truths of the world. I hope you connected on some level with the trials and tribulations of Jimmy, Meg and Clark. I know when I look at the pages I am overwhelmed with a tidal wave of 'Jesus, if I could only do things differently'. I'm not someone who is consumed with regret, but I am human and I have made mistakes. I mean this both on a personal level and on an artistic one. This feeling, however, is one of the core tenets of the book, I think. It's not something Nicole and I ever expressly discussed but it's an idea that I see on every page. If *Fuck Off Squad* is successful, it's because it functions on a level where you can see your own weakness within the characters.

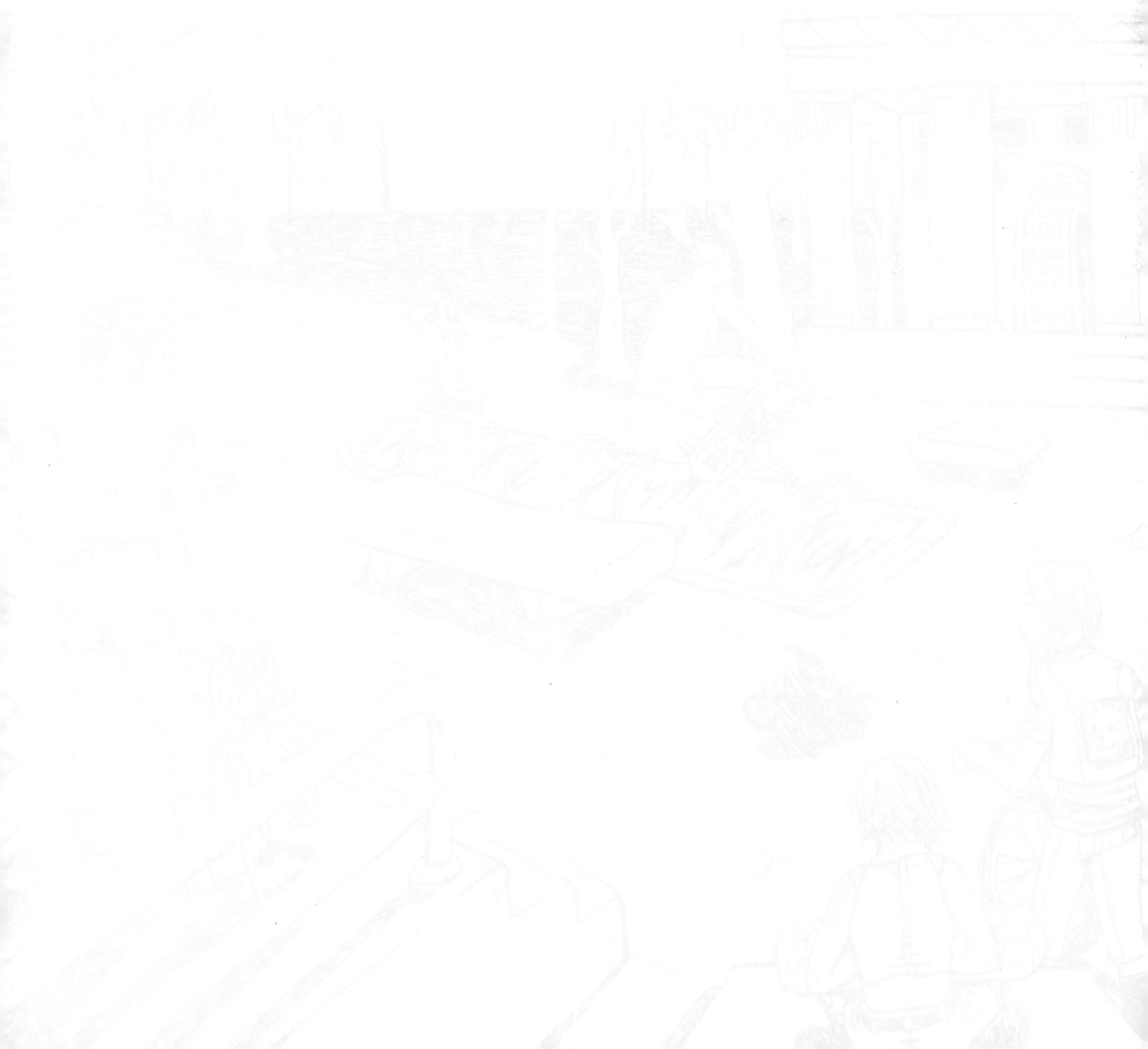

Let me be clear, when I say 'Nicole and I', I really mean Nicole. I just typed some words. The physical task of drawing comics is an undervalued and often misunderstood part of the process. I usually refer to it as the Exploding Cathedral Paradox. For some reason, we've collectively agreed that the writer who comes up with the idea of doing a splash page of a church exploding is the key creative force behind the image. Not the illustrator who is going to spend 25 hours rendering the fire, smoke, and molten brick. It seems pretty self-evident to me that if you give that image to an immensely skilled artist you're going to get one thing, and if you give it to someone who draws stick figures, you're going to get something else. This is just one of the reasons why, on this volume, Nicole's name is listed first. For some reason, most of the comics that are produced list the writer's name first, which has always struck me as slightly disrespectful. Why is the person who's job takes 1/6th the amount of time given the lion's share of the accolades? But I digress; let's get back on course.

We're here to talk about *Fuck Off Squad*. In the books that Nicole and I self-publish, we usually like to include an essay that details how we put the project together and what we were thinking about while doing so. I think this can help to demystify the arcane and ancient art of... putting drawings and words into boxes.

Self-effacing sense of humor aside, Nicole and I take the medium very seriously. We're always discussing what the parameters are going to be for the narrative mechanics we employ within our next story. And theoretically every book has a specifically codified set of mechanics that we're hoping to utilize.

As I'm sure you've noticed in *Fuck Off Squad*, the dominant narrative mechanic we employed was captions. Of course each issue has a sub-mechanic, skating, callout panels, and cell phones. Each issue was created with the idea of utilizing a unique storytelling device. I'm very proud of what we've accomplished. I think over the course of the books you can see us grow as creators but also you can see us unlocking the potential of what we set out to do narratively.

The only real constant within the medium of comics is the beautifully simple and frustratingly elegant mathematical equation: story + space = time. This is an inarguable fact. The comic book page, regardless of dimension, is a set canvas by which you are given space to tell your story. You can cram 35 panels onto a page or you can do a series of splash pages. Neither one is more admirable or compelling, they're just different ways to tell the same story. They are both bound by the deceptively simple mathematical equation above.

Despite what many would-be screenwriters who are attempting to get their screenplay turned into a comic will tell you, a comic book isn't just a movie on paper. It's a language. And if you don't speak it, it's very apparent.

This is something that Nicole and I wanted to expressly combat. We wanted to make a comic that utilized the medium to its furthest potential. We wanted to really push and pull things on a coldly mechanical level.

For *Fuck Off Squad*, we went into the first issue thinking about captions. Captions are often very frustrating to me. There seems to be a common agreement with the audience and the writer that in comics Exposition Dump Theatre is fine, as long as it's in a caption. This is something that I cannot support. Exposition is fine, necessary, and an inescapable part of storytelling. However, if your entire issue is just someone thinking exposition, you're fucking up. Hard.

So, Nicole and I decided to attempt combining a few disparate creative influences into a new way of using a caption mechanic. Those two influences? Chris Claremont and Drake. Stay with me. I know it sounds crazy, but I'm gonna get us there.

When we were making *Fuck Off Squad*, I was listening to *Nothing Was The Same*, essentially on repeat. I was obsessed with the production of the record. For those of you who don't know, Drake primarily works with a Canadian producer named Noah '40' Shabib. His production is stripped down, minimalist, and cold. All the songs are put together in a very delicate and intimate way. It's the meta textual antithesis of Drake's emotional vulnerability in the lyrics. Everything is simplified to its most basic and granular form.

Now, *Nothing Was The Same* is the first record that Drake put out that was only partially produced by 40. Producers like Mike Zombie, Nineteen85 and others picked up the torch. Which is an interesting modality to examine. You're looking at people making beats for Drake in the "40 Style" but still altering, improving, and reinventing it. It's a fascinating experiment. This made me think, "what's the simplest and smallest thing we can do?" How can we grind these captions down to the most minute detail?

And that's when I started to think about Chris Claremont, how in the beginning of many of his *Uncanny* issues, there were the 'Dramatis Personae' panels. Wherein each of the X-men who would appear in the issue would be drawn, standing in a row with their names floating below them in a little caption box. It all clicked for me. We should do the maximalist version of a minimalist idea. We should have callout panels detailing small elements of all of the characters. If done correctly, you could have a very intimate experience with characters that you only spent a little amount of time with.

Ultimately, I think that the mechanic was a resounding success. I've had more people come up to me and talk about it than practically anything else we've produced. And it just makes me happy to write that Meg wants to go home and watch *Hellraiser 2*. So, honestly, it's more a selfish desire than anything else.

As I'm sure you've noticed by now, the comics that Nicole and I make are really made by both of us. There's a real spark between the two of us. There's some real alchemy between us when we're creating the books. The work isn't about what's the shortest route we can take to get across the finish line. What's the best and most unique way we can tell an emotionally resonant story? How can we push the medium in a way that we've never seen before? How can we take advantage of what people in other creative mediums are doing and filter it through comics? These are simple questions with inevitably complex answers.

In closing, I'd just like to proffer a simple and self-evident truth. I love comics. I love them so much I've dedicated my life to making them and to proselytize for the medium to anyone who will listen. However, the greatest weakness that comics usually succumbs to is that it takes so much time and effort to create comics that the people making them often end up making comics about the act of making comics. That's not what I want for our book. Ultimately, I want this book to be a shining example of the truism 'the medium is the message', while still containing a human story. I want this book to be a vessel for all the pain and trauma and sacrifice that we all have to endure. That may be a lofty goal, but you know what they say about shooting for the moon, right?

I'm hoping that there was truth captured in these pages. Life isn't easy no matter who you are or where you come from. There's pain and heartache and beauty and triumph around every corner. In the end, it's just about where you put your time and energy and how hard you attempt to push yourself forward. The only thing that makes our collective journey a little more pleasant is some companionship along the way. I hope that these three idiots that you just read about have helped you in some way. I know they have for me...

Your friend,
–Dave Baker
Los Angeles, CA
June 11th, 2018

SKETCH BOOK

9 <u>MASK</u>: ||||||||
10 <u>SKULL</u>: ||||||||
8 <u>HOUSE</u>: ||||||||
7 <u>HAND</u>: |||||||
<u>HEADPHONES</u>: ||||||
14 <u>SPIDER</u>: ||||||||||||

19 <u>HEAD</u>: ||||||||||||||||||
4 <u>UNDIES</u>: ||||
6 <u>FIRE</u>: ||||||

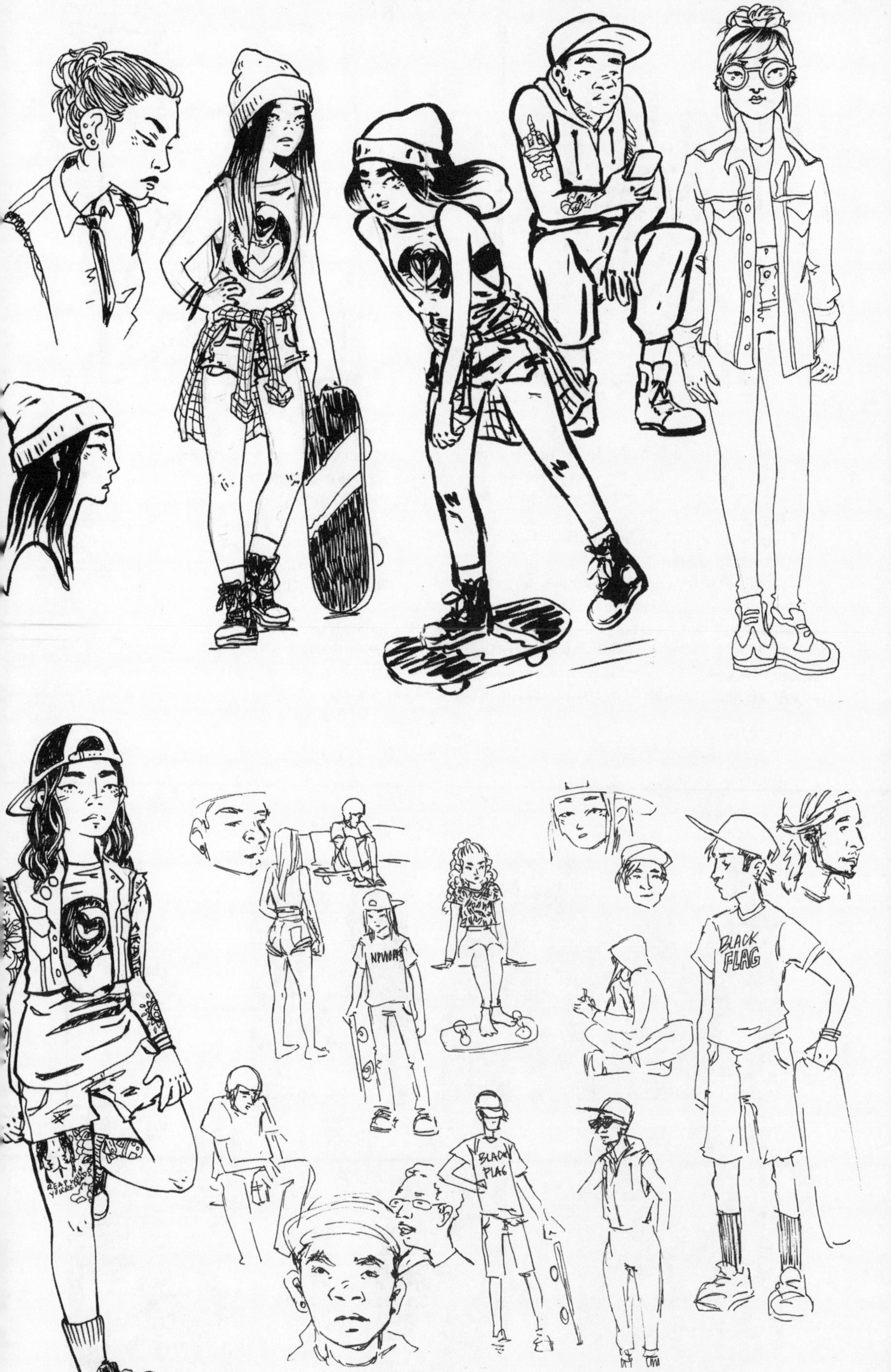
BLACK FLAG
BLACK FLAG

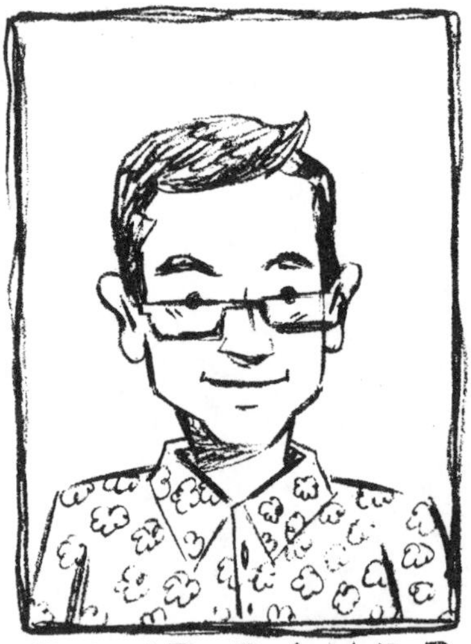

DAVE BAKER

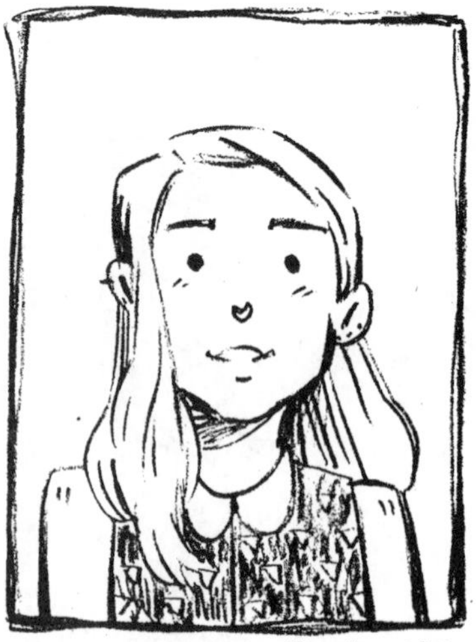

NICOLE GOUX

Dave Baker, originally from the barren wastes of Tucson, Arizona, lives and works in Los Angeles. He's written projects for Universal, Fox, and Disney XD. He's also produced numerous comics such as Fuck Off Squad, Action Hospital, Suicide Forest, Horrible Little People, and Professor Cuties, among others. When he's not touring the country selling said comics at conventions, he enjoys eating Peruvian food, internally debating which Starfleet uniform is the best, and taking long walks around his apartment.

heydavebaker.com
theactionhospital.com
IG:@xdavebakerx

When she's not binge watching Buffy The Vampire Slayer for the 47th time, Nicole makes comics. Her other books include Jem and the Holograms: Dimensions, Murders, Suicide Forest, Goodnight Honey, This Is Not A Girl Gang, This Is Not A Girl Gang: Northwest Edition, and Action Hospital.

nicolegoux.com
nicolegouxillustration.tumblr.com
IG:@ngoux

More from Dave and Nicole

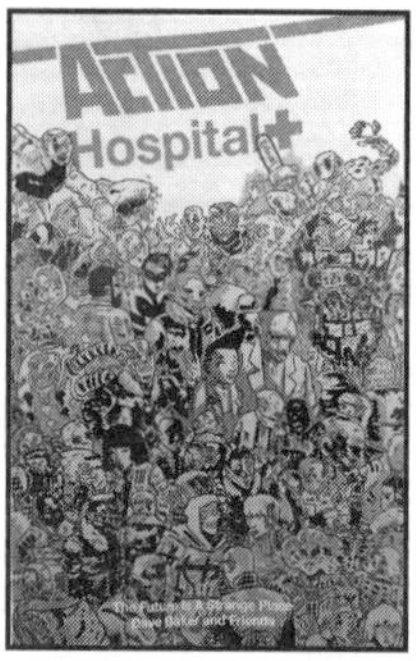
ACTION
Hospital

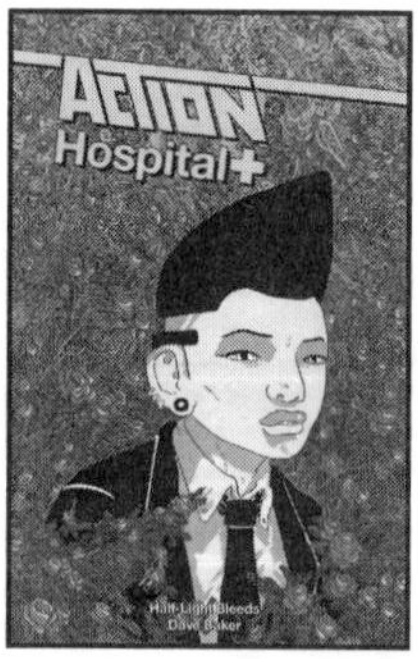
ACTION
Hospital

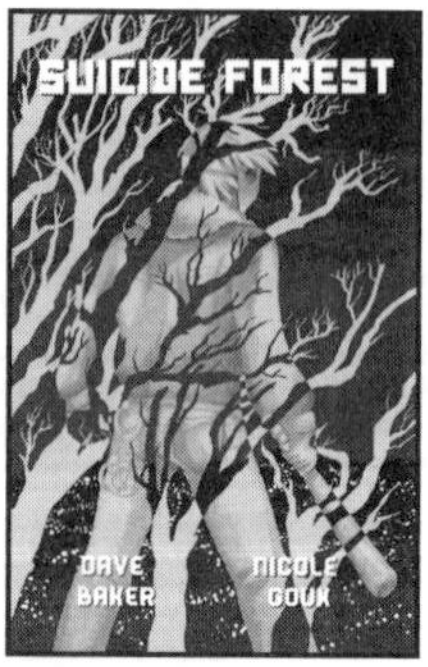
SUICIDE FOREST
DAVE BAKER
NICOLE GOUX

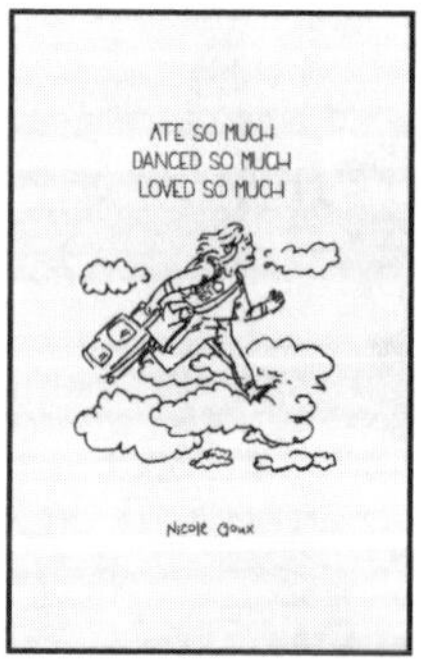
ATE SO MUCH
DANCED SO MUCH
LOVED SO MUCH
Nicole Goux

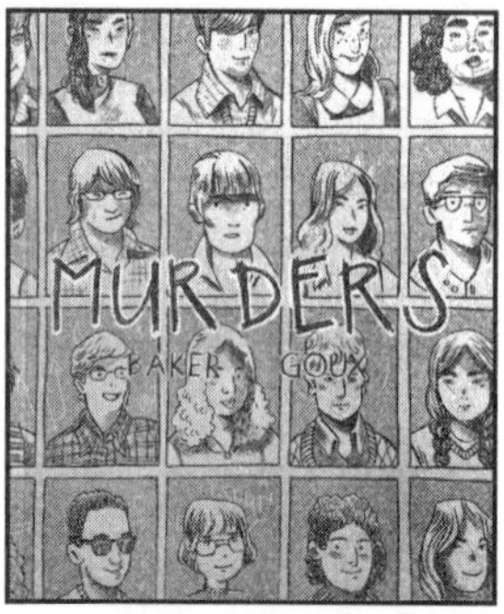
MURDERS
BAKER GOUX

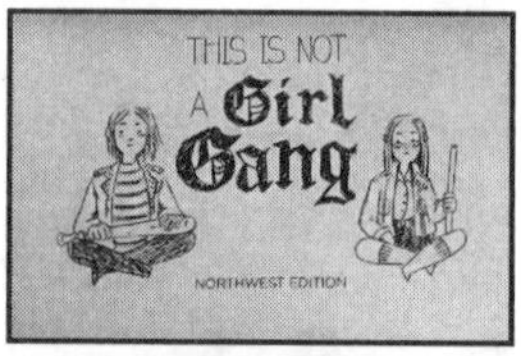
THIS IS NOT
A Girl Gang
NORTHWEST EDITION

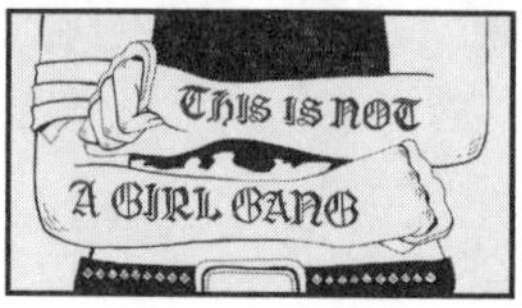
THIS IS NOT
A GIRL GANG

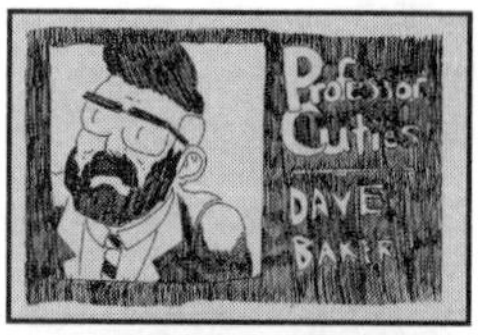
Professor Cuties
DAVE BAKER

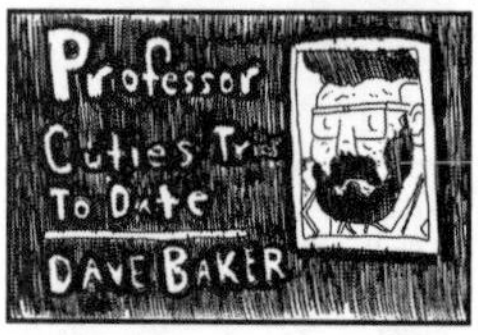
Professor
To Date
DAVE BAKER